T. F. Powys: Aspects of a Life

T. F. POWYS

dry-point etching by Frederick Carter, 1932]
[*courtesy of Richard Grenville Clark*]

T. F. POWYS
Aspects of a Life

BY
J. LAWRENCE MITCHELL

Our destiny, our being's heart and home,
Is with infinitude, and only there . . .

> Wordsworth, *The Prelude*

BRYNMILL

copyright © 2005 The Brynmill Press Ltd
first published 2005
by
The Brynmill Press Ltd
The Stonehouse Bishopstone Herefordshire HR4 7JE England
typeset by the publishers
printed by Print Solutions Partnership
88 Sandy Lane South Wallington Surrey SM6 9RQ

ISBN 0 907839 86 X

British Library Cataloguing in Publication Data: a catalogue record of this book is available from the British Library.

The right of J. Lawrence Mitchell to be identified as the author of this work has been asserted by him in accordance with the Copyright, Designs and Patents Act 1988.

www.edgewaysbooks.com

Contents

List of Illustrations	*page* vi
Acknowledgements	vii
Note on Sources	viii
Abbreviations	x
Introduction	1
1 The One Powys	5
2 The Education of Theodore Powys	33
3 "One Foot in the Furrow" Theodore Powys in East Anglia	59
4 Theodore Powys and the Mysterious Mrs Stracey	91
5 Getting into Print	115
6 Theodore Powys and John Death	141
Works Cited	165

Illustrations

T. F. Powys, dry-point etching by Frederick Carter, 1932 *frontispiece*

between pp. 90 and 91
I   The Powys Family *circa* 1896–7
II   White House Farm, Sweffling, in 1986
      Dorchester Grammar School
III   Mrs (Mary) Stracey as a young woman
IV   Theodore Powys and his eldest son "Dicky" *circa* 1910–11
      Dicky and Francis, 1916, in a photograph sent to Mrs Stracey
      Dicky, in a photograph sent to Mrs Stracey in 1923
      Theodore Powys outside Beth Car
V   Beth Car, East Chaldon, 1932
      Theodore Powys and American admirer Elizabeth Wade White, Mappowder, 1949
VI   David Garnett, 1934
      Bernie O'Neill
      Violet Powys, Theodore Powys, John Hampson, Charles Lahr, Francis Powys and Alec Bristow, September 1932
VII   two photographs of Theodore Powys and "Susie" *circa* 1938
VIII   T. F. Powys, photograph of the carving by Elizabeth Muntz, 1949–50

Acknowledgements

I am very grateful to all those individuals and institutions that have so generously given me access to their collections and archives, and to those who have helped me in ways too many to enumerate—offering hospitality as well as information about the Powys family. Specifically, I would like to acknowledge my indebtedness to the following: Philip Beetham of Shirley, Sylvia Belle, the late E. E. Bissell, Louise de Bruin, the late Gerard Casey, the late Francis Feather, P. T. Garner-Richardson, Richard Garnett, Richard Perceval Graves, Claire Harman, Cathy Henderson, Research Librarian at the Harry Ransom Humanities Research Center, University of Texas at Austin, the late Kenneth Hopkins, Belinda Humfrey, the late Mary Barham Johnson, Major B. G. Kirby, Robin Lindsay, the late Isobel Powys Marks, Stephen Powys Marks, Elaine Mencher, Hedley J. Morgan, Caryl Parsons of Bradford Abbas, Roger Peers, formerly Curator of the Dorset County Museum, Dorchester, Jacqueline Peltier, the late Gerald Pollinger, Laurence Pollinger, Ltd., the late Francis Powys, Peter Riley, Theodora Scutt, The Reverend Cyril D. R. Stevens, Rector, St Mary's Sweffling, Frank G. Robinson, Peter Tait, Headmaster of Sherborne Preparatory School, and Oliver Marlow Wilkinson.

Earlier versions of some chapters have appeared as follows:
Chapter 2: "The Education of T. F. Powys", *The Powys Review*, No. 19, 1986, pp. 3–19
Chapter 3: "'One Foot in the Furrow': T. F. Powys in East Anglia", *The Powys Review*, No. 23, 1989, pp. 3–24
Chapter 4: "In the Beginning: Theodore Powys and the Mysterious Mrs Stracey", *The Library Chronicle of the University of Texas at Austin*, Vol. 23.1, 1993, pp. 71–97
Chapter 5: "Getting into Print: from Mr. Tasker to Mr. Weston", *The Powys Journal*, Vol. IX, 1999, pp. 101–28
Chapter 6: "Theodore Powys and John Death", *The Powys Journal*, Vol. XIII, 2003, pp. 120–43

Note on Sources

Since the death of Theodore Powys in 1953, three major collections of Powys manuscripts have been developed: those of E. E. Bissell in England and Francis Feather in Zimbabwe, now both held by the Dorset County Museum, Dorchester, on behalf of the Powys Society, and the Powys Family archives in the Harry Ransom Humanities Research Center, Austin, Texas, the largest of the three. There are also rather smaller, but still important, manuscript collections at Colgate University and in the Sterling Library, University of London, as well as the material—letters or short stories for the most part—held by such institutions as Dartmouth College, Hofstra University, and Syracuse University in the United States and by the universities of Aberdeen and Reading, and the National Library of Wales in Great Britain.

In 1966, the University of Texas acquired the multi-author collection of T. E. Hanley, a Philadelphia banker and bibliophile. The work of all three Powys brothers is represented, including well over a hundred separate manuscripts, a substantial collection of letters, and seventy-five quarto and folio size notebooks containing diaries, essays, and stories. Many of the books in the collection are presentation copies. Among the TFP manuscripts in Hanley's collection, the star item is the 484-page autograph manuscript of *Mr Tasker's Gods*, the first written (though not the first published) and, in the opinion of some critics, the darkest in mood of all his published novels. This manuscript was the fair copy sent to Louis Wilkinson in New York in 1916, where it was typed by Frances Gregg, and first accepted, then rejected, for publication by Arnold Shaw, an English-born newcomer in the publishing world. Arnold Shaw, a genial Yorkshireman who met John Cowper Powys on the boat to America, first managed John Cowper Powys's lecture tours, before moving into publishing in

1914. The Gregg typescript into which many changes were later incorporated was lost some time after 1929, so the manuscript at the HRHRC alone now represents the earliest completed version of the work.

Between 1966 and 1970, a very large proportion of the TFP manuscript material still in the family—some had been sold during TFP's lifetime—was acquired through the agency of a major New York dealer, The House of El Dieff. In one batch came 442 letters from TFP to members of his family, including 165 to John, 87 to Llewelyn, 31 to Gertrude, 24 to Katie. There were also 76 to Louis Wilkinson and 59 to Alyse Gregory. In addition, there were manuscripts, typescripts and/or page proofs for all nine of the published novels, though only in two cases (*Unclay* and *The Market Bell*) were there complete fair copies. The Sterling Library of the University of London owns the fair copy of *Mark Only* and both the Bissell and Feather collections have fair copies of *Mr Weston's Good Wine*. From a scholarly standpoint, of course, early and intermediate versions, especially when heavily emended or corrected, are likely to yield more information about structure and development than fair copies only one step removed from the published work.

For a variety of reasons, it is harder to be precise about holdings of the short stories. To begin with, there are so many of them, published and unpublished. Of the 140 published stories, 121 have been collected in six volumes, and another 19 remain uncollected. The HRHRC holdings now include manuscripts or typescripts for 69, or 57% of these. There are also 129 separate short-story titles, some in multiple versions that remain unpublished. Some of these are fragmentary and others may prove to be drafts of published stories under different titles. "A Better Present", for example, on the HRHRC manuscript of which alternate titles, "The Wedding Gift" and "Simple Simon", have been deleted, may be an earlier version of "The Better Gift", a story which was first separately issued as *Goat Green* by The Golden Cockerel Press in 1937. Nonetheless, collation against the holdings of the Bissell and Feather collections suggests that at least 78 of these unpublished short-story manuscripts or typescripts are unique to the HRHRC; by contrast, the Feather collection has only five stories of which there is no version either in the Bissell or in the HRHRC collection.

Abbreviations

HRHRC = Harry Ransom Humanities Research Center
JCP = John Cowper Powys
LlP = Llewelyn Powys
PJ = *The Powys Journal*
PN = *The Powys Society Newsletter*
PR = *The Powys Review*
TFP = Theodore Francis Powys

Introduction

Soon after the death of Theodore Powys in 1953, his brother Littleton wrote an article about him for *John O'London's Weekly* and titled it "My Hermit Brother". The following year his son, Francis, dubbed him "The Quiet Man of Dorset" in *The Adelphi* and this seems more apt than "hermit", despite the title of his first regularly published book, *The Soliloquy of a Hermit* (1916) and his notorious reluctance to venture beyond the confines of his village. Though he sought and cultivated seclusion, he can hardly be described as a "hermit". Indeed, he had a wide circle of friends and admirers, many of whom made the pilgrimage to East Chaldon to meet him—artists and editors, as well as fellow-writers like Gerald Brenan, Rhys Davies, Liam O'Flaherty, and T. E. Lawrence. Sylvia Townsend Warner even felt impelled to move to the village and became a close friend; and the Garnett family were regular visitors. There was a quiet strength about Theodore Powys that drew such different people to him—what Louis Wilkinson described as "his presence".[1] David Garnett's first impression, later recorded in his autobiography, *The Familiar Faces*, was of "a grey-haired, elderly, heavily-built man with a big head and powerful rugged features . . . a moralist and a shrewd critic of men".[2] Yet, as Harry Coombes observed in his seminal study, *T. F. Powys*: "It is interesting that he, the quietest person of them all, and the quietest writer, incurred more general opposition than any of them."[3]

It is also surely significant that none of the six sons of the Reverend Charles Francis Powys took holy orders (only John even contemplated such a move) and most of the children unequivocally rejected traditional Christianity. Theodore Powys

1 *Seven Friends*, p. 98   2 *The Familiar Faces*, p. 4   3 *T. F. Powys*, p. 15

and Virginia Woolf would never have seen eye to eye on the subject of women (and she declined to take *The Left Leg* for the Hogarth Press); but the author of *Three Guineas* would have appreciated his perspective on one subject at least. In response to Louis Wilkinson's sardonic reference to the Church, the Army and Navy and the Bar as our only recognized "professions", Theodore dismissed them all as "Liars, murderers and thieves".[1] Not quite what one would expect from the son of a clergyman with a brother who had served—and died—in the Indian Army!

When he was called upon to provide background information for Alfred Knopf's celebratory *Borzoi 1925*, Theodore sent David Garnett a cryptic statement that included the following: "Powys believes in monotony. He is happy when he does the same each day. Writes from 11 till 1.30. Walks nearly always the same path in the afternoon, goes by the Inn to the hill." A decade later, in an essay on his reasons for giving up writing, he declared with discernible satisfaction: "I did nothing; I went nowhere; I met nobody."[2] While this statement does not altogether withstand scrutiny, it exactly reflects the *modus vivendi* Theodore had consciously adopted. Certainly there can be no comparison between the sameness of his daily life and the full and itinerant lives led for many years by his brothers, John Cowper and Llewelyn Powys. No wonder then that Belinda Humfrey concluded that "it is probable that there will never be a biography of T. F. Powys because his life was so uneventful."[3]

This study does not attempt the impossible; it is not a conventional biography but an attempt to approach its elusive subject from a variety of angles or perspectives. Necessarily it has involved a good deal of archival research in England and America that has yielded much hitherto unknown information—especially about his education, his experience as a farmer, and his extended apprenticeship in writing. A number of misconceptions and/or embellishments of the truth have also been corrected—for example, Theodore Powys never sat at the same desk as Hardy, he was never cheated by a bad bailiff, and Mrs Stracey was never his (or anyone else's) landlady.

John and Llewelyn were far more forthcoming about their lives than Theodore ever was; so there is a singular lack of published

---

1 In "Some Memories of T. F. Powys", *Theodore*, p. 11. Wilkinson first included this anecdote in *Welsh Ambassadors* and again in *Seven Friends*.
2 "Why I have given up Writing"   3 *Recollections of The Powys Brothers*, pp. 10–11

material available for those who would know "the secret self" of this enigmatic figure. John produced a remarkable self-critical autobiography of over six hundred pages (though he was infamously reticent about women in it) and a good selection of the thousands of letters he wrote have been published. He also kept a full diary that is gradually being published. Llewelyn's essays are almost reflexively autobiographical; and a competent biography of Llewelyn—who died in 1939—was penned by Malcolm Elwin as long ago as 1946. For Theodore, on the other hand, there are largely unpublished and often fragmentary sources such as the early story "Charlie",[1] a very sketchy "diary" for 1892, a Journal for 1910–13,[1] a few dialogues, "Cottage Shadows"[1] and the more substantial "This is Thyself".[1] His letters (mostly unpublished) have a cumulative value and are useful for dating events, despite often frustratingly abbreviated dating, but deal largely with everyday events and only rarely with his innermost feelings. The recent *Cuckoo in the Powys Nest: a Memoir* (2000) by his adopted daughter, Theodora Scutt, offers unique and invaluable eyewitness testimony about Theodore's later life after he had given up writing. It therefore complements the sketchier outline of his earlier life up to 1935 that can be extracted from Louis Wilkinson's readable but idiosyncratic *Welsh Ambassadors*. Inevitably then, if we are to approach the man behind the myth, we must rely far more upon the testimony of those who knew him—family and friends—and upon extrapolation from Theodore's own fiction, especially the early and more autobiographical material, than is the case for his brothers. When we set an early dialogue such as "Theodore Examined by the Brethren" against the early manuscript version of another dialogue, *An Interpretation of Genesis*, and note that the comments of Zetetes (the Seeker) were originally assigned to "Theodore", we will read the final product with a new alertness. Moreover, the dialogue form provided an important bridge from the earliest first-person material to the later fully realized fiction. Theodore's fictional preoccupations also seem to reflect fairly reliably his real-life views of the world and his place in it. For example, by their very existence, the two versions of "The Scapegoat" and the abortive play, *The Sin-Eater*[1] tend to confirm what John had obviously come to understand about his brother, as Malcolm Elwin points

---

1 now published in Selected Early Works of T. F. Powys

out in his *Life of Llewelyn Powys*: "Like Mr Quincunx in [John's] *Wood and Stone*, Theodore felt himself a pariah."¹ In his stories and novels, unsurprisingly then, the "outcast" figure is ubiquitous.

Did his feelings of inadequacy and rejection by society stem from his failure to follow his brothers to Sherborne and to Cambridge? From his lack of success at farming? Or were they simply the by-product of what, in old-fashioned terms, might be called his melancholic disposition—in modern terms, his long-term depression? We cannot be sure, but the evidence of his life suggests that he did not merely allow himself to be overwhelmed by "the bondage of fear" and "the moods of God". First he tried to shape for himself what is described in chapter three as "an alternative pastoral role, a way in which he might salvage something of his parents' unfulfillable dreams of the priesthood." When that failed, and failed to provide "the quiet seclusion" he imagined, he found solace—and, he hoped, a path out of the darkness—in the Bible and in a literature of consolation that embraced Boehme and Bunyan, Schopenhauer and Shelley, Wesley and Wordsworth. In 1936 he recalled tentatively: "I think it was a passage in Montaigne which finally turned my thoughts and habits to a life of contemplation."² In fact, manuscript evidence suggests that it was Hazlitt's essay "On Living to One-self" that was crucial in showing him the way to what he calls in *Fables* "the divine joy of philosophic meditation" and to finding a home in a landscape comfortably reminiscent of Bunyan's "delectable mountains". But even in that long period of elected silence after he stopped writing, his voice can still be heard from time to time, however indirectly. Such is the case when we encounter the sentence carefully underlined in his copy of George Fox's *Journal*: "I am become nothing in the world."

1 Elwin, *The Life of Llewelyn Powys*, p. 50   2 Riley, *Bibliography*, p. 63

I

The One Powys

There are a number of English families of the Victorian era whose collective literary and artistic success has made them legendary—among them the Brontës, the Huxleys, the Garnetts, the Stephens, and the Stracheys. In this distinguished company belongs the Powys family whose accomplishments within a single generation may be quite without parallel. Given their status as children of a Church of England clergyman of evangelical bent and their strong identification with a particular region of England, the Brontës would seem to afford the closest parallel, as R. H. Ward observed in *The Powys Brothers* (1935).[1] There are a few other intriguing points of contact between these Anglo-Celtic families—love of Nature and the inspiration of Bewick's *Birds*, a predictable clannishness, the loss of family members to tuberculosis, a strain of melancholy in one of the siblings associated with a fondness for William Cowper—but nothing that demands detailed scrutiny. Indeed, R. C. Churchill points out that "the clerical and Evangelical inheritance . . . worked in a contrary direction in the Powys brothers to that which it took in the Brontës."[2] Here he is alluding to an important characteristic—the range of heterodox beliefs embraced by the brothers, from John's firm repudiation of conventional Christianity in favour of a vague animism to Llewelyn's hedonistic atheism. The bedrock beliefs of Theodore (henceforth TFP) are harder to identify precisely. After some years of intensive study of the Bible (see

---

1 "These three brothers, John Cowper Powys, T. F. Powys, and Llewelyn Powys, together form a trinity no less interesting and remarkable than those three over-worked ladies, of whom we have lately heard so much, Charlotte, Emily and Anne Brontë, and their achievements are no less admirable." (*The Powys Brothers*, p. x)

2 Churchill, *The Powys Brothers*, p. 8

further chapter three), he proclaimed enigmatically: "I am without a belief;—a belief is too easy a road to God."[1] Nonetheless, he often attended his local church (though not always on a Sunday) and may have shared Walter Pater's view that the Ceremony is the important thing in Religion.[2] In "Some Memories of T. F. Powys", an essay written some years after his death, Louis Wilkinson called him "a born mystic . . . with his own heterodox mysticism".[3] It was also Wilkinson who referred jocularly to "the one Powys and the many" in *Welsh Ambassadors*, his early and important study of the family.

There were eleven children in the family of the Reverend Charles Francis Powys (1843–1923), the long-serving Vicar of Montacute, Somerset, but it was the three oldest—John (1872–1963), Theodore (1875–1953), and Llewelyn (1884–1939)—who made the biggest splash in the pool of life. In their time they published more than one hundred books of poetry, fiction, essays, biography, and autobiography, and earned no little fame on both sides of the Atlantic. Theodore Dreiser was a good friend of John and an admirer of his work, as was Henry Miller, who said "He was like an oracle to me."[4] Llewelyn's early essays in *Ebony and Ivory* (1923), *Black Laughter* (1924), and *Skin For Skin* (1925) provoked Stuart Sherman, in a *New York Herald-Tribune* review, to include him in the company of Charles Doughty, D. H. Lawrence, and R. L. Stevenson as a travel writer;[5] and TFP's work, especially *Mr Weston's Good Wine* (1927) and *Fables* (1929), won admirers as diverse as Clarence Darrow, Havelock Ellis, William Empson, F. R. Leavis, Augustus John, Arthur Waley, and Edward Sackville-West.[6]

In a lecture at Swansea, later incorporated into *Still the Joy of It*, Littleton Powys says of his family's history that "the genealogical table goes definitely back to the fifteenth century, to one William Powys of Ludlow."[7] He properly dismisses as fantasy the claim that the family could trace its descent through the Princes of

---

1 *The Soliloquy of a Hermit*, p. 1
2 His brother John certainly endorsed this view. See *Visions and Revisions*, p. 15.
3 *Theodore*, p. 11
4 Henry Miller, "John Cowper Powys: A Living Book", p. 190
5 Cited Elwin, *The Life of Llewelyn Powys*, p. 179
6 John Cowper Powys, for example, recalls that when he was living in Patchin Place, New York, Darrow asked him to read—not from his own work—but from TFP's *Mr Weston's Good Wine*. (*Autobiography* p. 536)
7 *Still the Joy of It*, p. 140

Powys all the way back to Rodri Mawr, King of Wales. Nonetheless, there were aristocratic, and not so distant, relations in the Powys family. One branch of the Powys family initially migrated to Shropshire and then to Northamptonshire, where Sir Thomas Powys, a judge, bought the manor of Lilford in 1711. His descendant, another Thomas Powys (1719–67), fathered two sons. One of them, Thomas Powys (1743–1800), became a Member of Parliament, and was made first Lord Lilford in 1797 by William Pitt; the other, Littleton Powys (1748–1825), was the first of many clergymen in the family and became Rector of Titchmarsh in his native Northamptonshire, a parish located to the south of the Jacobean family home, Lilford Hall. Lilford Hall was used as a hospital during the Second World War by U.S. 303rd Bomber Command despite the opposition of the fifth Lord Lilford whose quarters were latterly confined to one wing of the building. He reportedly said that he would "just as soon have a Nazi bomb hit the castle as seventy-five American Army nurses;" but he died in 1945 and the estate was sold to pay off death duties.[1]

The Powyses were also connected by marriage to the important Shirley family of Derbyshire that traces its lineage back to the twelfth century. A notable member of the family was Sir Hugh Shirley, celebrated by Shakespeare as one of the knights who helped shield King Henry IV by donning identical armour and getting slain at the Battle of Shrewsbury.[2] It was certainly the family connection to the Shirleys that persuaded the Reverend Charles Francis Powys to accept the living in Shirley, Derbyshire, so far from his father's parish and his own home, in Stalbridge, Dorset. No doubt too it was family pride in such connections that prompted Charles to keep a copy of Burke's Peerage in his study. The inclusion in that tome of reference to the much-vaunted descent of the Powys family from the "ancient Welsh princes of Powys" allowed him to share this story with his offspring. Yet there was nothing in the Powys ancestry that would explain the upsurge of creative talent so abundantly evident in the Reverend C. F. Powys's offspring. Malcolm Elwin ventures to summarize the gifts to posterity of this lineage as "love of the soil, loyalty to principle and affection, profound personal pride capable of unworldliness amounting to quixotry, and tenacity and strength of will enabling assertion of personality."[3] We can accept this bold

---

1 www.303rdbga.com/sp-hospital.html   2 See Joe Johnson, *Shirley Village*.
3 Elwin, *The Life of Llewelyn Powys*, p. 7

characterization, albeit with reservations about its evidential basis, because it accords rather well with what we know of the collective lives of the generation under scrutiny. But it is in particular the strain of "unworldliness" that seems most marked in C. F. Powys and in some members of the family, especially in John and in Theodore.

Their paternal grandfather, Littleton Charles Powys (1790–1872) was born in Titchmarsh, Northamptonshire where his father, the Reverend Littleton Powys (1748–1825), a graduate of Emmanuel College, Cambridge, had been Rector until 1805. Littleton Charles Powys went to school at Winchester, entered Corpus Christi College Cambridge in 1809, and held a fellowship there from 1814 until 1837 until resigning, as required, to marry "the beautiful Mrs Knight". According to JCP, his grandfather (whom he never met), as Bursar of Corpus, was in a position to give himself "the richest Living the College held"—i.e. Stalbridge.[1] When he became Rector, he hired three servants[2] and invited John Patteson, also a Corpus alumnus, to join him as curate. St Mary's Church had just been enlarged by some 200 sittings through the addition of galleries and yet the new Rector completely filled the church at three services every Sunday.[3] Patteson, by all accounts, flourished in Stalbridge too, and acted swiftly, even heroically, when a fire broke out in the church on 22 February 1840, destroying the organ. Amelia Powys wrote in her diary at the time: "Fire put out by 2 o'clock in the morning by [Patteson's] great exertions."[4] Patteson remained in the parish until 1844. Despite the evidence of Littleton Charles Powys's astuteness in securing for himself both a rich living and a rich wife, Llewelyn believed that his grandfather had both "an extremely simple nature" and "a deeply religious mind" on the evidence of some of his grandfather's "intimate scripts".[5] Llewelyn, the author of *A Pagan's Pilgrimage* (1931) and *Now that the Gods are Dead* (1932) sounds nostalgic about, even envious of, the "unquestioning Faith" on display. We are granted precious glimpses of Littleton Charles Powys's idyllic life: taking the country air in his carriage; carrying a purse full of half-crowns lest he met a needy villager; visiting Queen Victoria at Buckingham House; composing his

---

[1] JCP to Louis Wilkinson, 16 August 1955; Letters of John Cowper Powys to Louis Wilkinson, p. 320
[2] 1861 census [3] Jones, *The Stalbridge Inheritance*, p. 97 [4] *PSN* 25, p. 37
[5] "Stalbridge Rectory", pp. 373–4

weekly sermons while standing at his tall study desk. His wife, Amelia, some twelve years younger, was from an Anglo-Swiss family, the Moilliets.[1] Her father, Jean-Louis Moilliet, a banker originally from Geneva, but with a business in Birmingham, had anglicized his name to John Lewis Moilliet, probably around 1837 when he bought the historic Abbey Manor, Worcestershire, and had it rebuilt in the fashionable and grandiose Italianate style.[2] After Moilliet's death in 1845, his widow, Amelia (née Keir) lived there until 1861 when it passed to her son James as Abberley Hall.[3] The younger Amelia's first husband, Samuel Knight of Milton Hall, Cambridgeshire, had died in 1829 and in 1838 she married the Reverend Littleton Charles Powys who was already forty-seven years old. She brought both a considerable fortune and a daughter, Philippa or "Pippa", to this second marriage. By then she seems to have made her home at nearby Impington Hall, some three miles from Cambridge. Milton Hall was the seat of the Knight family—in All Saints Church, Milton, there is a monument by Chantrey to "Mr Samuel Knight, d. 1829".[4] Although Impington Hall had long been in the Pepys family, the two families were united when Samuel Knight, D.D. (1675-1746) married Hannah, the daughter of Talbot Pepys of Impington. Their only son, Samuel, who would become a fellow of Trinity College, Cambridge, used his considerable inheritance to buy Milton Hall and its estate. It must be this Samuel Knight, when Rector of Milton, whom William Cole (writing in 1769) describes as a "furious madman" whose parish registers were "very often ill kept". Here too may be concrete evidence for what is characterized as "a strain of masochism" in one branch of the Powys family.[5]

It was from their mother's side of the family that the brothers seem to have acquired their literary talent; for Mary Cowper Powys, née Johnson (1849-1914) came from an East Anglian family that claimed two poets, John Donne and William Cowper, among its forebears. The Donne connection is somewhat tenuous, it is true, and rests largely on heraldic evidence. Stephen Powys Marks offers the cautious opinion that the relationship "seems most likely but has not been proved."[6] Mary was the fifth child of

1 *Swiss Essays*, Ch. 6   2 There is a photograph of Abberley Hall in *Swiss Essays*.
3 Belinda Humfrey gives the date as 1857 in the family tree included in *Recollections of the Powys Brothers*, p. 275.
4 See *Kelly's Directory of Cambridgeshire*, 1929.
5 Letter from to JCP to Trevor Moilliet, 29 January 1957; HRHRC   6 *PJ* 13, p. 12

the Reverend William Cowper Johnson (1813-1893), Rector of Yaxham from 1843 until 1880. It was his father who took care of the poet William Cowper, a second cousin, in his declining years and who was affectionately dubbed "Johnny [Johnson] of Norfolk" by the poet. Such was his pride in the family connection with the poet that the father commissioned a large portrait of Cowper by Lemuel Abbott (1760–1802) in 1792—a portrait that "dominated the dining-room at Yaxham [Rectory] for three generations."[1] It had been incorporated into a specially made double frame, the second section of which traced the family pedigree all the way back to Thomas Mowbray, the Duke of Norfolk of Shakespeare's *Richard II*. William Cowper Johnson was given his middle name to honour this proud connection to the poet, thereby initiating a practice that would be carried forward into the Powys family. William Cowper Johnson's academic history parallels that of many of the Powyses, his future relatives by marriage. After attending Sherborne between 1827 and 1833, he went up to Corpus Christi College Cambridge, which was, until 1906, essentially "a seminary for the production of clergymen" according to the College's own history. The religious views of William Cowper Johnson's brother, the Reverend John Barham Johnson, became increasingly Low Church so that his daughter, Emily, wrote to her cousin Cowper (whom she would eventually marry): "Papa gets lower and lower every day, it all comes of reading the [*Church*] *Times*. I should not be surprised if he gave up the surplice altogether."[2] William Cowper Johnson shared these low-church views and clearly passed them on to the pupils he was preparing for study at Corpus, among them his future son-in-law. His equally committed wife, Marianne, was so anxious about her eldest daughter's exposure to High Church practices that she urged her not to go to St Margaret's church, Welbeck St, while in London.[3] When Mary's mother, Marianne Patteson, married, she could not have foreseen the consequences for her daughter; but, as Stephen Powys Marks points out, "It is through the medium of the friendship of Marianne's brother John with William Cowper Johnson and his curacy under the Revd Littleton Charles Powys [Mary's grandfather] at Stalbridge that ultimately Mary Cowper Johnson met the Revd Charles Francis Powys."[4]

1 *PR* 8, p. 61   2 Letter in Mary Barham Johnson Collection   3 *PR* 8, p. 60
4 *PJ* 13, p. 16

Mary seems to have been a rather diffident young woman with a serious interest in the life of the mind. When she was nineteen she was invited to stay with her relatives, the [Rev. Henry] Vaughan Johnsons, in London. As the daughter of the 1st Lord Campbell and former Lord Chancellor, her Aunt "Cecie" (Cecilia) was well-connected; so the family could afford to live in a style somewhat beyond that of the average Anglican clergyman's family. Thus Mary got to spend some three months (1868–9) in fashionable Curzon Street as well as in the family's country retreat in Esher, Surrey. They arranged for her to take drawing and painting lessons from a Mr Pileau in Woburn Square and to attend lectures at the Royal Institution three times a week. She also visited the House of Commons with her Aunt Cecie, and took trips with groups of young people including her cousin Hamilton —to the British Museum to see the Elgin Marbles and to popular concerts every Monday. "Nothing opens your eyes more than going to London, you see and hear so much that is new," she wrote to her brother, Cowper.[1] Her father wrote to her brother too, then on an extended tour of India, China and Russia, that she was enjoying her lessons, "but as usual is full of modest fears lest she should disappoint."[2] Mary was an avid reader who benefited for a time from access to her father's library (Virginia Woolf's free run of Leslie Stephen's library was by no means unique)—at least until he thought better of this privilege, because of the possibility of her stumbling across something unsuitable. In another letter to Cowper she enthused over Victor Hugo's *Toilers of the Sea*, which she read in French: "the language & the whole imagination & descriptions are so graphic and reading it in the original it seems more strong."[3] But Mary was not in London simply to advance her education and her social skills. Her parents were worried about her health, given her susceptibility to coughs and colds, especially since the death from TB of her older sister, Eleanor, in 1864 at the age of seventeen. So her father arranged for a course of treatment under a Dr Bell whom he also consulted about his own health. For Mary, the treatments seem to have consisted primarily of spinal "rubbings," to which her Aunt Cecie also alludes in a letter: "I believe she submits now to rubbings and feedings and

---

[1] *PSN* 24, p. 6
[2] William Cowper Johnson to Cowper Johnson, 25 February 1869; Mary Barham Johnson Collection
[3] Letter in Mary Barham Johnson Collection

resting and drinking."[1] She first encountered C. F. Powys when he arrived as a pupil under her father, probably in 1859, to prepare for admission to Corpus Christi College, Cambridge in 1862. Later she recalled that "I was 13 years old when he was a boy & my father's pupil for 3 years [at Yaxham]"—a somewhat puzzling statement since she would have turned thirteen on 11 September 1862, just before C. F. Powys went up to Cambridge.[2]

Charles Francis Powys was born in his father's parish, Stalbridge, and was called Charley by family members.[3] He seems to have been a distinctly late bloomer educationally, evidencing what we now recognize as neuro-motor developmental delays perhaps including dyslexia. These problems would explain why he did not follow his elder brother, Littleton, to Sherborne, and even his need for tutoring before going up to Cambridge. Most revealing are the cryptic comments of his mother, Amelia, in her diary or notebook behind which we may discern considerable anxiety: "Charley at 3 years old, does not speak plain" and "Charley at four years old cannot speak plain, knows his letters—can repeat a few little hymns."[4] Indeed, JCP asserts that "as a family we were all extremely slow in mental development."[5] Littleton, always a little more discreet about family affairs, nonetheless concedes that both Llewelyn and Willie, the youngest son, were "backward in learning when at school".[6] He is also the original source of the information that their father was first schooled in Mappowder, Dorset (destined to be the final home of his son, TFP) and later in Kenilworth.[7] The most likely scenario is that L. C. Powys would have sent his son to be tutored by a clergyman who took in pupils and came recommended by clerical acquaintances. Confirmation of this is found in Theodora Scutt's memoir: "He had often told me that his father had been tutored by the then Vicar of Mappowder."[8] In fact, by 1851 there was a small Free School in Mappowder, started jointly by the Earl of Beauchamp and the Rector (not Vicar), the Reverend John Henry Thomas Allen, M.A., a graduate of Brasenose College, Oxford, and supported financially by the two of them.[9] There was also a curate, the Reverend Henry Weare, M.A., and a resident school-

1 *PR* 8, p. 59   2 Letter in Mary Barham Johnson Collection
3 In Littleton Albert Powys's last letter of 20 July 1879 to his mother from the Northwest Frontier, he sent "love to Charley". See *PSN* 45.
4 *PSN* 25, pp. 40–1   5 *Autobiography*, p. 24
6 *Still the Joy of It*, p. 155   7 Ibid., p.143   8 *Cuckoo in the Powys Nest*, p. 91
9 Details from 1851 Census and 1859 Post Office Directory

mistress, Lydia Allice White.¹ C. F. Powys would probably have been Allen's pupil in Mappowder, though not attending the school, from about 1852 when he was nine. His name would not have appeared on census records since the groom from Stalbridge Rectory took him by gig each time. Though there are few surviving accounts of Charley Powys's childhood, it is striking how vivid his memory remained among his sons and how often they made reference to him. Llewelyn records the fact that his father "used to go [to Abberley Hall] for holidays"² and managed to secure tantalising glimpses of his father's boyhood from Henry Habershon, self-appointed local historian of Stalbridge, in an essay entitled "Stalbridge Rectory", that was first published in *The London Mercury* in 1935. It might just as well have been called "In Search of My Father". Habershon recalled:

> The first time I can remember seeing the two young gentlemen [Littleton and Charley] was when I was a small lad going past the old cross, I looked up Gold Street and I saw a large donkey with panniers on its back and one young gentleman in each and a man in charge, Sam Shepherd, who was living then in one of the Powys cottages on the top of Gold Street, known as the Knapp in those days.³

From the same source came the story of how Littleton and Charley were seen one winter's day on the Sherborne Road "beating the snow off the high hedges with their sticks."⁴ But it was Amelia Powys who reminisced about "little Charley's favourite oak tree" on the road to Marnhull, the earliest example of Powysian love for nature in general and for identifying a specially favoured tree, a kind of totem. John retained vivid memories of his father too. He is reminded of his father's habit of scooping up fresh water from a stream or lake during a fishing trip when they saw Lord Lilford, that is Thomas Littleton Powys (1833–96), fourth Baron Lilford;⁵ of his father's collection of birds' eggs—"he had a huge diningtable drawer-full of eggs;"⁶ and even of his father's turns of phrase which struck John as somehow distinctive: "out of commission", "taken aback", and "bowing & scraping".⁷

1 1859 Post Office Directory, p. 28   2 *Swiss Essays*, p. 36
3 "Stalbridge Rectory", p. 373   4 *Ibid.*, p. 372
5 JCP to Louis Wilkinson, 4 October and 2 May 1956; Letters of John Cowper Powys to Louis Wilkinson, pp. 377 and 353
6 JCP to Louis Wilkinson, 27 January 1953, *Ibid.*, p. 297
7 *Autobiography*, pp. 220 and 265; JCP to Louis Wilkinson, 7 February 1953, Letters, p. 299

After his three years with William Cowper Johnson, C. F. Powys must have been well enough prepared in Mathematics and Theology for admission to Corpus. But it is hardly surprising to learn that, at Cambridge, he followed many of his contemporaries in giving more attention to physical exercise—in his case boxing, rowing and walking—than to serious study.[1] As his son Littleton later observed: "No one could call him a man of letters."[2] Of course, it must be remembered that this was the heyday of that "muscular Christianity" associated with the Evangelical wing of the Church of England—the term was first used in a review of Charles Kingsley's novel *Two Years Ago* (1857) and later applied to *Tom Brown's Schooldays* by his friend Thomas Hughes—and C. F. Powys "had been brought up in the Evangelical School."[3] Many years later, JCP was even more specific and relates that his father was "definitely Evangelical and what when I was young used to be called 'Low Church'".[4] However, he was diligent enough to graduate in 1866, as eighth Senior Optime, with a respectable second-class degree in the Tripos[5]—still something of a disappointment to his father who had been a Wrangler, the cream of the crop.

He declined the opportunity to become a schoolmaster, despite the tempting offer of a position at Repton, a school in Derbyshire of some distinction, and opted instead to take holy orders. Many years later,[6] JCP claims that his father also turned down the offer of "a Mastership at Radley" before he went to Shirley, but JCP's memory may be faulty here, influenced by the coincidence of the same initial letter in both names and by the fact that Louis Wilkinson attended Radley. He was duly ordained in 1867[7] by the Bishop of Salisbury, and quickly found a post as officiating curate in Bradford Abbas, a village close to the Somerset border and just a few miles from Sherborne.

The church of St Mary the Virgin is an attractive building in the Perpendicular style dating from the fifteenth century, though the earliest records go back to the twelfth century.[8] C. F. Powys went straight to work. The baptismal register shows the newly ordained curate officiating for the first time in his new parish on 7 April 1867, baptizing John William, son of Elizabeth and Simeon Pavitt,

1 *Still the Joy of It*, p. 144   2 *Ibid.*, p. 145   3 *Ibid.*
4 *Aylesford Review*, Spring 1963, p. 82   5 *PSN* 25, p. 41
6 JCP to Louis Wilkinson, 28 September 1955; Letters of John Cowper Powys to Louis Wilkinson, p. 328
7 *Still the Joy of It*, p. 145   8 Garrett, *Bradford Abbas*, p. 56

baker, and burying John Clarke of Clifton Maybank. He presided over his first marriage, between Thomas Marchant and Elizabeth Stephens, on 24 April 1867. He was the fourth in a series of curates of the Reverend Robert Grant, the long serving (1825–86) but aging —and non-resident—Vicar, succeeding the Reverend Charles Neil. The Vicar had initiated such appointments in 1857 with the selection of his son, the Reverend Edward Pierce Grant, and subsequently "less was seen of him in the village than in the early years of his incumbency."[1] While serving in Bradford Abbas, C. F. Powys returned to Cambridge for the award of his M.A. in 1869, and made time to visit the Johnson family for a week. He participated fully in the life of the community—playing games of battledore, croquet, and shuttlecock and impressing his hosts with "a simple earnest gospel sermon" on Whit Sunday morning.[2] Marianne Johnson's detailed account of the occasion in a letter to her brother-in-law, Cowper, provides invaluable testimony: "His manner is solemn & devout. . . . He is grown a very strong looking man—he seemed to be so pleased with us & quite enjoyed the family party, after being so much alone in his lodgings—he has lost his shyness very much."[3]

Indeed, C. F. Powys seems to have lost his shyness sufficiently to see Mary, by then twenty, in a new light and to re-establish acquaintance with her on new terms. Perhaps there was more to his visit all along! At the time, he had been living quietly with his mother and elderly father, the Reverend Littleton Charles Powys, in Bellevin Cottage, Bradford Abbas. His father, who had retired in 1867 after thirty years as Rector of Stalbridge, was by then an eighty-year-old and "without Cure of Souls". Then in 1871, two years after his brief visit to Yaxham, C. F. Powys's feelings for Mary prompted him to write to her father seeking permission to marry her, only to learn that she was not at home—clearly an indicator that she was unaware of the impending proposal. In fact, she was staying with her aunt and uncle, the Vaughan Johnsons, in Esher, Surrey. Initially, her father wrote on 14 June 1871, asking her to return home, though without any hint of urgency save a firm "Do not stop beyond <u>Thursday</u> in next week." Impatient for a response, C. F. Powys wrote again to her father, begging him to forward the letter to Mary. In his cover letter of 19 June 1871, William Cowper Johnson revealed his position in stating that "You will be, I am sure, <u>pleased</u> to receive such a proof of the esteem of

---

1 Garrett, *Bradford Abbas*, p. 78   2 *PR* 8, p. 61   3 *PJ* 13, p. 25

a high-minded and good man" and encouraged her not to "break the poor fellow's heart" if she thought she could "love him as a wife ought to love a husband."[1] Her response to the proposal from Esher the very next day expressed surprise "that you should care for me at all" but hastened to add that "if you can trust me and really think that I will be a good wife, I will say 'yes'."[2] Thus her father was able to report on 21 June to Mary's maternal grand-mother, Mrs Patteson, that "she has most heartily accepted him" and describes him as "the best of sons and a right valuable clergyman". His account also verifies the reticence of the couple in what had hardly been a courtship: "Though neither of them gave the other any intimation of a growing regard, this same smothered fire had been lurking in the heart of both." Mary arrived home in time to receive a telegram from Bradford Abbas announcing C. F. Powys's impending visit to Yaxham on 22 June. Her own subsequent letters are brimful of enthusiasm about her intended, though she vacillates between calling him "Charley" and "Mr Powys": his love is "so strong and noble", she writes, and he is "very tall and strong". He gave her a photograph of himself and took the opportunity to share a good deal of information with his bride-to-be in a short time: he gave a vivid account of the large parish of 649 of which he had sole charge, of "the large Church Vicarage house" and "the beautiful river Yeo running through Bradford Abbas" (23 June 1871).[3] He recounted "a great deal about his Cambridge boating days, the Cups he won . . . [and] the excitement of bumping" and reassured her about moving so far from home with a promise that her sisters could come and stay. The marriage was very much a family affair and does not appear to have been particularly lavish: the couple were married in Yaxham on 4 October 1871 by Mary's father assisted by her clergyman brother and eight bridesmaids. After the ceremony, there was a Wedding Breakfast in the Parish Room and "a Village Entertainment" which allowed parishioners to partake of the celebration. William Cowper Johnson's former pupils later supplied another husband for the family when Mary's younger sister, Annie, married the Reverend Cecil Blyth.

C. F. Powys seems to have been well liked by the parishioners of Bradford Abbas; indeed, upon his marriage, he was presented with an inscribed twelve-inch silver salver in appreciation of his pastoral care. When he returned from his honeymoon with his bride, the newly-

[1] Johnson Collection   [2] *PSN* 24, p. 8   [3] Johnson Collection

weds moved into the Vicarage, and a village-wide holiday was declared. A contemporary report noted that "everybody appears to be looking at the arches, flags etc, which have been erected to welcome the return of the Rev. C. F. Powys and his bride."[1] Despite the inevitable disruptions associated with betrothal and a wedding, C. F. Powys did not neglect his pastoral duties: for example, he visited the nearby school, just beyond the south wall of the church, to hear classes read on 4 April 1871 and again on 6 July. But on 2 November, the school logbook records, "Mr Powys visited the school for the last time as curate of the parish." When C. F. Powys had written so enthusiastically to his bride-to-be about the allure of Bradford Abbas, he sounded like a man who was prepared to settle there for some time. Yet, within a short time, the lives of the young couple would be disrupted again and they would leave Dorset for the North of England—in fact, for Derbyshire. The last record of C. F. Powys performing any duties in the parish is from late October when he officiated at the baptisms of Angelina Bartlett and Bessie Parsons on 29 October 1871. A few months after they left for Shirley, C. F. Powys's eighty-year-old father died, on 11 February 1872.

C. F. Powys was appointed vicar of Shirley, Derbyshire, early in 1872, succeeding the Reverend Eardley Wilmot Mitchell who had been vicar since 1842 under the patronage of the tenth Earl Ferrers. Though Shirley was the ancient seat of the Shirley family whose ancestors had served the Crown since the twelfth century, it was a much smaller parish than Bradford Abbas, with only 281 inhabitants recorded by the 1871 Census. The living was in the gift of C. F. Powys's half-sister Philippa ("Pippa") Shirley (née Knight), whose husband, the Reverend Walter Waddington Shirley, D.D., Canon of Christ Church, Oxford and Regius Professor of Ecclesiastical History, had died young in 1866. Although the church retained traces of its fourteenth-century origins, it had been largely rebuilt in the mid-nineteenth century. The vicarage was an imposing nineteenth-century edifice, built in 1824 to the specifications of the then vicar, the Reverend W. A. Shirley, and boasted a striking Minton tiled floor and turned balusters on the staircase.[2] JCP remembers it as "as square whitish-yellow building surrounded by shrubberies and closely-mown grass"[3] with a "widely spreading

---

1 Bradford Abbas school logbook, 5 October 1871. Primary data concerning Bradford Abbas has been provided by Caryl Parsons. See also Garrett, *Bradford Abbas*, p. 78.
2 Joe Johnson, *Shirley Village*, p. 15   3 *Autobiography*, p. 4

Pirus Japonica that clambered up the front of the house";[1] there was also "some sort of summer-house in the garden."[2] Yet Shirley does not loom large in the history or the mental geography of the Powys family, despite the family connection and the fact that the first five children were born there. Mary Barham Johnson reports that when Mary Powys became pregnant for the first time "she was full of foreboding and did not expect to survive."[3] Such an attitude is hardly surprising in a young woman who had so long been treated as though she were "delicate". In fact her first child, John, was delivered without incident on 8 October 1872. Ten more children would follow in a span of eighteen years—evidence enough of a robust constitution—but child-bearing took its toll and she aged all too rapidly, as photographs show. With age, came a kind of weary resignation in the face of family troubles—surely a strategy for coping—that made her seem uncaring to some of her children.

Even in the first chapter of his *Autobiography*—ostensibly devoted to Shirley—JCP admits to "scanty memories of my Derbyshire birth-place".[4] Nonetheless, some of them are powerfully evocative. He recalls the surrounding countryside as "pastoral and undulating" and stored away the kind of details that would impress a child—a small stile, a large Scotch Fir,[5] a nearby pond,[6] "seeing the sky assume a greenish tint,"[7] and the "fleeting and fitful cuckoo flower".[8] He remembers Heber Dale, the postman, perhaps only because he was "a hydrocephalic dwarf", Stephen the gardener[9] and his father's tall dog-cart, but professes no memory at all of "the little grey church [St Michael's] in the midst of the village".[10] He mentions too a visit by his Uncle Littleton, "a dignified bearded man, with a square forehead"—probably in early 1878—whose beard he was invited to pummel.[11] At least one of JCP's "scanty recollections" (a phrase he uses twice) is also in error: his father was not succeeded as vicar by "Mr Linton, a nephew of his by marriage, who was a scientific botanist",[12] but by the Reverend Frederick Corfield who died in 1883. It was Corfield who was followed by the Reverend William Richardson Linton in 1886 or 1887—another alumnus of Corpus Christi College Cambridge.[13] Contact with the Shirley family was maintained over the years.

---

1 *Autobiography*, p. 30   2 *Ibid.*, p. 11   3 *PR* 8, p. 62   4 *Autobiography*, p. 14
5 *Ibid.*, p. 3   6 *Ibid.*, p. 14   7 *Ibid.*, p. 30   8 *Ibid.*   9 *Ibid.*, p. 11
10 *Ibid.*, p. 4   11 *Ibid.*, p. 11   12 *Ibid.*, p. 16
13 Sources disagree on the date. See *Shirley Village*, pp. 27–8 and *Kelly's Directory of the Counties of Derby, Notts, Leicester and Rutland*, 1891, p. 300.

JCP had high praise for his cousin Alice as a teacher and remembered with special fondness being taken by her to visit Frau Foster Nietzsche in Weimar where he was able to view Nietzsche's book shelves; Gertrude paid at least one visit to her relatives in Derbyshire. JCP, TFP, and LlP all had regular contact with their cousin, Ralph Shirley, later editor of *The Occult Review* and principal partner in William Rider & Son, a publisher that specialized in books on such subjects as the Kabala, Masonry, the Rosicrucians, shamanism, tarot cards, and other aspects of the occult. It was, in fact, these family ties—and some funding from C. F. Powys—that led Rider to publish JCP's first two books, *Odes and Other Poems* (1896) and *Poems* (1899). Poetry was hardly the focus of their list. JCP admits as much when he refers dismissively in his autobiography to "those two little booklets of copy-cat verse that Cousin Ralph published in London".[1] In time, books by all three brothers would be reviewed in *The Occult Review*—among them TFP's *Soliloquy of a Hermit* (1916) and John's *Wolf's Bane* (1916), both by Arthur Edward Waite, a founding member of the Order of the Golden Dawn and author of, among other books, *The Secret Doctrine in Israel: a Study of the Zohar and its Connections* (William Rider & Son, Ltd., 1913). Aleister Crowley and W. B. Yeats were also prominent members of The Order. John, always sensitive to family characteristics, real or imagined, detected something in common between Ralph Shirley and his brother: "there has always been observed by me in him something like Theodore, also of the *formidable* kind. I would love to know exactly what this is & how Theodore & he get it from their common Moilliet (Swiss from an Italian origin) blood."[3]

The Reverend Charles Francis Powys appeared to his children as a tall, energetic, and somewhat remote figure in "black trousers and grey flannel shirt-sleeves."[3] John detected in his father "enormous emotional and magnetic explosiveness" allied with an ability to hold his emotions "rigidly under an almost military control".[4] While he never resorted to physical violence ("that boxing of our ears") after they left Shirley, the threat of some verbal outburst was omnipresent. "In a thousand little things

1 *Autobiography*, p. 581
2 JCP to Louis Wilkinson, 17 May 1946; Letters of John Cowper Powys to Louis Wilkinson, p. 206
3 *Autobiography*, p. 3   4 *Ibid.*, p. 4

which touched his life he was liable to burst out with an intensity of emotion that was terrifying,"[1] John recalled. Only when he was an adult did John dare to tease his father by pretending to wax enthusiastic about the notorious Annie Besant. Predictably, his father, "trembling with fury", exclaimed: "She is a Demon . . . John . . . a Demon! *The woman is a Demon.*"[2] C. F. Powys's predilection for physical activity can thus be viewed as therapeutic— anger and frustration calculatedly or instinctively dissipated in long vigorous country walks. At the same time, his enthusiasms seem to have been equally intense, and John resorts once again to the language of eruption: "He was a man who derived . . . thrilling pleasure —a deep, massive, volcanic pleasure—from little natural things" such as a rare bird, butterfly, or flower,[3] Kimmeridge Clay or Purbeck Marble.[4] He was also unashamedly opinionated: anything "old-fashioned" was deemed praiseworthy while anything "newfangled" merited only reprobation. Llewelyn suggests that by these standards Thomas Hardy, of all people, was found wanting. The occasion was Hardy's impending visit to Montacute: "My father had not read a word he had ever written, but he had heard rumours enough of the freedom of his thought to qualify his enthusiasm for this new hero that his eldest son [John] had discovered."[5]

Richard Perceval Graves interprets John's account of his father's Spartan diet simply as evidence of "his efforts to be a good Christian"[6]: C. F. Powys "ate only the smallest quantities of fish and meat," abstained from alcohol "except as a priest at the altar", and subsisted largely upon bread and butter. Some such piety may well have influenced the behaviour of this devout clergyman, although John also recalls his father bringing out a bottle of sherry from the sideboard when the Bishop of Bath & Wells came to lunch.[7] But there is another, more mundane, reason for his general abstemiousness: he almost certainly suffered from an ulcer. Alyse Gregory, detailing the death of her husband, Llewelyn Powys, notes that "four of his brothers had had ulcers of the stomach;"[8] and Bertie died in 1936 after the kind of stomach hemorrhage—"the family stomach trouble" as Graves labels it— that eventually killed Llewelyn in 1939. Thus one facet of the

1 *Autobiography*, p. 16 2 *Ibid.*, p. 50 3 *Ibid.*, p. 14 4 *Ibid.*, p. 51
5 *Wessex Memories*, p. 63 6 *The Brothers Powys* , p. 3
7 JCP to Louis Wilkinson, 14 April 1946; Letters of John Cowper Powys to Louis Wilkinson, p. 201
8 Introduction to The Letters of Llewelyn Powys, p. 37

Powys brothers' genetic inheritance from their father was this predisposition for gastro-intestinal disorders. John's case was perhaps the most extreme—he had his first operation for ulcers in 1907 and subsisted for long periods on a very restricted diet.

    C. F. Powys's study was a kind of fortress against the world and the family, a sanctuary to which he would retreat almost daily. On his desk lay a quill pen and a stick of red sealing wax for letters and parcels. Apart from his books—most precious of which were his two-volume set of Bewick's *History of British Birds* and his massive Greek dictionary—the study contained a curious assortment of mementos and trophies: the ceremonial sword of his dead brother Littleton; two silver cups won at Cambridge for rowing and walking; an extensive collection of birds' eggs begun as a schoolboy; and, most bizarrely, an elephant's foot. To enter this sanctuary, his children were expected to knock on the door. Only through his deeply felt love of nature does C. F. Powys seem to have been able to communicate his genuine love for them, as they grew up and shared frequent long walks in the countryside. The strategy worked and all of them became enthusiastic amateur naturalists, knowledgeable about and responsive to the natural world in ways that are reflected in their fiction and their letters. More than thirty years after his father's death, John still recalled how much he liked "to walk with father & know birds and butterflies and wild flowers."[1] He was not without imagination: sometimes, in a more relaxed mood after tea, he would share "an interminable story about two mythic personages called Giant Grumble and Fairy Sprightly."[2] More rarely, he would read—John remembered in particular a reading of "The Passage of the Rhine" from that Victorian bestseller, Aytoun's *Lays of the Scottish Cavaliers* (1849). There were other occasions when this Victorian *paterfamilias* would unbend a little—he still enjoyed showing his athletic prowess by rowing at the seaside and he liked to ride the ferry at Weymouth during the annual Montacute Church Choir outing.

    C. F. Powys's speech retained a few West Country words and inflections,[2] that betrayed a fierce loyalty to his home county—John[3] cites the pronunciation "goss" for "gorze" (that is "gorse"); and so it was that, from casual hints, his children were made to understand *"the absolute inferiority... of* Derbyshire ways,

---

1 JCP to Louis Wilkinson, 15 November 1956; Letters of John Cowper Powys to Louis Wilkinson, p. 387
2 *Autobiography*, p. 4   2 Ibid.   3 Ibid., p. 52

scenery, people, customs, dialect, flora and fauna, to those of his native Wessex."[1] Littleton's memory of his father is typically more upbeat than John's; he insists that "we knew exactly where we were with him. He was the most honest and simple-minded man I have ever known."[2] By the time he wrote this, Littleton sounded and behaved rather like his father in many ways. But simplicity, with all it overtones of restraint, even sanctity, is the characteristic most often associated with C. F. Powys and it would later re-emerge most notably in TFP. John was almost in awe of his father's "astounding and disconcerting simplicity". Louis Wilkinson's observation about his speech is telling too: "the father rarely used words of more than three syllables, and he preferred those of one or two. He did not know many others, nor did he wish to know them. Any language but the simplest was to him an object of suspicion and contempt."[3]

Inevitably Mary Powys had to sacrifice her own intellectual and artistic interests for those of the family—her husband had no interest in music and soon even her beloved painting was set aside. The change is reflected in her commonplace book—laundry lists replaced quotations from books she had read and notes from her art classes.[4] With the advent of three children in four years—she "dreaded each birth"—there was simply no time for such self-indulgence, even granting the presence of the family nurse, Emily Clare. However, she maintained a subscription to Mudie's Library and took pleasure in reading aloud to the family in the evening while her husband reclined on the drawing-room sofa. Walter Scott was a perennial favourite as was the case in many Victorian families, among them those of Sylvia Townsend Warner and Virginia Woolf. Later she would listen while her children read to her. When his spirits were low in later life, Llewelyn liked to recall his mother reading *Tom Jones* to him;[5] and for John, the fondest memories of his mother were associated with being able "to sit by Mother and appreciate Poetry and Literature and how to read & recite."[6] C. F. Powys, of course, led the family and servants in "brief and simple" prayers[7] and daily Bible-reading before

---

1 *Autobiography*, pp. 31–2   2 *Still the Joy of It*, p. 143   3 *Welsh Ambassadors*, p. 5
4 *The Life of Llewelyn Powys*, p. 9
5 LlP to JCP, 7 November 1915; Letters of Llewelyn Powys, p. 80
6 JCP to Louis Wilkinson, 15 Nov 1956; Letters of John Cowper Powys to Louis Wilkinson, p. 387   7 *Welsh Ambassadors*, p. 3

breakfast, sometimes, of necessity, by candle light. Once in a while, in lighter moods, he would send one of the children to fetch the two-volume edition of Bewick from his study for consultation.[1]

Despite the family connection, Shirley must have suffered by comparison with Bradford Abbas, especially after the allure of new people and places had faded. Family came to visit—Mary's cousin Emily in 1873, her sister Dora for some months from late 1874 until January 1875, and her father in spring 1875. Yet as early as 1874, C. F. Powys was growing restless, and evinced some interest in moving back to the West Country, experiencing what his father-in-law diplomatically termed "a phaze [sic] of unsettlement". Specifically, he expressed a desire to become a curate under the new incumbent in his father's former parish of Stalbridge. William Cowper Johnson was horrified: "all very well for a single man to run about the church so—but a serious thing for a married man with two child[re]n, and no very long purse. Besides it is a serious matter to leave a parish of which you have become Rector or Vicar . . . and Derbyshire air suits him & his wife & chil[dre]n so well."[2] C. F. Powys never seems to have betrayed his private discontent and he was certainly not shirking his duties. Indeed, he was working hard and had taken on many extra obligations—he ran an evening school, conducted Home Mission services, and in one ill-fated week in November 1874 buried "two bright happy boys", victims of diphtheria. By the beginning of 1879, however, C. F. Powys seems to have quite tired of his posting in remote Derbyshire. He was also becoming increasingly concerned about the health of Amelia, his widowed mother, and the distance between them—she had retired to Weymouth—especially since his elder brother, Littleton Albert Powys, a Major in H.M. 59th Regiment, stationed in Kandahar, Afghanistan, was not even in the country. JCP recalls a visit which took place while the family was still in Shirley—probably in early 1878. TFP's single "memory" of his "rich bearded uncle from India", serves only to document the way in which family awareness of this exotic relative triggered an imaginative response in him—a muddled recollection of an idyllic walk "over the soft

---

1 JCP to Louis Wilkinson, 28 December 1955; Letters of John Cowper Powys to Louis Wilkinson, p. 340

2 William Cowper Johnson to Cowper [son], 11 July 1874; information and quotations from Johnson Collection

turf of the Wessex downs" that could never have occurred.[3] TFP's account, which includes visiting a "famous castle", is demonstrably wrong, since he was only two and a half at the time and his uncle visited Shirley not Montacute.[2]

Littleton and Charley had been close as children, according to their mother's diary,[3] and kept in touch with one another despite their very different careers. Yet whenever he mentioned his brother, it was "with a respect in which awe seemed to swallow up familiarity".[4] Extant correspondence shows that C. F. Powys informed his elder brother about his plans to make what would, in ordinary circumstances, have seemed a very curious career move: he had agreed (when he wrote to Littleton) to move to St Peter's Church, Dorchester, as a curate. Even John later recognized that taking "the subordinate position of a small-town curate" was "a rather unworldly move in a young priest's life"[5] and attributed it to his brother's death. Malcolm Elwin interprets the move as evidence of C. F. Powys's "preference for duty and natural affection and a contempt for worldly considerations"[6] and these were undoubtedly aspects of his character. But the evidence of his abandoned plan for a Stalbridge curacy five years earlier suggests other motives too. In any case, brother Littleton expressed his approval in a reply that survives.[7] Given its occurrence after his signature and its isolation, the relevant statement—"I am glad you are going to leave Shirley" —appears to be something of an afterthought rather than an issue to which he had given much attention. It is also likely that he had heard similar plans before. The body of Littleton's letter is understandably self-absorbed, addressing the uncertainty of the situation in Kandahar but remaining relentlessly upbeat: "we are making ourselves as jolly as possible, with sports every week, & cricket & football also." "Jolly" was evidently one of his favourite words and reflects his capacity to "maken vertu of necessitee". Thus, in a later letter to his mother of 20 July 1879 he diplomatically writes as though Charley's abrupt move back to Dorset had nothing to do with *her* situation: "It will be very jolly for the holy man to be down at Dorchester."[8] In Littleton's last letter to Charley, this same bantering tone leads him to address his brother, then the Vicar of Shirley, as "Dear Bishop". Unfortunately,

---

1 *PSN* 45, p. 19   2 *PSN* 45, p. 24   3 *PSN* 25, p. 39
4 JCP, *Autobiography*, p. 20   5 *Ibid.*, p. 42
6 Letters of John Cowper Powys to his Brother Llewelyn, vol. 1, p. 10
7 Littleton Powys to C. F. Powys, 31 March 1879, HRHRC   8 HRHRC

Littleton succumbed to cholera on 6 August 1879 at the age of thirty-nine, while "doing all his power in self denial & kindness for the Sufferers" in the cholera camp.[1] He was perhaps the only person who could have brought some continued levity into the life of his otherwise sober-minded brother. His had been a full and adventurous life, much of it spent in the army. Yet it was a choice that could hardly have accorded with his father's notion of a suitable career. After all, the Reverend Littleton Charles Powys had won a double first in Classics and Mathematics at Cambridge, and had been a fellow of his college for many years (1814–37) before settling into the sedate life of an Anglican clergyman. Unfortunately, Littleton had shown little inclination for either the academic or the ecclesiastical path in life. His headmaster at Sherborne, H. D. Harper, was remarkably blunt on the subject in a letter to his father:

> I am very sorry that he has chosen the army. I am always sorry for every boy who does so, not only because it is no profession in reality but also because of the temptations into which he is so thrust. However in many points your lad is fit for a soldier and will be a straightforward brave fellow under any circumstances.[2]

In writing this letter, the headmaster may have had in mind incidents similar to the one recalled by Henry Habershon, a long-time resident of Stalbridge, who witnessed a fierce "boxing-match" between Littleton, a "mere youth" at the time and "the worst poacher in Stalbridge" behind the wall of the Rectory garden. Though he sustained considerable punishment at the hands of his opponent and was eventually knocked out, Littleton demonstrated the kind of bellicosity and "bottom" (as courage was called in the prize-ring) that suggested he was indeed "fit for a soldier". He had first sailed for India on Whitsunday, 12 June 1859 at the age of eighteen. In the span of his career, he rose to Captain and was gazetted Brevet Major in January 1879;[3] he served in India and in the Second Afghan war; he survived skirmishes and battles in which upwards of eighty men were killed or injured; and his big game exploits included an encounter with a wounded tiger in a cave. That he was not oblivious to the dangers he faced daily can be gleaned from the "Christmas text" he inserted into a letter to his mother in 1878—he wrote cryptically: "*Deuteronomy* XX. V 3–

---

1 *PSN* 25, p. 41   2 "Stalbridge Rectory", p. 373   3 *PSN* 25, p. 41

4."[1] The message of the text itself is an unambiguous affirmation of faith in God, and reads in part: "Let not your hearts faint, fear not, and do not tremble . . . . For the LORD your God is he that goeth with you, to fight for you against your enemies, to save you." In his father's Stalbridge church, a black and white marble wall plaque still honours the "affectionate memory" of this soldier whose death was "deeply regretted by officers and men"—language that echoes the inscription on his tombstone in Kandahar. On a fishing trip with his father, JCP also once visited the parish church in Achurch in Northamptonshire (which had served the community of Lilford as well since 1778) "where our Uncle Littleton has a monument".[2] So the soldier who could cite scripture and the brother who found it necessary to hold his emotions "under almost military control" seem to have been closer in temperament than their sharply different vocations might suggest.

Recognition of these temperamental affinities will help us understand some of the otherwise puzzling characteristics of C. F. Powys's offspring. JCP certainly associated his father with the world of physical activity, contrasting "the great authority on Boxing or Rowing or Walking or Running or Playing Football" with his own "book-worm world of Macaulay and Elia & Hazlitt & Laurence Sterne or Scott or Wordsworth".[3] Because of Littleton's death too, his younger brother's life would be dramatically altered—Charley / C. F. Powys became sole beneficiary of Littleton's estate, a considerable fortune of some £40,000. In future years, this windfall would be put to good use in helping his own children— TFP included—as they struggled to make their way in life.

Despite his lowly status at St Peter's in Dorchester, C. F. Powys's newfound wealth enabled him to lease a very large newly constructed property, Rothesay House, in South Walks Road, for a family that by this time numbered five children. Since the house was not yet ready for occupancy, the family went first to the seaside town of Weymouth where their paternal grandmother, Amelia Powys, "a little old lady, exquisitely dainty, with cheeks flushed like the petals of dog-roses" (as Llewelyn remembered her), lived in Penn House at the end of Brunswick Terrace.[4] For

---

1 HRHRC
2 JCP to Louis Wilkinson, 2 May 1956; *Letters of John Cowper Powys to Louis Wilkinson*, p. 363
3 JCP to Louis Wilkinson, 15 November 1956; *Ibid.*, p. 387   4 *Swiss Essays*, p. 35

John she is the "aged relative" who gave him a tiny black and gilt cedarwood cabinet.[1] The family found lodgings just behind Brunswick Terrace and soon C. F. Powys began "almost daily" eight-mile treks across the Downs to begin his parish work and to monitor progress on Rothesay House.

C. F. Powys spent some six years as curate at St Peter's under the Reverend Mr Knipe, the "elderly Rector" of the parish church, a fifteenth-century building, "improved" in the nineteenth century by J. Hicks, under whom Thomas Hardy once worked. C. F. Powys took advantage of his wealth and engaged four servants, two of whom (Emily Clare and Kate Fairbairn) were nurses for the children. Mary's sister, Ann Johnson, also lived with the family for a time. For John, this was a period in which much of the unhappiness associated with life in Shirley seems to have vanished; he learned to read and, in his peregrinations with his brothers, first encountered the mysterious prehistoric monuments that would become such an important part of his mythology. For TFP, it was also a crucial, if less happy, period: he was only three when the family moved south, but about to turn ten at the time of the move to Montacute in December 1885.[2] Littleton had, understandably, bonded with his elder brother; so TFP created for himself a place apart, an outdoor sanctuary that he dubbed "Bushes' Home", first "beneath a curious pink blossoming bush"[3] at Rothesay House and later in the evergreen shrubbery at Montacute.[4]

C. F. Powys was offered the living of Montacute, Somerset, by William Robert Phelips (1846–1919), the principal landowner in the area, and was duly installed on 5 November 1885 in a ceremony at the fifteenth-century church of St Catharine's. Phelips resided in Montacute House which was close by at the edge of the village. This edifice, a magnificent example of the late Elizabethan country house, had been in the family since it was built between 1588 and 1601 by Sir Edward Phelips, a lawyer of the Middle Temple. It became a familiar part of the childhood world of the Powys children because they were given the freedom to explore it at their leisure. William Phelips and his family were the last generation to live there. In 1931, it became possible for the Powys family to repay their debt of gratitude to Phelips for bringing them to Montacute: A. R. ("Bertie") Powys, the sixth child of

---

1 *Autobiography*, p. 43
2 Littleton says "at the beginning of 1886". (*Still the Joy of It*, p. 149)
3 *Autobiography*, p. 64   4 *Still the Joy of It*, p. 149

the former vicar, and Secretary to the Society for the Protection of Ancient Buildings, was instrumental in persuading a benefactor to buy the property and donate it to the National Trust.

Montacute Vicarage was a large early-Victorian house to which a wing had been added so that it comfortably accommodated a family with eight children, a governess (Frances Beal), a nurse (Emily Clare) and three servants, among them Annie Geard and Herbert Rogers the gardener.[1] C. F. Powys always referred to the female servants quaintly as "the maidens".[2] Climbing plants, including honeysuckle and roses, covered the walls; and there were large sash windows that let in plenty of light. All around the house there were gardens—a walled kitchen garden, extensive orchards, plant beds and thick shrubbery where the children established private domains of their own. TFP went his own solitary way while Bertie, the future architect, constructed Maberlulu Castle from a lean-to shed, for Marian, Llewelyn, and himself. Such was his nostalgia for this lost domestic paradise that Bertie could not resist enclosing a sketch of the vicarage, with stick figures playing tennis and croquet on the front lawn, in his letter home from Sherborne. Inevitably, in surroundings so idyllic, it was easy for a large family to feel itself self-sufficient, beholden to none, a tendency hardly discountenanced by the fact that the Powys father had become less sociable than in his Bradford Abbas days and "always lived in splendid isolation."[3] By temperament or will-power, some of his children—notably Bertie, Littleton, and Marian—overcame their instinctive clannishness and found themselves able to assimilate into the hurly-burly of the world at large; others (John in particular) gave the appearance of so assimilating but retained a solitary core of inner solitude resistant to and even fearful of the diurnal round. John's reflection on this matter is instructive:

> Yes, it's interesting to think of our real real real reaction to people. I think *Fear* dominates with me.... And yet I was born so clever that I was clever enough to know how to deal with my weakness.... And I found that the best thing for a Funk to do is either to escape or to rush at the thing & hug it. "In the Destructive Element Immerse!" Was it Nietzsche who said that?[4]

Fear, especially in the milder guise of excessive caution, was

[1] JCP to Louis Wilkinson, 31 July 1944; Letters of John Cowper Powys to Louis Wilkinson, p. 154   [2] *Ibid.*, p. 101
[3] *Still the Joy of It*, p. 150
[4] JCP to Louis Wilkinson 15 November 1956; Letters of John Cowper Powys to Louis Wilkinson, p. 388

prominent in TFP too. Louis Wilkinson, a reliable witness in such matters, deems "inordinate caution in matters of personal conduct" to be a Powys family trait.[1] Whether we can take at face value his "evidence" is another matter: "They are true sons of the father who, during interviews with his lawyer, invariably sat on his strong-box."[2] "The Archangel", as TFP dubbed him, was never one to let facts get in the way of a good story.

By the time Louis Wilkinson came to know her, the Powys mother was a shadow of her former youthful, and intellectually curious, self—the self that enjoyed archery and croquet as well as drawing, literature, and music. But she had sacrificed herself, albeit willingly enough at first, on the altar of duty to husband and family, the quintessential Victorian angel in the house. She had to bear and bring up a large family while humouring her difficult, often taciturn, husband—Wilkinson's phrase for him is "repressed ferocity"[3]—who could at least find refuge from family in his study. No wonder that she became resigned to the tribulations of the world, and the family streak of melancholia she apparently shared with William Cowper made her suspicious, even resentful, of other people's happiness. How else are we to interpret Wilkinson's claim that she "hated success [and] with secret intensity, well-constituted people, or even people whose health was too good"?[4] Littleton found writing about his mother more of a challenge than writing about his father, since "she was as complex as our father was simple."[5] He identifies the contradictions in her character—moral courage but physical timidity; love of life crushed by fear of it; public support of her husband's faith but private doubts. Notoriously, John avoided mention of her and other women by name in his autobiography. Though she is not a sharply defined figure in her maturity, something of her youthful enthusiasm is still present at times in her letters. For example, she writes an upbeat letter on 17 May 1908 to Llewelyn tutoring in Wiltshire and takes care to include details she knows will interest him—the goldfinches that have built in the arbutus near Willie's tree, the eggs in the tree-creeper's nest, the peculiar cry of the corn crake at night. Temperamentally, TFP was closest to her, especially in his early adult years when success, of any sort, still eluded him. He would sit with his mother, Llewelyn mischievously reported to Louis Wilkinson, "in tragic communion, silent, with touching

[1] *Welsh Ambassadors*, p. 87 [2] Ibid. [3] Ibid., p. 5 [4] Ibid.
[5] *Still the Joy of It*, p. 145

hands, heartbroken . . . over nothing."[1] However, in time, his heterodox views or "religious heresies" caused her pain too. She would have read and perhaps even approved of his first venture into print, *An Interpretation of Genesis* (1908); but she died of cancer at Montacute on 30 July 1914, two years before publication in America of *The Soliloquy of a Hermit*. It is hard to imagine what she would have made of that work, never mind the brutal world of *Mr Tasker's Gods*. For Llewelyn, the unrepentant atheist, his mother's death marked a distinct break with the past. "It is curious how strange last summer seems to me in retrospect," he wrote to John from on board the R.M.S. *Dunvegan Castle, en route* to East Africa, "Mother's illness and death, the war, the uncertainty of everything."[2]

By now a sadly enfeebled man and no doubt anticipating the death of his wife, C. F. Powys made arrangements for his daughter Katie to return home from Holban's Farm in Heathfield, Sussex (21 May 1914). He carried on for a few more years but eventually retired from Montacute in April / May(?) 1918 after thirty-two years of service to the parish, and went to live at 3, Greenhill Terrace in Weymouth, with his eldest daughter, Gertrude. "I have much time on my hands" he wrote to Katie, then at Roper's Farm in Montacute, on 1 February 1919, and his letters show the effort it took for him to communicate at all. Gertrude took care of him until died on 5 August 1923. On his return from East Africa at the end of the war, Llewelyn found a temporary home at Greenhill Terrace too, and thus took afternoon walks with his increasingly silent and withdrawn father "over Lodmoor and the downs behind Preston".[3] But these were not the nature walks of his youth. Unable to write and sexually frustrated, Llewelyn felt trapped in this domestic environment and was impatient with his father's world in which every day was all too comfortably alike. Symptomatic is his complaint to John after hearing C. F. Powys, one Sunday, in that most innocuous of occupations—hymn-singing: "extraordinary that Father, even now, can put into these words so much exasperating unction."[4] In these later years, a series of small strokes seems to have contributed to C. F. Powys's condition, rendering him not only silent but confused and liable to get lost. On one occasion he somehow made his way back to his

1 *Welsh Ambassadors*, p. 6
2 28 September 1914; Letters of Llewelyn Powys, p. 65
3 *Ibid.*, p. 99   4 *Ibid.*, p. 108

childhood home in *his* father's old parish in Stalbridge and, with great aplomb, presented himself for tea at the Rectory. Llewelyn wondered about the impulse that prompted this adventure: "Did he simply wish to revive in his mind old memories of his childhood, to remind himself for the last time, before he entered the realm of dust and darkness, of the exact look of the mulberry tree, whose every bough he knew from climbing them as a boy?"[1] Llewelyn was in any case intrigued enough by the paternal past to make a kind of pilgrimage to his father's home village in 1927, and was delighted to be able to tell Thomas Hardy that he "had seen the daughter of the woman who had suckled father."[2] "That ... is *very* interesting," Hardy said over and over again. The episode is recounted with relish in "Out of the Past".[3]

By his bedside C. F. Powys had kept a mahogany case in which, every night, he would place his gold watch. In later years, Llewelyn still vividly recollected the way in which the very objects in his father's room seemed to absorb certain paternal qualities, in particular the "curious atmosphere of *austerity and reserve*" that emanated from the china utensils on his dressing table. In the last chapter of his *Autobiography*, John recalls proudly the occasion when he overheard Mr Phelips of Montacute House telling a guest "Yes, that's the Vicarage; Powys is the name; a very good family;"[4] this memory in turn conjures up a mental image of his father "seated at a solitary meal, with *The Spectator* on the table beside him"[5]—perfectly captured in Gertrude's 1920 painting of her father—and finally, it brings him to "the continuity of the human generations ... the way in which from father to son our life-sensations are handed down from the past, creating a sort of 'eternal recurrence' of the poetic mystery of the *little-great* rituals, the daily acts by which we all must live." It is to just such continuities that we must be alert.

---

1 "Stalbridge Rectory", p. 376
2 LlP to JCP, April 1927; Letters of Llewelyn Powys, p. 137
3 *Earth Memories*, p. 283
4 *Autobiography*, p. 629   5 *Ibid.*, p. 64

2

The Education of Theodore Powys

One of the peculiarities of T. F. Powys's style is the way in which he combines simplicity of subject and language with sophistication of literary and philosophical reference and allusion. A couple of random examples will suffice to make the point: ". . . John Pardy had never been able to agree with Voltaire that the only true happiness was found in cultivating a garden."[1] "A few days later, when the donkey was feeding contentedly and philosophically, considering in the manner of Bishop Berkeley that the moor could never have had an existence unless he had been there, the mother rabbit stepped out of her burrow and thus addressed the ass."[2]

That his wide and eclectic reading should be so self-consciously displayed some critics have found a fault. Yet one can take delight in the insouciance with which TFP scatters his learning before us. Given, however, the obtrusiveness of that learning, it is strange that so little attention has been directed to its source, or even towards his motivation for incorporating it into his fiction. In other words, should we not ask: What sort of education, broadly speaking, made TFP the writer he became? Here, I will attempt an answer to that question, based upon my examination of many unpublished documents, as well as upon the published data. At the same time, I will reconstruct an entirely new chronology of TFP's early years.

The early schooling of TFP has never been presented in anything but the sketchiest of outlines. Even so meticulous a biographer as Graves found very little to go on, and has as a result some-

[1] "John Pardy and the Waves", *Fables*, pp. 82–3 and 84–5
[2] "The Ass and the Rabbit", *Fables*, pp. 67–8 and 70

times slipped in his reconstruction of the details of the first twenty years of TFP's life. Of his schooling in Dorchester, Graves writes only: "Theodore, eight and a half years old in the summer of 1884, had been attending a school in Dorchester."[1] His failure to mention that the school was Dorchester Grammar School probably reflects unwillingness to grant credence to unsubstantiated reports of his attendance there—especially at the age of eight and a half. In one account, Francis Powys tells how his father attended Dorchester Grammar School and sat in the very seat once occupied by Thomas Hardy. Elsewhere the story gains embellishment, and we are given to understand that TFP carved his initials below those of Hardy. The earliest version is Francis Powys's account in "The Quiet Man of Dorset": "And later the family moved to Dorchester, the county town of Dorset where he attended the Grammar School, occupying the very seat that Thomas Hardy had used many years before."[2] The most recent version is to be found in his "Mr. Weston's Good World" in *Recollections of the Powys Brothers*: "Theodore now attended the Grammar School at Dorchester, occupying the very seat that Thomas Hardy, the great Wessex novelist who afterwards became his friend, had used many years before. Hardy had carved his name on the desk and Theodore was caught carefully cutting out his own beneath it."[3] In the last of these essays it is also suggested that TFP's home in East Chaldon, Beth Car, was built by Hardy's brother (Henry), and that the architect was Hardy himself. This is not altogether implausible, although Hardy gave up the practice of architecture in 1872. After all, Hardy designed Max Gate himself, and hired his father and brother to build it; and as late as 1893 he designed Talbothays as a home for his brother, to whom, Millgate says, "Hardy had long been in the habit of giving occasional assistance . . . in what he no doubt still regarded as the family business."[4] On the other hand, Beth Car is not marked on the 1900–1 large-scale (25 inches to a mile) ordnance survey map of East Chaldon. Sylvia Townsend Warner says that the house was built at Mr Cope's command but that Mr Cope died while the house was yet a-building and for some time stood unfurnished and abandoned.[5] This information helps us to date the house, since the Reverend Joseph Staines Cope died in

1 *The Brothers Powys*, p. 14
2 "The Quiet Man of Dorset", p. 53
3 "Mr Weston's Good World", p. 124
4 *Thomas Hardy*, p. 345   5 *PR* 7, pp. 66–7

1901. But even if Henry Hardy were the builder, why would Thomas Hardy have concerned himself with the project? There was no known bond of friendship or family between Cope and Hardy, and the house was in any case originally said to have been intended for a curate or a gardener. The story is surely apocryphal. It is a fine story with a nice symbolism that places TFP squarely in the tradition of as well as the seat of Hardy. Alas, it is quite without foundation, as Graves no doubt detected. Not that TFP never attended Dorchester Grammar School—he did, though later than 1884. But Hardy never attended Dorchester Grammar School. He went to the Dorchester British School, under Isaac Glandfield Last, in Greyhound Yard, from 1850 to 1853. Then he moved to Last's new school, an independent commercial academy until 1856, when he left school for ever.[1]

Now this is just the kind of story that TFP would have been capable of perpetrating in mischievous mood, but only, one suspects, if it had somehow cast him in a bad light. As it happens, he does seem to have been the ultimate source for the Hardy connection, though not with any intention of self-glorification—which would have been quite uncharacteristic. Asked by Charles Prentice of Chatto and Windus for some autobiographical material for publicity purposes, TFP sent a typically short and generally un-illuminating statement—the sort of thing that reflects nothing quite so much as the author's unwillingness to say anything at all to reveal himself. Nonetheless, David Garnett later incorporated it into an article on TFP in *The Borzoi 1925*. In this short paragraph TFP does say that he was at Dorchester Grammar School for a year or two, and adds parenthetically: "I think that's Hardy's school too." From this casual observation there seems to have grown a legend of sorts, with TFP represented as following in the footsteps of the master, Hardy. There *are* affinities between the two—both were certainly pessimists of sorts, both wrote short stories as well as novels, both used dialect in their work, both left school around sixteen, and both are rather prone to show off the learning later acquired. The mistaken notion about Hardy's attendance at Dorchester Grammar School almost certainly derives from the fact that Dorchester Grammar School was endowed in 1579 by one Thomas Hardye of Frampton. Moreover, Thomas Hardy, the novelist, was for many years a

---

1 See Millgate, *Thomas Hardy*, pp. 49–53 for further details.

governor of the school (1909–25), and was always mindful of the role his namesake had played in its foundation.[1]

The dates of TFP's attendance at the school may be, and have been, seen as relatively unimportant within the larger biographical framework. Hitherto critics have considered it sufficient merely to note his attendance before passing on to an equally fleeting reference to his unhappy days at Sherborne Prep and his sojourn at the school in Aldeburgh run by the father of Louis Wilkinson. Yet there are a number of reasons why we should pay closer attention to this period of TFP's life. First of all, the factual and chronological details of one whose life was so markedly uneventful ought at least to be documented with scrupulous care, if for no other reason than that later events may be erroneously dated from the earlier "facts". Secondly, as can be amply demonstrated, ferreting out apparently trivial details can help reveal inconsistencies in the established "facts" and assumptions, and can lead to more important issues. Finally it is arguable that since TFP's formal education can reasonably be judged a failure, we ought to know as much about it as possible. How otherwise are we to explain the fact that he did not follow his father and older brothers to Cambridge? And how can we ignore a phase of his life that more or less determined his future for him, that excluded him from the professions, and that led him to try the life of a farmer? His relative lack of education cast a giant shadow across his life; it was never far from his consciousness, as is evidenced in the attack upon him that TFP puts in the mouth of Llewelyn in "Theodore Examined by the Brethren": "You are not intelligent, you don't know the world, you don't know French, you can't spell;"[2] it contributed in no small measure to his negative self-image, his feelings of inadequacy, of being an outcast and persecuted—even perhaps to his choice of a wife; and it certainly helped shape his career as a writer. In a letter to John Cowper Powys, some of his pent-up feelings about his education surface: "Do I say things that you don't like, do I? Very likely I do—but remember that I have been to a different kind of school to you and to Lulu. And not a very pretty one either—so forgive me."[3]

Of course, TFP has in mind what we might call the school of hard knocks or life itself. Sometimes, then, it suits him, in the role

---

1 See Millgate, *Thomas Hardy*, pp. 49–53, for further details.
2 *Recollections of the Powys Brothers*, p. 268
3 TFP to JCP, 24 September 1917; HRHRC

in which he cast himself, to exaggerate the differences in their education. It is this fact that colours some of his not altogether reliable observations about his schooling or the lack thereof. But it is also outbursts of the sort cited above that encourage one to treat TFP's education as a topic broader than a listing, however precise, of the institutions attended.

But, to begin with, we must establish firmly the period of TFP's attendance at Dorchester Grammar School. While the Rev. Charles Francis Powys served as curate to the Rev. Mr Knipe at St Peter's Church, Dorchester (1879–85), the family lived in Rothesay House, South Walks, just a short distance from the church. Some two years after they arrived, JCP and Littleton began attending a dame's school near the Great Western station. Recalling his education in a letter to Louis Wilkinson, John alludes to this school: "The mathematics I was taught by a Miss Osborne in Dorchester (where by the advice of Colonel Oldfield we learnt French by reading the 'Malheurs de Sophie')."[1]

It is likely that John did not begin at this school until the autumn of 1882, by which time he would have been approaching ten, since he refers to the happiness of his school-free eighth and ninth years.[2] TFP never attended this school, though the family did not move to Montacute from Dorchester until the autumn of 1885. But could an eight- or nine-year-old have been attending Dorchester Grammar School? Yes, according to the records, pupils could begin as day boys or boarders at eight. However the *terminus a quo* is determined by the fact that the school had been closed since 1879 and did not re-open until 18 January 1883. TFP would then have been eligible to attend by January 1884. So Graves's assertion that he had been attending the school in 1884 is a perfectly reasonable one. It just happens to be wrong. There are two important sources of information about TFP at Dorchester Grammar School—a single paragraph in "This is Thyself",[3] and a letter to TFP's sister Gertrude, written on 7 May 1941. "This is Thyself" I would date around 1914–15 in that it is part of the autobiographical piece TFP began in response to JCP's call for a contribution to the abortive Three / Six Brothers Project. In the end, TFP's contribution evolved into *The Soliloquy of a Hermit* (1916). In the crucial manuscript he gives the following account:

1 JCP to Louis Wilkinson, 14 June 1959; Colgate
2 See *Autobiography*, pp. 56–7.
3 Selected Early Works

> So far the world was a cake to be eaten by me, tea and dinner came to me and I ate. And sadness I did not know until I went to school. I was ten when this began. There was a country vicarage I went out of, and a Grammar School I went into. It was in the old town where we had once lived, but how changed—I saw all things with new eyes, eyes that were learning to fear.[1]

If he was ten, this traumatic change in his life could have taken place no earlier than January 1886, and probably not until September 1886. The country vicarage could only be St Catharine's Vicarage, Montacute, and the Grammar School none other than Dorchester Grammar School. Independent corroboration is provided by the letter of 1941. TFP tells us that "I was at Dorchester Grammar School in the lowest form, taken there by Aunt Philippa [known as Pippa, she was Ralph Shirley's mother] and taught by a Mr Kingdon who died aged 92 two years ago." Now this Mr Kingdon was, according to the evidence at the Dorset County Library, not just a teacher but H. N. Kingdon, the first Headmaster of the re-opened school. He held this post from 1883 until 1898.

Who could have guessed that TFP would be sent *back* to Dorchester to school when his two elder brothers had already been enrolled for two years at Westbury House, Sherborne? Had he joined them at Acreman House, to which the headmaster and proprietor, Blake, had moved the school in 1885, he would at least have enjoyed some comfort from the presence of his brothers, if not actual protection against the kind of bullying described by JCP in his *Autobiography*. And Sherborne was far nearer than Dorchester, too; it was only about ten miles or so from Montacute. Why, then, was young Theodore sent off by himself to Dorchester Grammar School? Earlier critics have, to some extent, chosen to interpret the facts of TFP's education as early evidence of a desire to be different and of a stubborn determination to seek his own solitary path. But it is unlikely that a ten year old who had never been to school at all could be so single-minded. It is far more likely that TFP was not sent at once to Acreman House (at that time it only had informal status as Sherborne Prep), because his parents knew from John's experience exactly the kind of reception he would get from the other boys. Littleton, on the other hand— by all accounts a far more robust character—flourished in the new environment and was perfectly happy at school. So the family

1 Selected Early Works, p. 332

must have decided that TFP, who was at least as sensitive as John, was simply not temperamentally suited to such a school. As later events proved, he was not. Dorchester, on the other hand, was a place comfortably familiar. Almost all TFP's childhood memories until that time were associated with Dorchester: Rothesay House, his own Bushes Home, and St Peter's Church, etc. Moreover, Dorchester Grammar School was located in South Street, next to the almshouse, Napper's Mite, in an area with which he would certainly have been familiar, since it was so close to his former home. Alas, things did not work out as they might have; the change of circumstances profoundly altered TFP's perception of Dorchester. Of this first, unhappy experience of formal education, TFP tells us little save a grotesque vignette of Mr Kingdon's mother in which she is identified with Madame Bubble, the seductive enchantress (and representative of the world) in *Pilgrim's Progress*:

> Odd things come to my mind, odd people. An old woman, the headmaster's mother, who taught us the Bible. She made at every lesson a rumbling noise somewhere in her belly. Her dress was silk and widely braided with black lace. Her body took up a great round place in the room. I saw her once in a picture—she was Madam Bubble trying to beg a thin, tired pilgrim to go with her to bed. I wondered while I listened to the Bible when the next rumble would come. And this noise is the only thing that I think is worth remembering about my school life.[1]

According to the chronology given in his 1941 letter to Gertrude, TFP only spent three terms at Dorchester Grammar School, and during most of one of those terms "I was ill of jaundice." Unfortunately, it has not been possible to verify from the Dorchester Grammar School archives the dates of TFP's attendance. According to Major B. G. Kirby[2] many of the earliest records were lost or destroyed. Even TFP himself is less than certain about the duration of his stay at Dorchester Grammar School, saying cautiously: "I think I was there three terms." But his tenth birthday fell on 20 December 1885, so he may have begun in the second term (January 1886) or, more likely, started with the new academic year in September 1886. In any case, there is documentary evidence of when he began at Acreman House (to which Sherborne Prep had moved in 1885); so it is clear that

---

1 "This is Thyself", p. 332   2 personal communication

either he spent longer at Dorchester Grammar School than he recalls or that he was out of school altogether for more than one term. If he began, as I suspect, in September 1886, there is only one extra term to be accounted for (that is, he was at school for four terms or he was out for two).

When Littleton Powys returned to Sherborne Preparatory School in 1905, succeeding W. H. Blake as Headmaster, he began to compile a school log or diary of sorts, which is still extant.[1] At the back of this book there is a list of the dates at which boys joined the school, going as far back as 1880, arranged by term. The parents' address is given, and the names of day boys are marked with a star. Theodore Powys is entry number 122 for the second term of the academic year 1887–8 (i.e. January 1888). He was one of three new boys that term—another, interestingly, being Chas. A. W. Pope of South Walks, Dorchester, the son of Alfred Pope, original member of the Dorset Natural History and Antiquarian Field Club, J.P. for Dorset, and author of *The Old Stone Crosses of Dorset* (1906). Could he have been a friend of TFP's, also transferring from Dorchester Grammar School? This documentation is consistent with TFP's statement in the 1941 letter that he was twelve by the time he went to the Prep. Now we know from the Potocki typescript[2] that TFP left the Prep in April 1889, since he received a *Book of Ballads* from Headmaster Blake, inscribed: 8 April 1889, leaving Sherborne Prep. Therefore TFP's recollection in his letter to his sister that "I went to the Prep for three terms . . . I had measles one of those terms and went to Weymouth to stay with Cousin Mary and I suppose Grandmother" is only slightly off the mark. In fact, he was a pupil at the school for four terms. This is a very different picture from that established by Graves, who has TFP attending the Prep from 1885 to 1889, though his would be a perfectly reasonable reconstruction in the absence of the details now available from the school log.

---

1 photocopy courtesy of Robin Lindsay, former Headmaster of Sherborne Preparatory School

2 This typescript, entitled "Portrait of T. F. Powys", by his adopted daughter Theodora Gay Powys, is signed and dated by Count Potocki of Montalk: "Lovelace's Copse, Plush, Dorset, 30. iv. 65". In the introduction Count Potocki explains that he played the part of a tape-recorder to Theodora, as she in effect dictated to him an account of her adoptive father. However, Mrs Scutt (the married name of Theodora Gay Powys) has expressed reservations about the document, particularly as to her role in its compilation. For her views, see her letter in *PR* 16. Richard Perceval Graves, who was kind enough to allow me to read the document in his home, has presented the biographer's view in *PR* 17. Theodora Scutt's own official account has now been published as *Cuckoo in the Powys Nest*, 2000.

What sort of experience did TFP have at Acreman House? The only eyewitness account is that of JCP in his *Autobiography*, a record that has to be treated with caution in matters of fact and in dates, but is nevertheless useful here for the precious glimpses it affords us of life at school. John and Littleton had spent three years at the Prep (1883–6), and had acquitted themselves well, albeit in different ways, in spite of initial bullying. John had proven himself as a scholar, graduating Head of the Prep—that is the best boy academically; and Littleton, a natural and enthusiastic athlete from the beginning, had captained both the rugby and the cricket teams in his last year. Perhaps, then, there were expectations at the school about the new Powys boy that TFP could not possibly have fulfilled. But at least TFP was not entirely isolated from his brothers, who were after all in the same small town. JCP conjures up a vivid picture of his younger brother: "In his Prep straw-hat and his Eton jacket he would await us at the top of the hill for our Sunday afternoon walk." If only there were a photograph! John obviously felt sympathy for his brother, describing how "those mournful grey eyes under that straw hat . . . used to turn to us as we came hurrying up that hill."[1] And he asked with passion: "If I suffered when I first went to school, what must Theodore, so much more predisposed to suffering, have gone through?"[2] It may be that TFP was never even subjected to the overt bullying reported by John, but he seems to have been decidedly unsuited to the communal life, or at least to the sporting variety thereof which flourished at Acreman House under a headmaster who had been a Cambridge Rugby Blue.

No wonder that John and TFP could agree, as they reclined in the Lenty meadows one day, that it would be far better to be a navvy on the railway track than to be at school;[3] and no wonder too that Littleton, to whom school life was professedly congenial, chose to omit any reference to his younger brother, Theodore, in his chapter entitled "School Days" in *The Joy of It*. Yet it would be unfair to leave the impression that Headmaster Blake was nothing but an unthinking "hearty". He also had literary inclinations, and encouraged reading and the appreciation of poetry among his pupils; he would even read to them himself. A. B. Gourlay[4] describes him as a man of enterprise and vigour; and it appears that he may have been distantly related to the Powys family. He

1 *Autobiography*, p. 349   2 *Ibid.*   3 *Ibid.*, p. 99
4 "The Powys Brothers at Sherborne School"

was a Norfolk man and a descendant of the famous seventeenth-century Admiral Robert Blake, as was Louis Wilkinson. In *Swan's Milk*, Louis Wilkinson refers to the brave rebelling blood of Robert Blake [because he served under Cromwell?] in his family, or rather in that of his alter ego, Dexter Foothood,[1] and claims that he himself and the Powyses were related vaguely by a descent from Admiral Blake. The only record of Blake's treatment of TFP is the book he gave him as a going-away present, apparently a personal gift, not a school prize; but in light of the tenuous family connection and the encouragement he offered to John, it is reasonable to assume that Blake took a more than ordinary interest in this latest member of the Powys clan. It cannot have been the fault of Blake that TFP did not manage to stay the course at the Prep.

Graves's account of the circumstances of TFP's departure gives the impression that he left when it was time for him to leave and directly (i.e. at the beginning of the next academic year) "went on . . . to a boarding school at Aldeburgh in Suffolk."[2] In fact, he did not finish the academic year at all, but left at the end of the second term—*prima facie* evidence that his departure was precipitated by something out of the ordinary. Whether it was further illness, TFP's state of mind, or merely parental unhappiness at his lack of progress, we cannot be absolutely certain. However, there are indications that psychological stress was probably the major factor. Theodora Scutt states (private correspondence) that his experience at Sherborne nearly drove him to a nervous breakdown; and we have his own testimony that "sadness I did not know until I went to school." The observations of JCP in his *Autobiography* and of Louis Wilkinson in "Some Memories of T. F. Powys" are in substantial agreement on this matter. So the painful pattern established at Dorchester Grammar School had now been repeated.

Just how much TFP learned at the Prep it is hard to say. The school offered Latin and French; and one can only presume that he took these subjects there. "When I look back at the past . . . I do not care . . . whether I have ever learned Latin,"[3] TFP himself remarks in *The Soliloquy of a Hermit*—a statement which suggests some exposure to the language. Even the loyal Littleton conceded that in those days the standard of work at the Prep was not very

1 *Swan's Milk*, p. 22   2 *The Brothers Powys*, p. 19   3 *The Soliloquy of a Hermit*, pp. 64–5

high, and that Mathematics was not well taught. So TFP's later claim that "I never reached a form in which anything but simple arithmetic was taught" may not be far from the truth. It is very doubtful whether he was academically well enough prepared to follow his brothers to Sherborne School itself, even had he wished to do so.

What was to be done? The fragility of his mental health and the uncertainty of his parents as to an appropriate solution no doubt contributed to the length of time he was kept out of school. For rather more than a year he remained at home, though his education was not entirely neglected. TFP recalls with pleasure, for example, doing lessons with Gertrude under the guidance of Miss Frances Beales, governess at Montacute.[1] Perhaps it was during this period that the ties of special affection between TFP and Gertrude were firmly established. John and Littleton, despite their differences of temperament, had always been at school together, and this was a bond between them, and an experience from which TFP was excluded. Graves suggests a growing affinity between John and TFP while they were both at school in Sherborne: "When Theodore was so desperately unhappy at the Sherborne Prep . . . John had tried to cheer him up by reading out to him the first chapter of a dashing romance in which Theodore appeared, under another name, as the head of a band of smugglers."[2] Now this example is drawn from a letter of John's to Llewelyn dated 12 October [1931]; and John places the writing of the story from "the first year we were at Montacute when Katie was about to approach to birth"—that is 1886. At this time, the reconstructed chronology shows, TFP was not at the Prep; early in the year he was probably at home and quite happy, and later in the year he was at Dorchester Grammar School, and not so happy. Yet the date itself is by no means as certain as John's statement seems to suggest; for, in his *Autobiography,* he locates the composition of the story after TFP had been transferred to the Wilkinsons' School at Aldeburgh,[3] in which case the date would have to be no earlier than June 1890.

It was after the Summer half-term break that TFP arrived in Aldeburgh to begin attending Eaton House School, as the Wilkinsons' school was called. The choice of Eaton House for

---

1 Letter from TFP to Gertrude Powys, 21 July 1893; Bissell Collection
2 *The Brothers Powys*, p. 21   3 *Autobiography*, p. 141

TFP proved a lucky one. Although the school was far from the family home, it was within relatively easy reach of TFP's maternal grandparents in Northwold and his uncle at Yaxham (the Rev. William Cowper Johnson was Rector of Northwold from 1880–92; his son, Cowper Johnson, Mary's brother, took over his father's parish at Yaxham in 1881 and remained there until 1915). The Headmaster and proprietor of the school was the Rev. Walter G. Wilkinson, with whose family there was also a connection of sorts through TFP's mother. There had been contact between the Johnson and the Wilkinson families for many years, going back to the days of Johnny Johnson, William Cowper's benefactor, and earlier. For example, young Walter G. Wilkinson read the lessons for the Rev. W. C. Johnson at Yaxham in 1844. But the link between the Johnsons and the Emras (Mrs Wilkinson's maiden name was Charlotte Elizabeth Emra) is far less certain. For a time one of Mrs Wilkinson's sisters was governess at Yaxham (perhaps Maria, the eldest, who never married). But it is highly unlikely, given the disparity in their ages, that Mrs Wilkinson, who was born in 1842, and Mrs Powys, who was born in 1849, could have been friends in girlhood, as Louis Wilkinson describes them, in "Some Memories of T. F. Powys" or "best friend[s]" as Graves, citing a letter of John's, puts it. Louis Wilkinson is a little more credible in his account in *Swan's Milk*: "His mother [that of Dexter Foothood, the *alter ego* of Louis Wilkinson] remained a romantic figure of her past [Mary Cowper Johnson's]; with her she read poetry, with her she first realized it. Those were the days of Mrs Powys's courtship."[1] As well as can be reconstructed, the two women never met until after the Wilkinsons' marriage in 1867; Mary Cowper Johnson, as she then was, visited Mrs Wilkinson in Lowestoft in 1869, when the latter would have been pregnant with Christabel, and reported her well. In her letter of October 1869, writing to her brother, Mary also makes some less than kind remarks which hardly confirm an impression of friendship. She writes: "Fancy Mrs Wilk. having an infant, only think of it with hooked nose and screwed mouth!" But more than twenty years later, it must have been with relief that Mrs Powys remembered the Wilkinsons and their school, as she and her husband wrestled with the problem of TFP's education. Louis Wilkinson's full account of what happened is

1 *Swan's Milk*, p. 238

worth including at this point, because it has been the basis of almost all other statements about the circumstances of TFP's transfer to Eaton House:

> Why T. F. Powys, at his age, was at a Preparatory School I did not know and I was not curious enough to enquire; but the reason was that his mother and mine had been friends in girlhood and Theodore had not been happy at the school where he formerly was. So his mother asked if he could come to my father's in spite of his age.[1]

It is true that TFP's presence at a prep school well beyond his fourteenth birthday would ordinarily constitute something of an anomaly, if we think in terms of the modern prep school. But nineteenth-century preps were not so bound by regulations as they became in the twentieth century. Moreover, TFP was by no means the only over-age boy at Eaton House, then or in later years. When he first arrived, there was already one fifteen-year-old there, who was admitted in the Autumn term to Bradfield College in the fifth form. And photographs taken no more than four years after TFP left show a number of suspiciously big boys, at least one sporting a moustache!

TFP was placed in the third form. With him he brought a cricket bat (he had at least a mild interest in the game), and, he wrote to Gertrude, "I was treated with respect owing to that bat and owing to my being fourteen years old." The eight-year-old Louis Wilkinson had begun at the school just over a term earlier, in January 1890, and two forms lower, in the Remove. One could hardly expect that either boy would remember much of the other, even in a school which never had more than thirty-five boys. But Louis Wilkinson recalled: "It was only because of the unusualness of his age that I took notice of him . . . I remember him as a big, heavy boy because I was a small one. I remember his gravity, his slow movements, and his low-toned voice."[2] TFP, with a characteristic sense of mischief, claimed to remember punching Louis Wilkinson because he was the headmaster's son, but the alleged victim discounts the story as a Theodorian invention. However, TFP was happy at Eaton House, as his letters revealed. He told John, for example, that he was "treated as boys should be treated."[3] Perhaps it was the high quality of the food (notoriously bad at English boarding schools) that prompted this remark; he

1 *Theodore*, p. 1   2 *Ibid.*, p. 9   3 *Autobiography*, p. 266

told Louis Wilkinson that it was so good that he didn't think Louis' father could have made much money from the school. But his pleasure at being left largely to his own devices may also have been a contributing factor. "Some of my time there I spent in writing in a plain simple copybook. That seemed a quiet employment and I enjoyed it," he recalled for Gertrude in 1941. Thanks to TFP's frugality and hatred of wasting paper, this very copybook has survived.[1] It is a black soft-covered notebook, 7 by 9 inches, containing an odd jumble of entries. After writing "T. F. Powys / Montacute / Bob Powys" (an affectionate name used only by family members) on the paste-down, he began copying Lord Macaulay's "Battle of Lake Regullus"[2] on the first page, in a large, careful, but manifestly immature, hand. The poem required nearly thirty-seven pages, and at the end of it, just before he began Longfellow's "Psalm of Life", TFP inscribed the date "1890 / 8 of December". He was in his second term at Eaton House. Like many a schoolboy, his copying was by no means faultless; and careful scrutiny of his work reveals evidence of pencil correction in an unknown hand—no doubt the work of a teacher. It is unlikely to have been the work of the headmaster, who was indeed something of a recluse, and only took real interest in those who showed ability in Latin and Greek.

TFP followed "A Psalm of Life" with "The Song of Hiawatha", and later added Kipling's "Mandalay" and "Tommy Tomlinson". Such poems would have been in vogue at the time, so their selection for copying is not necessarily indicative of TFP's taste in poetry. Yet, given the dearth of material on his early life, especially at school, these poems at least deserve mention. "The Battle of Lake Regullus", however, seems to have been a standard assignment. Louis Wilkinson recalls how an imaginative friend told him, as they broke stones on the beach, that inside were impressions of scenes attended by the stones in their earliest existence.[3] The interior of one, he insisted, was "The Battle of Lake Regullus".

By way of contrast, John was reading Tennyson in 1890–1, and Littleton, perhaps the most avid of the brothers for Nature and obviously in training to be a schoolmaster, was preoccupied with books about fishing. Twelve years later, when TFP did some lecturing at two South Coast girls' schools in Eastbourne and West

1 now in the Bissell Collection   2 from *Lays of Ancient Rome*   3 *Swan's Milk*, p. 9

Brighton,[1] he included Macaulay and Longfellow among his authors. In the notes of those lectures, perhaps drawing upon his own experience, he makes special mention of Macaulay's Suffolk time, and offers the opinion that "we can admire but not love [him]." Longfellow he sees as "a kind of old priest". One assumes that Kipling would have been deemed too indecorous for schoolgirls, for by then TFP owned a copy of *Barrack Room Ballads* (11th ed., 1897), and could certainly have lectured on Kipling too. In any case, TFP's earliest literary leanings seem to have been towards poetry rather than fiction. But this predilection is not unusual in the budding fiction writer as one can see from JCP's first two books, both volumes of poetry. However, the Kipling influence, if we can call it that, involved more than the reading of his poetry. There is one remarkable unpublished story from the World War I period, "The Coward", which suggests that Kipling's short stories made some contribution, albeit minor, towards TFP's development as a writer.[2]

The whole time TFP spent at Eaton House—three and a half terms in 1890 and 1891—he remained in the third of six forms. Only one other boy shared this dubious distinction. For the most part, there seems to have been a great deal of movement from form to form—a fact which, when coupled with the smallness of forms (on average, five to six), suggests the kind of openness of structure and flexibility possible in a small school. Louis Wilkinson's progress provides an interesting example; in the space of a little over a year he moved from two forms below TFP to one form above ("Shell"). Obviously TFP was *not* up to scratch academically, even in comparison with much younger pupils. Yet careful reading of the record shows that he did in fact make considerable progress in his new school, giving credence thereby to Walter Wilkinson's claim that "the experience of many years has, I think, taught us how to interest boys in their work."[3] School records, obtained through the kind offices of Mrs Sylvia Belle of Orwell

---

1 There are two letters in the Bissell collection from the Headmistresses of these schools. One is from Mary Wallder, St Aubyn's House, Wilbury Road, West Brighton (now Hove); the other is from Helen N. Inman, Endcliffe, Meads, Eastbourne. The text of these letters is printed in Michel Pouillard's "T. F. Powys Conferencier à Eastbourne 1902–03", p. 349.

2 One critic detects parallels between TFP and Kipling in the published work too. Clare Hanson says: "It is tempting to link, for example, Kipling and T. F. Powys's love of symmetry in the short story with a similar belief in a universal purpose or design." (*Short Stories & Short Fictions, 1880–1980*, p. 5)

3 Quoted from a pamphlet dated June 1884 distributed to parents and friends of the school, announcing the move from Crespigny House to Eaton House

Park School (the successor to Eaton House), show that in his first term TFP was placed fifth out of six in his form, and based on total marks, twenty-sixth out of thirty-one pupils in the school. However, at the end of the Autumn Term, 1890, he was second in his form, had the sixth highest marks in the school, and won first prize for English History. Quite a transformation! In the Spring Term, 1891, he was again second in the class (this time to the fast-rising Louis), and moved up to the third in the school, behind Louis, who also took First Prize for Industry and First Prize for Classics. Perhaps it was about this time that TFP felt like punishing his future friend, even if he never actually did so. Again, in his final term, TFP was second in the class (Louis had been promoted), fifth overall, and won, appropriately enough for the future author of *An Interpretation of Genesis*, First Prize for Scripture History, probably *Lion Hearted: The Story of Bishop Hannington's Life* (1890).[1] In later years, Littleton paid tribute to his mother's role in the family knowledge of the Bible, pointing out that "each of us had won Scripture Prizes at school."[2] But until now there has never been any documentation of TFP's success in this or any other academic area. TFP's father also, of course, contributed significantly to his biblical knowledge. Perhaps TFP was thinking of his own father when he writes of John Glidden's father in the story, "In Good Earth":

> He had taught his son at an early age ... to read from an old book that, until recently, had been the constant evening companion of both the son and the father. There was a certain short story written there that had always pleased John which he had read often enough and knew by heart—the story of a sower who went forth to sow his seed.[3]

Eaton House School was situated at the north end of Aldeburgh in a quiet area not far from the sea. It occupied two adjacent properties, Eaton House and Darfield House, with some two acres of garden on the slope behind them. Eaton House itself was, and remains, a large, ornately columned, and rather unattractive, three storey sandstone edifice; it contained the dormitory, and, in a flat-roofed annex, the schoolroom, originally built as a museum.

---

1 Peter Riley saw a book while working on his bibliography of TFP which in an unpublished segment he records only as "Dawson's Life of Bishop Hannington. A school prize". So it is possible that the book in question was *James Hannington, D.D., F.L.S., F.R.G.S., First Bishop of Eastern Equatorial Africa. A History of His Life and Work, 1847–1885*, London: Seeley and Co., 1887, rather than the children's edition described here.

2 *Still the Joy of It*, p. 142   3 *The Two Thieves*, pp. 24–5

Darfield House contained a recreation room, a gymnasium, and staff rooms. The school rented some nearby land as a cricket field (so TFP would have had the opportunity to try his cricket bat). Tennis, golf, and cycling were also available to the boys. The school had begun at Lowestoft, the earliest reference to it being an entry in a Johnson family diary for 1869: "Their school is increasing so much they have scarcely room in their house for 18 boys." It moved to Crespigny House, Aldeburgh in 1870, and was formally organized as a school of 24 boys. It had only been at Eaton House for six years when TFP arrived, but was flourishing, and sent its pupils on to such distinguished public schools as Eton, Haileybury, Uppingham, and Wellington, as well as to many of the minor public schools. There must have been a distinctive sense of community, even family, at the school that endeared itself to TFP. In some ways, it *was* a kind of extended family in that Louis Wilkinson had no fewer than five cousins attending while he was there, the children of his mother's married sisters and brother: Roderick and Alexander McDougall, Richard Ferrand, Eustace Jones, and Cyril Emra. Christabel Wilkinson (1869–95), Louis Wilkinson's elder sister, also taught at the school, and Mrs Wilkinson served as Head Matron—though she had an under-Matron, Mrs Rimmer.[1] Mrs Wilkinson made a deep impression on young TFP, providing the kind of maternal warmth that he so badly needed. His letters to Louis Wilkinson in subsequent years repeatedly allude to Mrs Wilkinson with fondness and appreciation. In 1916, after she had read *The Soliloquy of a Hermit*, TFP told Louis Wilkinson: "It means a great deal to me that she likes it."[2] In 1923 he recalled playing cards with her at Deepdene [the family home]; and after her death in 1931, he wrote to Louis Wilkinson: "I shall always remember her kindness to me."[3] In the flirtatious Christabel, TFP found his first love. She was a beautiful young woman (as photographs confirm) with hair of an auburn undertone. Of course, TFP's could have been no more than a schoolboy crush, the education of the heart. She was already nearly twenty-one when TFP first arrived at Eaton House; he was fourteen and a half. She was a tutor, as the teachers were called, and he was a pupil. She was regarded by the other mistresses as an unsettling influence, and probably was! According to Louis Wilkinson nearly all of the older boys were more or less in love

---

[1] She appears as Mrs Ringer in *Swan's Milk*.   [2] 24 April 1916; Colgate
[3] *Welsh Ambassadors*, p. 202

with her.[1] Alas, she died of tubercular laryngitis in Davos, Switzerland, in November 1895.

Just before she left England for the sanatorium in Davos, Christabel received a photo-album as a present from one of the older boys, James or "Jammy" Swinburne. He overlapped with TFP for only one term, and won a reputation as a keen amateur photographer. The album is inscribed "Chris E. Wilkinson from J. K. Swinburne / 10 March 1895"; so the photographs themselves can safely be dated around the same time. One of them shows a school group reclining on the grass after lawn tennis, with Christabel in the centre in a white blouse and boater, and Swinburne nearby in white flannels and striped blazer. Most interesting, perhaps, is the photograph of the dormitory. The resolution of the original is excellent, and shows details that would hardly have changed in the four years since TFP left. Along each wall of a half-panelled and wood-beamed room ran a row of beds; in the centre aisle stood a row of washbasins. There were no cupboards, just hooks behind each bed on which to hang belongings. And upon the walls were emblazoned a series of morally uplifting injunctions —among them "Whatsoever ye do, Do all to the glory of God," "Overcome Evil with Good," and "Not My Will But Thine Be Done." Even the slanting wooden beams were not ignored; each bore a single word: Diligence, Sincerity, Humility, etc. It is intriguing to think that such messages may have had some subliminal effect upon TFP, or to imagine him gazing up at the one above his head—Humility perhaps?

In his adult years, TFP did not forget Eaton House, Aldeburgh, or the people he met there. Responding to some observation by Louis Wilkinson, he writes: "I remember Eustace Jones [Louis Wilkinson's cousin, and a pupil at Eaton House]. I commend him for leaving the Bank. . . . His father I remember too. He had thick black garments and a soul somewhat dormant."[2] Commenting upon as trivial a matter as the stamp on one of Louis Wilkinson's letters, he writes: "What a fine old fellow in the stamp! He looks like the King of Siam in the poem that you rejoiced your heart in at Eaton House."[3] And a reading of *Swan's Milk*, that quirky fictional autobiography, evokes a flood of memories: "All of your early life brings back to me so much of my own that I seem to have another life given to me as I read of these happenings at

1 *Swan's Milk*, p. 94   2 27 December 1910; HRHRC   3 20 February 1915; HRHRC

Eaton House. Had that old Gardener—I have forgotten the name—a hand in the picture?"[1] The picture referred to was an obscene drawing in the latrines at Eaton House, the scandal of which is enthusiastically described in Chapter 2 of *Swan's Milk*. There, Louis Wilkinson dismisses TFP as a possible culprit on the grounds that he could not draw well enough, and besides, could never have had that pagan candour.[2]

Apart from his unsurprising success in Scripture History, what are we to make of TFP's final experience of school? Well, his work improved dramatically in what seems to have been the right climate of learning for him. And his self-confidence must have increased dramatically too. No child likes to fail, after all. Perhaps that was the wisdom of keeping him in the same form—better to succeed at a lower level than to fail at progressively higher levels. Yet, no serious estimate of his accomplishments, however dramatic in the context of earlier failure, could have disguised the fact that TFP still lagged behind his peers. No doubt after consultation with the school and soliciting TFP's own views, his anxious parents reluctantly determined to end his formal education. The decision would not have been reached lightly; for it meant the end also of any possibility of his entering the professions, especially the Church. TFP's father, it will be recalled, had also been a late developer, as Gourlay points out, and did not go to Sherborne as did his elder brother, Littleton. The profile of TFP's educational problems (among them, spelling problems with simple words, fainting, and some evidence of "awkwardness" perhaps attributable to motor-coordination) strongly suggests that he suffered at least marginally from some form of learning disability. His father's own late development can also be seen as a specific indicator. At a reading of this chapter, the late Peter Powys Grey independently suggested dyslexia as a possibility. Nonetheless, C. F. Powys's patchwork education did not seriously impede him, and he obtained a Second Class degree in Mathematics from Cambridge. For TFP, however, it would barely be an exaggeration to say that his real education did not begin until after he left school.

When TFP returned to Montacute in the summer of 1891, he knew that he had reached an important turning point in life, for his schooldays were unequivocally over. But what did the future

1 2 February 1934; *Welsh Ambassadors*, pp. 206–7   2 *Swan's Milk*, p. 44

hold? That remained to be decided by him and his parents. At least he had acquitted himself well enough at Eaton House to erase some of the self-doubt and parental anxiety that must have been provoked by his experiences at Dorchester Grammar School and at Sherborne Prep. While at home, he spent a good deal of time with John. They enjoyed the "adult" pleasures of tobacco, made nighttime expeditions into Stoke Wood and began "fooling with firearms," as John put it.[1] John had secretly bought a revolver as protection against the anticipated intrusion of College rowdies into his room at Cambridge, and shared his secret with TFP. John says that TFP by this time had left the Wilkinson School in Suffolk, and had gone, as "a pupil in farming", to a village in that same county.[2] Here again we see the unreliability of John's dating of events. He went up to Corpus Christi College, Cambridge in the Autumn of 1891; but TFP did not begin his farm-training until 1 March 1892, on the evidence of his diary for that year.[3]

For some understanding of why TFP went back to Suffolk, and only a few miles from the school he had just left, we are once again indebted to Louis Wilkinson. In "Some Memories of T. F. Powys" he writes:

> A few years later, he decided to be a farmer, and again his mother wrote to mine, asking if she knew of any farm where Theodore could learn the business. My mother's sister's husband had a farm about ten miles from us, at Rendham in Suffolk, and it was there that Theodore went. This uncle-by-marriage of mine was very much an amateur farmer, losing money steadily year by year, so he could hardly have been a competent instructor. But Theodore did learn something about farming.[4]

Who was this unnamed uncle-by-marriage whose pupil in farming TFP would be for more than two years? Louis Wilkinson's mother had five married sisters, but only one, so the electoral rolls show, farmed in Rendham—Arthur McDougall, whose sons, Roderick and Alexander, had been TFP's contemporaries at Eaton House. The McDougall family lived at Hill House, a substantial property set back from the road and secluded by trees, on a road that ran north-east out of Rendham (population 336 in 1891). South of the house was the Smithy, and just to the north, Rendham Green. Arthur McDougall was a considerable property-

---

1 *Autobiography*, p.164 2 *Ibid.*, p. 164 3 HRHRC 4 *Theodore*, p. 10

holder in the neighbourhood and active in local affairs, eventually becoming a Justice of the Peace. He also owned the historic Dernford Hall Farm in Sweffling, the site of the Manor of Dernford. This fact is of some importance in the history of TFP's farming activities because Dernford Hall Farm is just up the Glemham Road from White House Farm, where TFP was to begin farming for himself some three years after his arrival in Rendham. TFP in fact spent some of his time at Dernford Hall Farm, helping James Ellis, McDougall's bailiff there. So the choice of White House Farm placed TFP conveniently close to the property of his mentor, Arthur McDougall. However, by 1895, the bailiff was one John Row. It is reasonable to suppose then that the fictional John Roe who figures so prominently in *Mark Only* and *The Two Thieves* had his genesis in TFP's next-door neighbour, McDougall's bailiff. In an interview with Claude Luke, TFP recalled in 1936: "I wrote one story around a real character, a Suffolk labourer named John Roe [sic], who undoubtedly had the noblest spirit of any man I have known."[1] Now we know just who he was.

TFP has, atypically, left us three accounts of his arrival in Rendham. His diary entry for Tuesday, 1 March 1892, is the most cryptic: "Arrived here, snow, beginning of bad weather." But in the same black notebook into which he had copied poems at school, he wrote a fuller account: "Arrived safe at Rendham / Spent a happy evening Went / to bed. Good beginning." Finally, there is a much fuller, albeit slightly fictionalized, account in "This is Thyself", in which Mr McDougall appears as Mr Elsley:

> I did not go to a farmer to learn farming; I went to a gentleman who always tried to farm and never could succeed. This poor man found farming a continual drain upon his capital, and he was forced to make burrows into his capital like a rabbit every time he had a bad harvest, which was almost every year.
>
> The groom met me at the station the first night I arrived, and for supper I tasted beer for the first time. I thought it very nasty. In the morning I was shown the room where breakfast was to be, and where Mr Elsley read prayers.[2]

The diary provides the best account of day-to-day activities on the farm. It is clear that TFP was to learn both by observation and by participation; so from the first we find him sharing in all

[1] "Why I Have Given up Writing" [2] Selected Early Works, p. 333

the humdrum tasks of the farm: cutting wood, dressing sheep, setting folds, spreading molehills, chopping beets, etc. And with the solemnity of youth, he faithfully records useful tips to be remembered: "Single lambs have to have their tails cut off earlier than doubles because they soon grow fat." "Always be careful to cut off young shoots off beets as they kill lambs as quick as anything."

TFP took a particular interest in sheep, and often visited Mr [Alfred] Chambers on the adjoining Grange Farm to learn more. Even at this early date, it seems, he was planning to include sheep on his own farm, when he got one. The vision of himself as shepherd is a persistent one, and probably had something to do with his desire to go into farming in the first place. It is part of the sense of self he was shaping, as well as a mission in life, an alternative pastoral role. We see it most vividly and explicitly in the moving description of his first efforts at White House Farm:

> I intended to begin farming with sheep, with ewes and I would tend them myself. I bought them at the further end of the county and they arrived by the Cattle train at 1 in the morning [at Saxmundham station]. As I drove these tired beasts the three miles to my farm my thoughts were in the East. I was David and was watching my Father's sheep in the plains. The beasts and I were alone under the stars, they were friendly and loved me and filled the road with the soft pattering of their feet, my heart was bubbling with hope, I longed to pass my life as a shepherd watching the sheep, and I shut the gate of their field and leaned over it watching them lying down, and they formed a half circle round the gate, and looked at me with their pleading tired eyes.[1]

No wonder, then, that images of sheep / shepherd / flock recur throughout *The Soliloquy of a Hermit*, many sections of which had their origin in "This is Thyself". Some are vividly remembered impressions direct from TFP's farming experience:

> And I remember a night in winter when I saw a white lamb lying quite dead under a clear moon.[2]
>
> ... and in one place I saw the half-eaten carcass of a sheep.[3]

Others are rather more figurative, as in: "The priests who also know their duty have to keep the gods away from the flock, for

---

1 "This is Thyself", Ch. 2, pp. 346–7
2 *The Soliloquy of a Hermit*, p. 54   3 *Ibid.*, p. 74

fear the flock might give away some of its wool or perhaps even a ewe lamb, here and there, without a priest's blessing."¹

Inevitably too, the self-as-shepherd makes an appearance in his fiction. What, for example, is the usual name of the shepherd in his short stories? Shepherd Poose—that is Powys with a Suffolk accent! Often this character has a minor role, but in two stories— "Thy Beautiful Flock" and "A Pretty Babe" (both Christmas stories, not coincidentally)—he is central to the plot. And in the fable of "The Dog and the Lantern" Shepherd Poose is seen by his dog as a truly God-like figure, as he puts a lame ewe out of its misery: "Here indeed . . . is God Almighty because he saves or destroys as he chooses."²

To help in grasping the full import of this point, it is necessary to cite JCP's profoundly insightful statement in a letter to Louis Wilkinson: "He took God or projected God out of himself and made God his *other self*, and, as God was made out of himself, God's character and God's peculiarities were Theodore's. God in fact was another Theodore."³

There was not much time for recreation at Rendham, but occasionally there is mention in the diary of a walk with Mrs McDougall in Deadman's Lane (a place that crops up, so to speak, in "The Painted Wagon" and "The Suet Pudding"), a bird-shooting expedition, or a visit to church (sometimes even twice!) on Sundays. However, it was while he was learning to farm in East Anglia that TFP began a broader programme of self-education, of literary and philosophical reading. In the beginning, at Rendham, he seems to have thrown himself purposefully into reading such "practical" books as *Morton's Handbooks of the Farm, No 11. The Crops*, 5th edn, April 1892, which he purchased soon after publication, and annotated with an alternative cycle of crop rotation.⁴ If the the Bissell collection is fairly complete, the shift of interest from ploughing to poetry is first observable with a gift from Gertrude in November 1894, of Shelley's *Lyrics and Minor Poems*. By 1896, now established in Sweffling, TFP became one of the prime movers to establish a Library in the village. At first, he

1 *The Soliloquy of a Hermit*, p. 81   2 *Fables*, p. 97
3 JCP to Louis Wilkinson, 24 October 1956; Letters of John Cowper Powys to Louis Wilkinson, p. 382
4 After TFP had given up farming he lent this book to Katie, who had herself become interested in farming. In a letter of 17 December 1902, she asks him to bring another farm book to Montacute, and says she will return *The Soil*, but keep *Crops* a little longer. (Bissell Collection)

was asked to serve as librarian and to keep the books at his place. The Parish Council minutes record his acceptance, and his continued involvement with the Library until 1901. The culmination of the project came with the establishment of a Reading Room (so marked on early large-scale ordnance survey maps) to the north of the windmill. Without discounting the desires of working men for access to books, it is hard not to see in the Library project a strategy of TFP's to cultivate his mind as well as his fields. During his six years at Sweffling (1895–1901) in fact he says: "I fear I was too often in the shade of a tree, reading, when I should have been among the furrows."[1] Even if we do not accept this statement entirely at face value, there is still irony in the fact that it was in the isolation of the countryside that TFP should have found the inspiration towards self-education. And because there he was his own teacher, his books became a part of him in a way that might never have occurred, had he followed his brothers to Cambridge.

Most of his own early acquisition of books appears to have occurred in the years 1895–1901, while he was farming for himself. Thus in June 1897, he purchased a white-bound volume of Fitzgerald's *Rubaiyat*, a work that moved him enough to pay a visit to Fitzgerald's grave at Boulge in August 1901, just before he left Suffolk and farming for ever. No doubt he had in mind Fitzgerald's pronouncement from Boulge Cottage: "Here I sit, read, mope, and become very wise." He also bought the copy of Kipling's *Barrack Room Ballads* already mentioned, and was given another gift, *Selections from Plato*, by Gertrude, who kept house for him for some time from mid 1896 onwards. In 1898, he bought his first volume of Nietzsche, *Thus Spake Zarathustra*. John acknowledges in his autobiography that TFP "discovered and appreciated [Nietzsche] long before I did," and surmises that his courage on the farm was sustained by nocturnal readings of the works.[2] That comment of John's merits reflection; it means that a young man without the benefit of higher education who had been stuck on a remote East Anglian farm for some years had read a contemporary philosopher essentially unknown to his university-educated older brother. Whence came TFP's enthusiasm for Nietzsche? one may ask. JCP attributes it to Dr Bernard O'Neill:

1 "Why I Have Given up Writing"
2 *Autobiography*, p. 194. JCP put the matter even more strongly in a letter to Louis Wilkinson of 8 November 1956: "Theodore read Nietzsche before I even heard of him." ("Some Memories of T. F. Powys", *Theodore*, pp. 10–11)

"he, from whom I first heard of Dostoievsky, Theodore of Nietzsche, Llewelyn of Montaigne". Since Elwin (1946) says that JCP first met O'Neill in 1897 (possibly through Harry Lyon), it is not impossible that in the same year he should have talked to TFP of Nietzsche. But TFP was farming in Sweffling, so their discussion would either have occurred during a visit by JCP and O'Neill, or during one of TFP's rare visits to Court House in Sussex. Whatever the case, how could JCP have remained in ignorance of Nietzsche, as he represents himself? The other possibility is that TFP discovered Nietzsche for himself—a possibility by no means to be discounted. The edition of *Thus Spake Zarathustra* that he owned is the very first English translation, by Alexander Tille in 1896, part of a projected but never completed Collected Works of Friedrich Nietzsche; and the English translations were very widely reviewed when they began to appear in 1896.[1] In 1896 too, Havelock Ellis wrote a series of three enthusiastically sympathetic articles on Nietzsche in *The Savoy*, the gist of which could easily have been conveyed to TFP by the likes of his cousin, Ralph Shirley, even if TFP himself did not read them. In 1899, TFP bought another volume of Nietzsche, *The Case of Wagner* (in which, perhaps as an act of homage, he pasted a photograph of the philosopher) as well as Boswell's *Life of Johnson*, De Quincey's *Confessions of an English Opium Eater*, and Henley's anthology of *English Lyrics*. The late developer was blossoming remarkably in the congenial air of Suffolk. Finally, in 1900 and 1901, he purchased no fewer than ten volumes: Sir Thomas Browne, Carlyle, Heine, collections of Essays by De Quincey, Johnson, and Lamb, Voltaire, etc. Perhaps the best indicator of his future plans was the purchase of G. H. Lewes's *Principles of Success in Literature* in January 1901. It was no longer sufficient to be like Milton's shepherd in *L'Allegro*, telling his tale "under the hawthorn in the dale". The glow-worm in "John Told and the Worm" asks the drunken farmer the very questions that TFP must have posed to himself at this crucial juncture in life:

> But have you never considered that there are other joys in the world than the mere pleasure of possessing corn, sheep and bullocks? . . . Have you never considered the divine joy of philosophic meditation, the seeking after Truth, or the practice of lovely Goodness?[2]

1 Bridgewater, *Nietzsche in Anglosaxony*, p. 14   2 *Fables*, pp. 158–9

He had learned enough from the land to know that there could be but one answer for him, one path to follow. It would be many years before he learned his next lesson—that there are no principles of success in literature. There is only the solitude of writing, and the stamina to confront failure. In that, at least, he had had much practice.

3

"One Foot in the Furrow"
Theodore Powys in East Anglia

"A young man believes in himself, an old man has found himself out."—"This is Thyself"

Theodore Powys never could have written the kind of expansively self-indulgent autobiography that brought John, his older and more loquacious brother, such well-deserved acclaim. Nonetheless, *The Soliloquy of a Hermit,* his first "real" book, is a work that is insistently and obsessively autobiographical; and in it, to borrow the words of Graham Greene, occurs "that moment of crystallization when the dominant theme is plainly expressed, when the private universe becomes visible even to the least sensitive reader".[1] One facet of TFP's private universe is revealed in the remarkable persistence of a group of related images in his work: images of field and farm, of earth and clay. They are all but ubiquitous in *The Soliloquy,* as the following samples suggest:

> A priest *has his roots in the deep darkness of* human desires.[2]
>
> The common man...talks about..."*driving pigs to market*", "*sowing red wheat*".[3]
>
> *His* [the priest's] *is the soil* in which God practises His divine moods.[4]
>
> I love a *broken roller left in a field* that belongs to a *crippled farmer,* a weakly tottering old man, crooked and bent; all his *farm tools are broken* and tied up with string.[5]
>
> God often rests by the side of the roller and watches my little boys play and the *old farmer at plough.*[6]

---

1 "Henry James: The Private Universe", p. 23
2 *The Soliloquy of a Hermit*, p. 1   3 Ibid., p. 3   4 p. 4   5 p. 6   6 *Ibid.*

It is the priest's duty to *dig in the clay* through which the moods of God pass.[1]

Man is a collection of atoms . . . but always deeply *rooted in the soil.*[2]

The people of the earth are *clay* pieces that the moods of God kindle into life.[3]

We shall not, however, recognize the import of such rustic imagery until we erase from our minds that persistent and powerful picture of TFP conjured up by his brother: "of a windy November afternoon, making his way, like Christian with his forlorn pack, to his weekly purgatory at Saxmundham Market". John has summoned this "symbol of ultimate desolation", not from TFP's experience, but from the furthermost reaches of his all-too-sympathetic imagination. The allusion to Bunyan (whom John knew to be one of his brother's favourite writers) betrays the literariness of the image just as his admiration for his brother's alleged "courage in giving orders to those difficult East Anglian peasants"[4] reflects his own fear of the inarticulate farm-workers in Sussex from whom he so evidently shied.

Once John's misleading vision of TFP in purgatory is set aside, the agricultural, earthy images in *The Soliloquy* reveal themselves as markers of TFP's buried life; they suggest how much TFP the writer draws upon TFP the farmer of yesteryear. So to understand the former, we must search out the unknown TFP—and we will find him in East Anglia, the "country of his past", to borrow D. H. Lawrence's phrase, where the topography of his imagination first found shape.[5]

Norfolk Interlude

The Powys family had East Anglian connections through their mother Mary Cowper Powys (née Johnson), whose father, the Reverend William Cowper Johnson, was Rector of Yaxham, and, from 1880, of Northwold, Norfolk. He was also a Canon of Norwich Cathedral. Both John, in his *Autobiography,* and Littleton, in *The Joy of It,* have recorded memories of holidays spent with their Johnson relatives, recalling with particular affection the devotion of their maiden aunts, [Theo]dora and [Henri]etta. "Aunt Dora

---

1 *The Soliloquy of a Hermit*, p. 7 2 *Ibid.* 3 *Ibid.* 4 *Autobiography*, p. 190
5 "The Shades of Spring", The Tales of D. H. Lawrence, p. 104

was never a teacher, she was *one of us* . . . my father and all us sons simply adored Aunt Dora; & I do still," wrote John in a letter to Louis Wilkinson.[1] TFP visited Yaxham at least once, in 1878, at the age of three, in the company of his older brothers; but Northwold and its environs became, in Littleton's words, their boyhood Earthly Paradise.[2] Here they spent three glorious weeks of many a summer, obliged only to report for meals on time, to participate in post-breakfast bible-readings, and to attend church on Sundays. Their days were filled with the kind of activities beloved by children of any generation: boating, fishing, and exploring the world of nature. Since their grandfather had thoughtfully bought a punt for them to use, they could paddle lazily along the tributary of the river Wissey which abutted the Rectory garden, or brave the waters of the swift but shallow "big river", as they called it. The waters themselves seem to have been a fisherman's dream, to judge by Littleton's account; he mentions the presence of chub, dace, gudgeon, perch, pike, roach, and trout. Littleton was, of course, the main enthusiast, when it came to fishing, and soon became the family expert too. John once presented Littleton with a little notebook in which to record his observations; this still survives in the Bissell Collection, together with the impressive pen-and-ink drawings with which Littleton embellished his notes—evidence that like his sister Gertrude he had inherited some of his mother's artistic talent. And, one summer, when Littleton was for some reason not going to Northwold, he conscientiously drew a map of the river for young TFP, detailing the location of various kinds of fish and the best way to catch them.[3] Perhaps it was the memory of these idyllic boyhood summers as much as the family connection that drew TFP back to Norfolk in 1894. In a letter to JCP, moreover, we have explicit testimony to the lasting impression Northwold made upon him. The letter was in response to one from JCP who was with "Old Littleton mostly in our ancient haunts at Northwold", as JCP had described his plans to Llewelyn in a letter from Patchin Place, dated 19 April 1929.

TFP writes movingly and in surprising detail:

> I have often dreamed that I was at Northwold again. But I don't expect that I shall ever get there. And now that the little pond where the water lilies and the frogs used to be is filled up,

---

1 8 November 1956; Letters of John Cowper Powys to Louis Wilkinson, p. 385
2 *The Joy of It*, p. 80   3 *Ibid.*, p. 87

I almost feel as if Northwold is buried like a corpse and the grave filled up like the pond with earth. I remember those Horse flies. But I should like to have smelt the pig sty again where we used to get those little pink worms.[1]

After nearly two and a half years as a farming pupil in the friendly haven of Rendham, why should the nineteen-year-old TFP have moved so far north (relatively speaking) into a different county? For one thing, there were those strong family connections in Norfolk; and it is likely that he had determined or been persuaded to set up as a farmer there. Of course, it would be necessary to know more about local farming practice and conditions, before he could begin to investigate the availability and cost of farms in the area. He was, in any case, still rather young to begin farming for himself, given that he was not from a farming family. So it made sense to attach himself once more to an established farmer in an area not too far removed from the familiar childhood terrain of his grandparents' former Northwold home, or from the parish of his uncle Cowper Johnson in Yaxham. And there were other relatives now in Norwich, among them his beloved Aunts, Dora and Etta.

Warham was, in a number of ways, a happy choice of location, especially for a prospective farmer. It lay close to the heart of that area which had gained so much from the beneficent efforts of the agricultural pioneer, "Coke of Norfolk". He had urged upon his tenants the virtues of marling the light soil, the use of the Norfolk four-course rotation system (pioneered by "Turnip" Townsend of Raynham earlier in the eighteenth century), and the folding of sheep on arable land—all efforts to increase fertility and productivity. Moreover, he was the kind of enlightened landlord who saw the advantage of giving his tenants long leases, often up to twenty-one years. His descendant, the Earl of Leicester, was Lord of the Manor and sole landowner in Warham St Mary (an area of 2,067 acres); he was also the principal landowner in the contiguous parish of Warham All Saints (1,121 acres). The twin parishes had a combined population of 340 in 1891, rather larger than Rendham even a decade later, but not so different in character. There was a post-office, a bakery and a wheelwright in Warham All Saints, and of course, a pub, the Three Horse Shoes, whose landlord was Henry Ramm. The blacksmith, Isaac Tuck,

---

1 TFP to JCP, 7 August 1929; HRHRC

lived in Warham St Mary, as did the Reverend Charles Tilton Digby, long-time Rector of Warham All Saints. A memorial to his forty-nine years of service (1874–1923) is to be found in the modest hilltop church, and he himself donated the ornate alabaster reredos which graces the altar. However, the Rector is important in this account not for his pastoral accomplishments but for his connection with the Powys family. He was a contemporary and schoolfellow of TFP's maternal uncle, Cowper Johnson. They both attended Tittleshall School (later Clapham School) then run by a Mr Sayer. The young Digby's father, Rev. the Hon. Kenelm Digby, was then Rector of Tittleshall, and a Canon of Norwich Cathedral, contemporary with another distant relative, Canon F. Patteson. The Digby family was, incidentally, related to the Digbys of Sherborne Castle, Dorset.

Since Cowper Johnson's father, William Cowper Johnson, was at that time Rector of Yaxham, only about ten miles or so southeast of Tittleshall, contact between the two families, once established, would not have been difficult to maintain. And in both families there were seven children; but while all were boys in the Digby household, Cowper was the only boy in the Johnson home. Cowper first went to Tittleshall School in 1856, when he was twelve, and was later joined by his cousins, Henry and Hamilton Barham Johnson, who thereby also became part of the circle of friends. Many of the Norfolk families took their holidays in Cromer, and in 1857 the Johnsons and their friends, the Digbys, were at the resort, according to the diary of Mrs J. Johnson. For later years there is evidence of continuing contact among the families. In 1868, for example, the Rev. William Cowper Johnson preached for the Rev. Kenelm Digby at Tittleshall, and in 1887 Mrs Barham Johnson "heard good Norfolk stories" from Charles Digby, by then well established as Rector in Warham.[1]

Clearly then it must have been her brother who suggested to TFP's mother that Warham would be a suitable place for her son to finish his farm training. The village was not far from Yaxham and the Rector was an old school friend, known also to the Barham Johnsons of Welbourne. What could be better, Cowper may have argued, than to have such a man to watch out for TFP's spiritual, as well as his physical, welfare. Mary Powys must have been much reassured. At the same time, she may have begun to

[1] Information from unpublished diary and letters in the Mary Barham Johnson Collection and in "The Powys Mother"

envisage a possible future for her apparently wayward son. Perhaps he had disappointed his father (and himself) by being disqualified academically from pursuing the priesthood; but were he to establish himself as a farmer in Norfolk, might he not make a good life for himself and help strengthen the ties with her side of the family? In the absence of any testimony from Mrs Powys herself, this vision of a future long past must remain mere speculation. Yet it does provide a plausible explanation for the fact that each of TFP's decisive moves into and around East Anglia—to Eaton House, to Rendham and to Warham—was at the initiative (and this may be just the right word for it) of Mary Powys. She would seem to have been particularly close to TFP (the testimony of Llewelyn about their being in "tragic communion" may be recalled here; it is all the more convincing because it bears the taint of fraternal jealousy) and might therefore have been more than ordinarily anxious to see this son set up in the world. As best one can judge, mother and son showed marked temperamental affinities: both took life very seriously and both inclined to a Cowperian melancholy. John's "Cowperism", as he called it, is a different characteristic, a self-revelatory impulse to "tear away the portentous mask of comic dignity which conceals the tragic dignity of every human soul," as he himself analysed it.[1] In the circumstances, it is not surprising that Mrs Powys should be unusually attentive to her son's welfare. Certainly, none of her other sons was so privileged. Later, when Willie, the youngest son, decided that he wished to be a farmer, he was sent for his training to nearby Abbey Farm in Montacute. Could it be that his parents regretted allowing TFP to stray so far from home at so tender an age, and determined not to repeat this "mistake"? If so, it is ironic that Willie, after a mere five years farming for himself at Witcombe, just north of Montacute, found himself a life-long haven far more remote and exciting than any East Anglian farm, in East Africa. Here he became the successful sheep-farmer that his elder brother had yearned to be a generation before.

    TFP's new home in Warham was Church Farm, the property of Edward Nelson (1848–1924). There was a longstanding relationship between the Johnson and Nelson families that no doubt accounts for TFP being where he was: the Reverend John Nelson (1793–1867) had been a pupil of Dr John Nelson's school in

[1] *Autobiography*, p. 625

Winterton in 1824–5. It was from the Reverend John Nelson's paternal uncle that Edward Nelson, the farmer, descended; so it was quite fitting that in 1894 TFP should come under the tutelage of this member of the Nelson family. Edward Nelson was forty-six at the time of TFP's arrival. He was well established, and had been farming there at least since 1883, as *Kelly's Directory* for that year shows. He and his wife, Lucy (1858–1934) had one son, Edward Russell (1891–1917), destined to be killed in action in Njimbwe, East Africa, on 3 February 1917, at the age of twenty-six.

It seems appropriate, at this point, to indicate how we can be sure that TFP went to Church Farm rather than one of the others in the village. To begin with, ownership and/or tenancy were established for all the farms in the village for the relevant period. The only name at all connected with the Powys family was "Nelson". There is an interesting anecdote about a Mr Nelson in the same 7 x 9 black notebook (now in the Bissell Collection) that TFP had used for poems while in school at Eaton House, and later for notes and farming accounts. A few of the entries are clearly rough drafts of those that appear in TFP's 1892 diary of the HRHRC, and refer to his first days in Rendham. Others are dated and refer to his own farming affairs at Sweffling, of which more later. The Nelson reference occurs immediately after the last Rendham entry, and could easily be misinterpreted as part of it. Indeed, Michel Pouillard, the only other scholar who seems to have examined the notebook, makes just this mistaken assumption. He takes Mr Nelson to be the "uncle-by-marriage" ("beau-père") of Louis Wilkinson with whom TFP began his farming apprenticeship in Suffolk, and incorrectly has him beginning this phase in 1893 rather than in 1892.[1] In fact, as has been established earlier, Arthur McDougall was the man in question; and the name "Nelson" appears nowhere in the electoral rolls or other records for Rendham or surrounding parishes. Nor could he even have been McDougall's farm bailiff; that post was held by James Ellis at least until 1896, and then by John Row. Only with the establishment of these facts did it become clear that the TFP–Nelson connection had to be a Norfolk one, not a Suffolk one. The anecdote itself describes in the sketchiest of terms the confrontation resulting from Nelson's decision to install "barb

---

1 *T. F. Powys*, p. 55

wire"; it tells how "the wire scratches everything" and "two individuals swore to rid the community of the pest." This is perhaps TFP's earliest attempt to record an incident which might later be transformed into fictional form; it is certainly also the only piece of his own work he illustrated himself, albeit crudely.

Church House Farm lies directly opposite the Church of St Mary Magdalene in Warham St Mary, at a bend in the road, and on the south side of it. Behind the house and barns, the fields slope gently upward; the land is "of rich loamy nature, producing excellent crops of wheat, oats, and barley", according to *Kelly's Directory of Norfolk*, 1896. The house itself, like the church across the road, is of flint construction, and faces away from the road on to an enclosed yard and the fields beyond. A line of wooden shuttered horse-stalls (more recently occupied by cattle) is the only reminder of the stalwart horses that drew the plough in TFP's day. The barn with its red pantiled roof looks deceptively modern from the outside; but inside, the rough-hewn timbers of the high beams provide impressive testimony of its great age. It was in this building, almost certainly, that the nineteen-year-old TFP helped to crush mangolds in the hand-operated mangold crusher. Some forty years later, he still remembered the experience, and recalled it vividly for Theodora, his adopted daughter. At about seven or so in the morning, he would go out to a load of cold and frost-encrusted marigolds; they hurt his hands to touch and, in the mangold crusher, sounded like pebbles on a beach as the waves sucked them in and out. The mangolds were used as fodder for the sheep and cattle.

For some strange reason, TFP never learned to milk, in spite, apparently, of a strong desire to do so. Perhaps he was too nervous in his approach to the cows; the animals would detect that, and make things difficult. He did learn to plough, but never, he said, achieved more than "passable ploughmanship". However, he acquired a life-long admiration for a truly expert ploughman, and loved to see a good team in action. Theodora (known as "Susie" as a child) recalls being taken to witness a field in Mappowder being ploughed by just such a professional ploughman with his two dapple-grey Shires. "Remember this, Susie," TFP advised solemnly, "You won't see this sight any more in a year or two."[1]

1 *PR* 9, p. 70

This anecdote illustrates nicely how irrevocably changed TFP was by his farming experience. There is no indication here of bitterness, only of forgivable nostalgia. TFP's farming past has been indelibly etched upon his memory.

Were it not for the existence of a few letters from TFP to his sister Gertrude now in the HRHRC, it might not ever have been known that he spent a year in Warham. Alas, the letters are not very revealing about his day-to-day activities on the farm; they are valuable rather for giving us his location on notepaper with the printed heading "Warham, / Wells, Norfolk" and for fixing, at least approximately, the time-span of his stay in Warham. The earliest letter is dated "8th of August 1894", the second "17th of Feb 1895"; and the last, "19th of May 1895", announces his plan to visit Montacute for about three weeks, beginning on 24 June. He must then have returned to Warham to help with the harvest before heading for his own newly acquired farm in Sweffling. His move to Sweffling had already been more or less settled by the time of his second letter, for in that he talks of having Gertrude visit him for a week at the end of October or November, and of wanting her to be his first visitor. There exists but one other item of evidence pertinent to TFP's time in Norfolk: a short story, "Charlie" in the Bissell Collection.[1] This three-thousand-word story, written in 1913, was one of a group that Frances Wilkinson had typed and tried in vain, for the best part of two years, to get taken by a magazine in America. Although it conforms to a well-established Theodorian pattern in its ending, suicide by drowning, it is atypical in being an old-fashioned frame story and in being transparently and revealingly autobiographical in its main character. Charlie Blackburn is described as "one of those castaways thrown out by the upper classes" because he "could not pass his exams as a boy." A man of forty, with a reddish moustache and hair already grey, he loved long walks. His father had been a well-to-do clergyman who had so many children that none of them was left much of a legacy. Charlie lived with a farmer in "a little village near the sea in Norfolk" who, so the narrator observes, "must have made a good thing out of him for he did the work of a labourer" in spite of the fact that most of his income "was handed over to the farmer . . . to pay for his lodging." There is an edge to this comment that raises the suspicion that TFP may just have

[1] now published in Selected Early Works

been remembering his own treatment on the Nelson farm. And while we must not forget that it is presented as fiction, the story does offer credible details of the very activities in which the real-life TFP would have engaged. There are references to "Autumn evenings in a snug Inn", to playing cards with a neighbouring farmer, invitations to tennis, haymaking, and to walking in the salt-marshes. These last, TFP evokes with particular vividness: "the curious yellow marshes with their mud creeks and wooden bridges", the sand-hills, and the wild, strange cry of the redshanks overhead. The claim that Charlie attended church twice on Sunday might seem piously implausible to the TFP most readers know. But in fact his own 1892 diary reveals that while he was at Rendham he often attended church twice on a Sunday; so there is no reason why the practice should not have been continued in Warham. In rural communities, the church was still a social as well as a religious centre for the community. One minor detail of TFP's description suggests how well he recalled the Church of St Mary's. In the story we are told that "Charlie always sat in one of the old high-backed pews;" in fact, the nave is still filled with just the kind of high box-pews that TFP described. The story makes no mention, however, of the enormous and impressive three-decker pulpit with projecting reading stands, a canopy, and a flight of eight steps.

Warham is only two miles from Wells and the sea. Along the coast here stretch miles of flat, wind-swept salt-marshes, barren to behold, it is true, but a haven for wild-fowl in bewildering variety: ducks, widgeon, wild geese, curlew, snipe, partridge, terns and stately blue herons. Today, much of the area is part of a nature reserve; in TFP's day it was largely open for shooting. And here TFP continued to engage in another activity that must surprise those who know his regard for the sanctity of all life in later years—shooting. TFP's own first experience of shooting seems, in fact, to have been gained in Rendham, and he appears to have assumed the unlikely role of adviser to his elder brother in the matter of firearms, if we accept JCP's account. The gun itself was to be for JCP's protection against the intrusion of College rowdies into his room. However, the purchase of the weapon took place while both boys were at Montacute during the summer before JCP went up to Cambridge, that is, in 1891. But TFP did not begin his farm training in Rendham until March 1892; so he would have been as innocent of firearms as JCP at the time. Still, in JCP's account, we have the earliest reference to any interest in weapons on the part of TFP. And soon after his arrival in Rendham, he was given the opportunity to use a gun himself. In his diary for Thursday, 10 March 1892, TFP records offhandedly that "I shot two or three small birds in the morning." So by the time he arrived in Warham some two years later, he would have been an experienced marksman, and no doubt, eager to test his skills on the abundance of wild-fowl in the coastal area. His earliest surviving letter from Warham confirms that "I spent all yesterday afternoon in a creak [sic] close to the sea on the salt-marshes waiting for duck or wimbrell but only shot one redshank."[1] He also indulged in some rabbit-shooting among the sand-hills by the coast, where rabbits in their thousands scampered. In retrospect, TFP regretted this youthful enthusiasm for shooting, though his love for nature and wildlife remained with him the rest of his life. One detects, for instance, an apologetic note in "Charlie". The narrator comments that he never could understand Charlie's liking for following the hounds, and tries to excuse it or explain it away by adding "He never got near the 'kill' . . . he thought that a hunt was a harmless game, like a paper-chase, for he certainly never saw anything killed." Significant, too, is the anecdote Theodora Scutt remembers her adoptive father recounting about his time in East Anglia. Out on a shooting party, he brought down a snipe, but did not kill it clean, so that when he approached "it looked up at me . . . with a look of human reproach," he said. He never shot another bird, and in telling the story—characteristically for the mature TFP—expressed regret rather than pride in his achievement. Given the evidence that he sometimes went hunting with his foreman, Nunn, in Sweffling, this anecdote must refer to TFP's later Suffolk years, though the location is given as Norfolk. In any case, when TFP's son, Dicky, was old enough to want a gun, TFP was very much against it, so much had his attitude changed. And Theodora Scutt says that "his intense dislike of firearms" amounted to a phobia. "Daddy had a phobia about guns, and you can't argue with a phobia."[2] But *his* view on guns did not altogether prevail with the next generation; for there survives a photograph, sent by TFP to Mrs Stracey, the boys' godmother, of Dicky and Francis proudly posing with their rifles before them.

1 TFP to Gertrude Powys, 8 August 1894; HRHRC
2 *Cuckoo in the Powys Nest*, p. 181

TFP's love of nature did not, of course, begin in East Anglia; it was an important inheritance from his father. JCP tells in the *Autobiography* how "every phenomenon he [the father] referred to, whether animate or inanimate, became a sacrosanct thing, a privileged object";[1] of how he would return home from walks with a bunch of wild-flowers, and of his pride in his "formidable" collection of birds' eggs. As a child, TFP never seems to have manifested particular interest in the world of nature in the public way that John and Littleton did, each of whom became a collector. It was John who followed his father in collecting birds' eggs— though he intimates that it was a pursuit born of filial piety—while Littleton concentrated on butterflies and fossils. But if TFP resolutely collected nothing, as JCP asserts, he was nonetheless indelibly marked as his father's son.[2] For, in his maturity, it was TFP who would return from his walk with a buttonhole of wild flowers, and who treated every aspect of nature as if it were indeed sacrosanct. His habit of tapping his favourite oak (a habit he may have copied from his Rendham mentor, Arthur McDougall), of moving errant worms from his path, or of throwing a pebble on a pond—gestures of acknowledgement to other sentient beings— provide direct testimony of his reverence for nature. His reformed attitude to birds is evidenced in a number of ways—he really liked the cuckoo (no doubt in its role as harbinger of spring), used to feed jackdaws in Mappowder, and became extremely angry when someone in the village shot a heron during the war. And, inevitably, one recalls TFP's fondness for birds and bird imagery in his stories and novels. There is the Nellie bird (*Diomedea spadicea*) in *Mockery Gap*, the death-dealing cormorant and the foolish guillemot in *Innocent Birds*, the Holy Dove sent to stir things up in "The Dove and the Eagle", not to mention the diplomatic crow in "The Coat and the Crow" who manages to persuade the coat that the seeds in Mr Facey's field are really "the crumbs of the Holy Sacrament" there to be "religiously consumed" by a thousand waiting crows. Among characters of note are Parson Sparrow, Luke Bird, a St Francis-like character who preaches to the animals, and the Reverend James Duck, the Rector of Goat Green. But most widespread of all are incidental images in which

---

[1] *Autobiography*, p. 51

[2] "It was of course unthinkable that a son of my father should collect nothing. No doubt it was for precisely this reason that TFP, always so terrifyingly original, did actually collect nothing." (*Autobiography*, p. 50)

we see how thoroughly TFP has assimilated his youthful experience as a hunter. For example, in "The Dewpond", we encounter the Reverend John Gasser "stepping the ground like a sportsman looking for a *jacksnipe*";[1] in "Abraham Men" Mr Pring, the roadmender, has "the troubled expression of a *plover* that would lead a child away from its nest",[2] while Mrs Dunell "waddled about her front room like a *duck* on unsafe ice."[3] These are not just the incidental images of a gifted writer but the observations of a keen-eyed countryman. No wonder that TFP claimed modestly in an interview in *John O'London's Weekly* that "Whatever inspiration I had came from Nature and from one or two other writers."[4]

There has been very little substantive information about TFP's years as a farmer. For example, Louis Wilkinson asserted that "when he was about twenty-four [i.e. 1891], his father bought a farm for him at Sweffling, near Rendham."[5] Graves, usually quite precise about dates (one of the strengths of his book), is uncharacteristically vague about almost all matters pertaining to the farming years. In the head-notes to Chapter 2 (1885–1894), he writes: "apprenticed to a farmer, 1891–93, then to his own farm at Sweffling in Suffolk"; in the body of the chapter, he asserts: "Theodore was capable, and, despite being only seventeen, he managed his labourers with authority."[6] In fact, neither Louis Wilkinson nor Graves are accurate. TFP did not begin his "apprenticeship" until 1 March 1892, and remained at Rendham until 1894, when he moved to Warham, Norfolk for a year. So it was not until October 1895, when he was a few months shy of twenty years old, that he eventually took up residence at White House Farm, his own master at last. For nearly three years he had prepared himself conscientiously for this moment of independence, and his moving vision of the life he planned, a pastoral idyll no less, shines through his retrospective account in "This is Thyself" of the harsh reality he in fact encountered: "I wanted to love my home, to work with my hands in the fields, to use the workpeople kindly, and to settle with my books into a quiet seclusion."[7]

It was from the first, an impossible, and curiously Wordsworthian, dream of "Man free, Man working for himself, with

---

1 *Bottle's Path*, p. 209   2 *The Left Leg*, p. 241   3 *Ibid.*, p. 244
4 "Why I Have Given up Writing"   5 *Theodore*, p. 10   6 *The Brothers Powys*, p. 32
7 Selected Early Works, p. 346

choice / Of time, and place, and object . . . ."¹ In his youthful desire to succeed he must have persuaded himself that he would not suffer as had his mentor, Arthur McDougall, who as we have seen "was forced to make burrows into his capital like a rabbit every time he had a bad harvest, which was almost every year."² Yet the odds were heavily stacked against the young farmer; for he had chosen to begin farming at an extraordinarily inauspicious time in farming history—in the middle of that long period between 1870 and 1914 which agricultural economists term "The Great Depression". Prices for cereals, livestock, and land fell dramatically. An estate purchased in 1874 for £4,000 was sold for less than £900 in 1897; another property acquired in 1870 at £45 an acre went for a mere £16 an acre in 1897. Within this period of forty years and more, there were two acute phases, both associated with severe drought: the 1870s and the first half of the 1890s. The year TFP began his apprenticeship in Rendham, 1892, was a drought year, as was 1893; and his first two years at Sweffling, 1895 and 1896, were also drought years. Even wet years brought their problems, notably liver fluke (sheep rot) which had reached epidemic proportions in 1879–81, and which was in part a result of poor drainage.

Such heavy clay soils as were found on TFP's flat and low-lying land ("a country of poor heavy land" he calls it) were often too expensive to cultivate profitably. P. J. Perry provides a useful summary of the situation:

> It cannot be doubted that more farmers failed in some areas than others—in *Suffolk* than in Somerset, for example,—but it is more important to recall that *more farmers than usual failed* in nearly every locality.³

A careful reading of "This is Thyself" will yield clues which confirm the testimony of these facts in more graphic terms: the inroads into "Mr Elsley's" capital, the uncut hedges, the "dingy, poverty-stricken cottages", and the despairing labourers driven to suicide.

For a time in the last quarter of the eighteenth century, George Crabbe was curate in charge of the adjoining parishes of Sweffling and Great Glemham for the incumbent, the Reverend Richard

---

1 "Retrospect—Love of Nature leading to Love of Man", *The Prelude*, Book 8, 104–5
2 Selected Early Works, p. 333
3 *British Farming in the Great Depression*, p. 33; my italics

Turner of Great Yarmouth.¹ Initially he lived in Parham, but on 17 October 1796 he moved into Great Glemham Hall just south of Sweffling, as a tenant of Dudley North, the Whig M.P. In the mid-nineteenth century, Sweffling also became known in a modest way as the home of Jonathan Smyth, who, with his brother James of Peasenhall, developed the Suffolk corn-drill, which featured adjustable coulters and other technical innovations. One of his descendants (a son or grandson) was still listed in *Kelly's Directory*, 1896 as "drill manufacturer".

It is little wonder then that TFP's own sojourn in Sweffling drew him to a writer who shared not only something of his own melancholy disposition but who had walked the self-same country paths. TFP purchased his copy of The Poetical Works of George Crabbe (1888) in 1901, his final year in Sweffling, and wrote on the end-paper, as though from his own experience in the village: "When all the finer Passions cease . . . / Tis then we rightly learn to live." In an essay of 1925 in HRHRC on his development as a writer, TFP acknowledges his reading of Crabbe: "I was better prepared than I supposed myself to be for the task I set myself—to write a country novel. I knew Crabbe very well, his *Tales of the Hall, The Borough*, etc."²

Suffolk

Sweffling is a village in the valley of the Alde, three miles west of Saxmundham. According to Skeat, the name records a settlement of the sons of Sweftel or Swæftel, a name not otherwise known.³ There appears to have been a Roman outpost in the area; a dig in 1909 turned up some Roman pottery, and two years earlier a well-preserved bronze head had been found in the river Alde. The soil is rather mixed: sand, clay, and subsoil. When TFP arrived in 1895, most of the 1,350 acres were owned by the Duke of Hamilton (who died that year), by Colonel A. Bloomfield, by Arthur F. McDougall (TFP's mentor in Rendham), and by the Trustees of the late Miss Shuldham. The population had been declining since the mid-nineteenth century; in 1845 it stood at 308, according to *Lewis's Topographical Dictionary*, 1845, but by 1891 it had shrunk to 282,⁴ and by the time TFP left in 1901, it was down to 271.⁵ The church of St Mary, a fourteenth-century foundation, stands on a

1 *The Life of George Crabbe*, p. 133   2 Selected Early Works, p. 442
3 *The Place Names of Suffolk*   4 *White's Directory*, 1891   5 *Kelly's Directory*, 1904

slight rise and is the focal point of the village. From 1890 until 1898 the rector was the Reverend Holmes Buxton, also vicar of Bruisyard. He was succeeded by the Reverend George Clennel Rivett Carnac (vicar 1898–1913). There was an inn, *The White Horse* (proprietor Robert Elvin), two mills (wind and steam), a smithy (James Knights, blacksmith), and a grocery-cum-sub-post-office (Oliver Newsom).

TFP never bought his farm, as Louis Wilkinson claims; like most farmers, he was a tenant, and thus far more vulnerable than any landowner. His landlord was Colonel Alfred Bloomfield, J.P. (d. 1915), who lived in The Grove, Great Glemham, described as "a house of considerable antiquity" in *White's Directory*, 1891, about a half-mile south of White House Farm. TFP did socialize with Colonel Bloomfield from time to time, on the evidence of a letter from Gertrude to her mother in which she writes "Tonight—dinner at Bloomfields."[1] Bloomfield must also be the inspiration for the "Colonel Alfred" in TFP's unpublished story "Jane".

White House Farm is in low-lying land about one sixth of a mile west of the river Alde. TFP succeeded Thomas Burrows as tenant, and paid £376. 16s 2d for his lease under the Suffolk Farm Covenants system.[2] Under the Suffolk system, it should be noted, the incoming tenant was disadvantaged, because he had to pay all costs, including labour, for the cultivation of the root crops, even if the value of the crops had sunk beneath production costs (as could easily happen in a depressed economy). Under the more progressive Norfolk system, the incoming tenant only had to pay the value of the crops as fodder. It does not appear that TFP kept any detailed systematic accounts, but few farmers did in those days. However, we are fortunate that some evidence survives from which it is possible to reconstruct a good deal about the economics of TFP's farming. In the original draft of "This is Thyself", he wrote "I hired a farm *and my father advanced the money to stock it.*"[3] The italic portion he deleted in the final version, but we herein have confirmation of what JCP said in his *Autobiography* about his brother "acquiring, with my father's help, a small farm of his own at Sweffling in Suffolk."[4] "Acquiring"

1 October 1897; HRHRC
2 See the *Inventory and Valuations of Farm Covenants*, 30 September 1895, in the Bissell Collection.
3 HRHRC   4 *Autobiography*, p. 189

does not necessarily imply "buying", no matter how little John knew of the transaction. TFP employed five, and occasionally six, farm labourers: Fred Nunn (foreman), John Sherwood, Ben and Bill Pond, Bill Tie and John Hall. Both Nunn and Sherwood are mentioned in TFP's Rendham diary of 1892; so it is likely that they were taken on, with Arthur McDougall's blessing, as experienced hands well equipped to help the fledgling farmer.

In 1841, when the tithe maps were drawn, White House Farm, which was originally part of the Manor of Sweffling, was owned by one John Smith. He died in 1847, leaving his 152 acres of land to his two sons, Samuel and Wingfield. The property was conveyed to Colonel Bloomfield in 1872 from the estate of a relative (father?), the Reverend E. Bloomfield, who must have acquired it from the Smith family. At some point, two fields were sold, so that by TFP's day the farm was no more than 120 acres. With the aid of the 1841 tithe map and TFP's crop-planting records, it has been possible to determine many of the relevant facts about the operation of White House Farm. There were eleven arable fields, comprising 107 acres, a hay meadow (Barn Meadow) of about three acres, an orchard, the house and barns, etc. On average, TFP would sow eight of the eleven fields, or some two thirds of his arable land—a conventional enough pattern (see Tables 1 and 2). For the two years for which data are available, he sowed only wheat, barley, beans and peas, alternating wheat and barley as the largest crop. Elsewhere there are references to buying turnip seed, cow grass, and chemical fertilizer or "46 manure" (perhaps super phosphate). He also raised sheep and cattle, evidence that he was following the arable–livestock system then prevalent in East Anglia.

Table 1: White House Farm

1896			1897		
Acres	Crop	Name of the Field	Acres	Crop	Name of the Field
8	Wheat	Seven Acres	8	Beans	Seven Acres
7	Wheat	Brick Kiln Field	7	Beans	Brick Kiln Field
8	Beans	The Five Acres	7	Wheat	[The] Five Acres
8	Barley	Kiln[s]hill*	5	Beans & Peas	Pisty Brook
5	Barley & Peas	Pisty Brook	13	Wheat	Barn Field
13	Barley	Barn Field	12	Wheat	Oak Hedgerow*
14	Barley	The Walk*	9	Barley	Eight Acres*
6		Cottage Field*	12	Barley	Cart Shed Field*
68		8 fields	73		8 fields totals

*See in the text.

TFP kept a payroll record of sorts for some eight weeks in his first year (18 October–6 December 1895), which shows a weekly payroll total average of around £3. Nunn was paid 15s per week, and the others between 10s and 12s. These rates are well below the 1895 national average of around 13 shillings, but they are comparable to the rates in Dorset in the early 1890s; so it does not seem that TFP was overpaying his farmhands. He also provides a synopsis of his total outlays for his first year of operations (11 October 1895–11 October 1896): Implements = £200. 8s 9d; Livestock = £554. 11s 6d; Labour & Covenants = £526. 12s 6d; Furniture = £35. 7s 6d. In all, it seems, out of the £2,000 advanced

Table 2: Crop Production for 1896 and 1897 Seasons

Crop Production	1896	1897	Subtotal	Percentage
Barley	33	21	54	38%
Wheat	15	32	47	33%
Beans	14	18	32	23%
Peas	6	2	8	6%

by his father, he spent £1,602. Unfortunately, there are no comparably detailed figures listed anywhere for TFP's income. However, there are some figures available in TFP's black notebook, which appear to show his crop and livestock income for 1896. His wheat paid only £48, his barley £98, and his beans & peas £60—a total of £206. He also earned £155 for cows and lambs; so total income was £361. Against these earnings, he paid out some £315: £200 for labour, £85 in rent, and £30 for a loss on ewes. He would seem, then, to have survived the year with a slim £46 profit; in fact, he records, without providing specifics, an "actual loss" of £80. Nonetheless, in September 1897, just two years after he began, he actually leased a second property, Gull Farm, from the estate of the Duke of Hamilton. For this smaller farm he paid £235. 9s 6d. It is reasonable to assume that at this point TFP was not operating at a loss, and may even have been doing moderately well—well enough at least to justify cautious expansion with the remainder of his father's advance. Corn prices had bottomed out, and TFP must have felt experienced enough to run a larger farming operation. Ironically, the apparently sensible decision to expand may have contributed to TFP's ultimate "failure". In his contribution to *The Victoria History of the County of Suffolk* (1907), Herman Biddell outlines a likely scenario:

The small holder, who has no bank reserve, and has all his available savings invested in tenant's capital, is the first to go under when the wave of bad seasons and low prices sweeps over the land. Many such have succumbed in this manner in Suffolk during the last twenty-five years.[1]

P. J. Perry cites from documents that make the same point in a slightly different way: "Worst off was the group too high in the social scale to use their own labour, too low to possess more than a little capital."[2] TFP certainly matched the profile of such under-capitalised individuals, though there is no evidence that he was actually losing money. The marginality of his operation, and his vulnerability, rather than any catastrophic failure, no doubt contributed substantially to his decision to leave farming—but other more personal factors were probably decisive. However, embedded in his story "When Thou Wast Naked", is the proverb "one farm do make, but two do mar a man;"[3] so here he may be giving belated recognition to what must in retrospect have seemed a decisive mistake.

Just over a year before he began farming for himself, TFP gave serious consideration to the kind of farm operation he would run. It was 10 August 1894, and he was newly arrived in Warham, when he sat down and penned "Rules of the Liberty Farm 145 acres". This extraordinary document reveals TFP's vision of a system that combined strict discipline with a generous profit-sharing scheme. The farm labourers would be guaranteed employment for the year, providing they swore "to work honestly and well to the best of their abilities". However, an individual could be dismissed at a week's notice, if he "misbehaves himself or shirks his work or in any way disobeys." The "shareholders" or labourers would collect their shares in October or November (after harvest), would have at any time "a perfect right to look into all accounts of the farm," and would be entitled to participate in a public vote on "any difficulty" faced by the farmer. No doubt, this is what TFP meant when he said in "This is Thyself" that he intended "to use the work people kindly." There is no evidence that he ever tried to implement this scheme born of youthful idealism. Had he done so, he might have provoked a revolution, and become immortalized as a great agricultural reformer. Yet traces of the compassionate

1 Vol. 2, p. 390   2 *British Farming in the Great Depression*, p. 102
3 *Bottle's Path*, p. 68

farmer in him can be detected in such characters as Farmer Anton of "Soppit's Sabbath", who provokes local ire because "he forgot to lower wages same as all the others, and didn't charge Nellie for milk."

TFP was himself on good terms with his men, especially John Sherwood and Fred Nunn, his foreman. From the first, in Rendham, he "made friends with the men and worked with them nearly every day."[1] But the testimony of "This is Thyself" points up an ambivalence in TFP's attitude towards the farm labourers. On the one hand, "their quaint clothes and rustic speech made them seem to me like pictures;" on the other hand, upon closer acquaintance, they proved uncomfortably human in their failings, since "greed and jealousy and hatred lived in them."[2] And TFP evidently found it more difficult in reality to give orders than he had envisaged in "Rules of the Liberty Farm". "The most ignoble task is to compel the labourer to work,"[3] he writes with obvious distaste. He claims that he was therefore "forced to hire a foreman to protect me from the other wolves; and the foreman took his blood price."[4] Now the appointment of a foreman would have been perfectly normal procedure, and is referred to as such in "Rules of Liberty Farm". So TFP's over-dramatic explanation does not ring quite true here. Clearly, he found it more effective and less offensive to his sensibilities to put someone else in charge of the day-to-day giving of orders. But the statement itself must be read in the context of that sense of disillusionment that permeates the whole of "This is Thyself". It cannot be read as a specific indictment of Fred Nunn, whom he had obviously selected from among McDougall's men as his foreman when he first moved to Sweffling. Fortunately, there are still extant a few letters which lend credence to this interpretation of the situation. From some of TFP's casual remarks to Gertrude in a series of letters in 1896, it appears that the Nunns were actually living in White House Farm for a period, with Mrs Nunn acting as housekeeper. After TFP had given up farming in 1901, Nunn took over as tenant at White House Farm, and another man, King, at Gull Farm. From Nunn's letters, it is clear that he was doing his very best to get decent prices for TFP's unsold crops, and was, in effect, acting as his agent. Although the letters are primarily concerned with crop yields, buyers and prices, one can discern both respect and

1 Selected Early Works, p. 335   2 Ibid., p. 348   3 p. 355   4 Ibid.

affection in them too. One letter of 10 January [1902] (for which the original spelling and punctuation are given) reads in part:

> You must have felt very lonely when you were by yourself. I should have like to have had a Chat with you then but I am very pleased to tell you I have saved one pound for my journey. I am saving my tobacco money so I hope I shall have the pleasure of seeing you.[1]

Another letter (n.d. but *circa* October 1901), from Mrs Nunn to Gertrude, soon after the sale of livestock, machinery, and household goods, is happily domestic in detail:

> It seem so sad to see the horses and cows go away because they had a good home. . . . I bought the red chair I could not let anyone else have it as it remind me of you as it did look quite nice after you put the new stuff round it . . . . we do miss Mr Powys very much. . . . I hope he is comfortable settle in his new home. . . . I have lost all my cats but three, two black ones are left which you were so fond of.[1]

There seems then to be no substance at all to Sylvia Townsend Warner's belief that TFP had suffered "the mortification of being cheated by a bad bailiff".[2] TFP never employed a bailiff, in spite of Louis Wilkinson's equally mistaken claim that "he, like my uncle, employed a bailiff," and TFP obviously maintained warm relations with Nunn—enough to invite him down to Dorset on at least one occasion.

Among his few comments about TFP's farming days, Wilkinson reports: "He told me then that it [the farm] had just kept him and that he just didn't sell it at a loss."[3] The first part of this statement accords with the available evidence; the second part, the matter of selling at a loss, is another matter. The White House Farm valuation was sold to Colonel Bloomfield for £251. 3s 6d; that is for some £125 less than TFP had paid six years earlier. Gull Farm, a little more favourably situated, went for £256. 19s 0d, some £20 more than originally paid. That the White House valuation was sold to TFP's landlord is itself something of an indicator of the hard times. It may be that no new tenant could be found; or perhaps rents had sunk so low that the landlord found it more economical to hire Nunn to run the farm for him. Garrard, the

---

1 Bissell Collection
2 letter to Alyse Gregory, 22 June 1967; Graves, *The Brothers Powys*, p. 49
3 "Some Memories of T. F. Powys", *Theodore*, p. 10

Estate Agent who handled the transaction, anticipates TFP's reaction in a letter of 16 October 1901: "I am afraid, looking at what you paid on entry, you will be rather disappointed with this amount, but you had a very small quantity of hay and your fallows work out rather low on this farm."[1] The observation about the hay and fallows was more than just a polite excuse; Nunn made much the same point in one of his letters to TFP. In a second letter, giving TFP the news about the Gull Farm valuation, Garrard usefully puts TFP's experience in a wider perspective:

> I can assure you valuers never had a more unsatisfactory year to face under Suffolk covenants both for buyers and sellers; in one valuation out of ten we can hardly realise the amount paid on entry or anything like it . . . I am afraid your experience of Suffolk farming has not been over successful. I hope your next venture may be more so.[1]

To those who knew him in later years in Dorset, TFP's "failure" as a farmer must have seemed inevitable. How, after all, could the retiring and bookish individual they knew or thought they knew, ever have expected to succeed? But the fact is, there was once another TFP, almost a different kind of man, whose shadow we may discern in fleeting glimpses into the unrealized past. It is almost as though one of the unrealized versions of the self that Joyce offers in *Dubliners* had actually existed. TFP had not yet acquired the almost pathological aversion to travel that marks his maturity; and so we find him travelling to Southwold in June 1896, to Bungay with Littleton, 9 September 1897, and planning "excursions to various eastern coast places for short periods" in Summer 1897.[2] Nor had he fully come to terms with his own impetus towards solitude and silence. It is true that in going to Sweffling he sought "a quiet seclusion", but he still craved the affection of family and friends, as is evident from a letter to Gertrude, asking her to keep house for him: "You see after all with all my boasting about liking to be by myself I do get most awfully lonely at times."[3] More surprising is the fact that he joined a local Tennis Club, which met once a week "on other people's lawns"[4] and that he enjoyed shooting with Fred Nunn, his foreman—even blasting away at a flock of curlew on one outing.[5] His social life

---

1 The letters from Garrard and other information about financial transactions are in the Bissell Collection.
2 letter to Gertrude, June 1896; Bissell Collection   3 5 May 1895; Bissell Collection
4 TFP to Gertrude Powys, 16 May 1896; Bissell Collection   5 See *PR* 4, p. 9

was inevitably limited, given the demands of the farm and his relative isolation from people of his own class. However, he received visitors almost from the beginning of his stay in Sweffling; John was perhaps the first, and reported that "Theodore's farm is splendid and his house quite picturesque."[1] His younger brother, Bertie, destined to be an architect, produced a good pencil sketch of the house in 1895, when he was just fourteen. And when Gertrude arrived in October 1897, Colonel Bloomfield and his wife invited the two of them to dinner.[2] Nor was TFP's life entirely devoid of romantic interludes. Sweffling was only seven miles from Aldeburgh, where he had attended Eaton House School, and where he had come to know a number of Louis Wilkinson's cousins, both male and female. Wilkinson says that TFP fell in love with two of his cousins "in quick succession".[3] One of them was almost certainly Louie Ferrand, whose family lived close to Eaton House. Nearly fifty years later, in a letter to Wilkinson, TFP's memories of her were still strong:

> I should think I do remember Louie. Would she allow me to kiss her now? She was a splendid creature. I galloped my pony to Saxmundham to catch her up and never did. And if I had, she would have only mocked. I remember a warm straw stack / alas / nothing—nothing! The last time I saw Louie was seeing you two together on the platform at Ipswich.[4]

At a time when he felt "the earth was slipping away from me," TFP even asked a local girl to marry him. But this seems to have been more an attempt to integrate himself into the community than a love affair: for, as he admits in "This is Thyself", "She was one that I hardly knew at all,"[5] and she quickly turned him down.

Other attempts to integrate himself into the community were far more practical and successful—albeit no less surprising to those who are aware only of his later distaste for community involvement. Notably, TFP became actively involved in the affairs of the parish in 1896, when he was elected to the Library Committee, the role of which was to investigate the formation of a library under the Public Libraries Act. But then on 17 April 1897, he was elected to the Parish Council itself, and made treasurer to boot; from 1898 to 1899 he also served as clerk and overseer. He

---
1 JCP to Gertrude Powys, 21 October 1895; Bissell Collection
2 Gertrude Powys to Marian Powys, 12 October 1897; Bissell Collection
3 *Theodore*, p. 11   4 24 December 1947; HRHRC
5 Selected Early Works, p. 353

was diligent in attending meetings (all five in 1897–98, for example), and remained on the Council until 14 March 1901, when he resigned, no doubt in anticipation of leaving his farm. Throughout the Sweffling Parish Council Minute Book for this period, "Mr Powys" crops up with great regularity, proposing and seconding motions of all sorts: "that everyone should employ an able body [sic] man when possible" on 17 April 1897, "that the Clerk write to the Charity Commissioners" on 15 October 1897, "that the Clerk be ordered to get the Public Libraries Act" on 27 January 1898, and so on.[1] Serving along with him were Robert Woodard and John Sherwood, two of his own men, who were, the record suggests, staunch supporters, and John Row, by then his neighbour at Dernford Hall Farm, whose memory is enshrined in the protagonist of *Mark Only*. At the time, TFP must have observed that Sherwood had problems with writing, because, years later, he invokes his name in a letter to JCP dated 18 August 1926: "I haven't written a letter even for a fortnight, so, like John Sherwood who worked for me at Sweffling, I can hardly hold a pen."[2] Trivial as it is, this recollection, like the vivid memory of Louie Ferrand, suggests that many of TFP's youthful experiences in East Anglia were not forgotten. Clearly, there *were* bad times; the problem is that the few published reports of TFP's farming days give the misleading impression that there were *only* bad times. TFP himself knew better, as we learn from a note scribbled in pencil on the free end paper of his black notebook: "my life is full of weary days, yet good things have not kept aloof." Even the darkness that permeates "This is Thyself" occasionally gives way to moments of nostalgia for "those old days", and for "the golden wheat straw and the sun that shone in March".[3]

The years in East Anglia must be reckoned as much a search for the self as an attempt to earn a living from the land. TFP invested far more than money in his farm; his vision of himself was at stake. He wanted to be a sheep farmer in part because it provided, in his eyes, an alternative pastoral role, a way in which he might salvage something of his parents' unfulfillable dreams of the priesthood. It is no coincidence that in *The Soliloquy of a Hermit* he characterizes himself as a priest, and claims that "It [Religion] is

---

1 Sweffling Parish Council Minute Book and other local records consulted at the Suffolk Records Office, Ipswich
2 HRHRC
3 Selected Early Works, p. 346

the only subject he knows anything about."[1] So his early failure as a sheep farmer (the problems he had with his rams in his first year and the subsequent decision to get rid of his flock altogether) had a symbolic significance that far outweighed any economic losses. The decision to abandon farming completely could not then have been an easy one. Although he would escape "the dismal fields and the days of worry", he would also have to relinquish some of those dreams that give meaning to life.

Fortunately, TFP had discovered in his programme of reading and self-education a source of solace—a philosophy of life that helped draw him away from the fields. The moment of discovery is recorded for us in the essay already cited. Writing sometime in 1925 (*Innocent Birds* is mentioned as not yet published), TFP says:

> A day or two ago I read again an essay of William Hazlitt's that I remembered very well reading with extraordinary interest nearly 30 years ago. I was then young but no means free for I was become involved in a pursuit, agriculture; that was tiresome to[o], at least the crude manners and habits of it. The time was harvest. I took out a paper book with daisies upon the cover, Bohn's cheap series, now extinct I expect, into my little orchard all lovely now and apples at a ripe appearance, and hearing the loaded wain of corn pass along the lane to the stackyard I read the essay "On living to one self". I read then. (Haz. p. 123) I felt that Hazlitt was right and that I would imitate him. I gave up business and I gave up farm[ing] that had led me to consort with all of my kind.[2]

Hazlitt's essay, written at Winterslow Hut, 1821, advocates a conscious retreat into "a world of contemplation, and not of action"; it warns of "the repeated disappointments and vain regrets" that await those who "go in search of realities." This seems to have had an extraordinary impact upon TFP and provided, in effect, a virtual blueprint for the rest of his life. Of course, he could not act upon Hazlitt's advice immediately; for, in his words, he "was by no means free." If we allow some latitude in TFP's estimate of reading the essay "nearly 30 years ago", we can assign it to 1896-8; so it would be at least three years before he could put into action what Hazlitt advocated. "What I mean by living to one's-self," Hazlitt wrote,

---

1 *The Soliloquy of a Hermit*, p. 5
2 Selected Early Works, pp. 441-2

is living in the world, as in it, not of it: it is as if no one knew there was such a person, and you wished no one to know it: it is to be a silent spectator of the mighty scene of things, not an object of curiosity in it.[1]

Had TFP followed Hazlitt's essay in every detail, he never would have become a writer; for Hazlitt portrayed the man who lived wisely to himself as relishing an author's style "without thinking of turning author". But TFP in fact began writing while he was still in Sweffling. Louis Wilkinson saw "a few short pieces" in dialogue form, on his first visit there, in the summer of 1900, after he had left Radley and was waiting to go up to Pembroke College, Oxford.[2] None of these first efforts appear to have survived, and there remains only a single sonnet, presumably the work of TFP, incongruously lodged among farm accounts and other mundane matters. However, some nine years of East Anglian farm experience had left an indelible mark upon the would-be writer. So, although Dorset supplanted East Anglia in the topography of his imagination, East Anglia was never forgotten. Reviewing his qualifications for writing *Mr Tasker's Gods*, TFP wrote: "I knew the ways of the land, village customs, and the right time to plant and to sow, and I knew my Bible."[3] No, he had not forgotten the land he left behind.

There are, for example, a few Suffolk references in the novels and the short stories that can be linked to real-life places or people. Responding to Elizabeth Myers's praise of his work, TFP volunteers the following: "The story, the short one you liked in *Bottle's Path* was nearly a true one. I heard the unhappy woman crying in Deadman lane [*sic*] near Sweffling in Suffolk."[4] The story itself is not identified in the letter, but it must be "A Suet Pudding". Did we not know from this letter and from TFP's diary that there was a lane by this name, we might have been forgiven for assuming that it was another allusion to Bunyan's *Pilgrim's Progress*. Of course, knowledge of the Suffolk locale adds nothing to our appreciation of the story: rather it provides rare evidence that TFP did in fact draw specifically upon incidents from this

---

1 Hazlitt, Selected Essays, ed. Keynes, p. 25

2 "I wish that one at least of them had survived. This was a dialogue between God and himself, and it expressed this same sense of the immanence and omnipresence of Divinity."(*Theodore*, p. 12)

3 "This is Thyself", Selected Early Works, p. 442

4 TFP to Elizabeth Myers, 1 March 1946; in *Theodore*, p. 71; one of a series of letters to Elizabeth Myers in 1945–6

phase of his life. There are but two other cases where TFP acknowledges the use of Suffolk material in his work. John Row, already mentioned as TFP's neighbour and fellow council member in Sweffling, appears as the persecuted ploughman, John Roe, of *Mark Only*, and also features in "The Two Thieves" and "A Strong Girl". And there is a letter in which TFP complains about Louis Wilkinson's assumption that the two singularly un-engaging clergymen in a suppressed episode of *Mr Tasker's Gods* are modelled on his father, the Rev. Charles Francis Powys:

> What a dog old Louis is to be sure, because he must needs make fun of his mother he thinks everyone else does it. When, I should like to know did father ever eat a pickled onion? When did he ever need to be woken up to attend holy communion? I chose for my type two Suffolk clergymen that I saw once stepping round the corner of a street—near the Butcher's shop at Saxmundham.[1]

However, even without verification of this sort, we would have to recognize that TFP's fiction commands a range of knowledge about the rural world that derives not from mere observation (as in Dorset) but from working the land itself (as in East Anglia). Farming is the backdrop against which many of his little dramas are performed. So his stories are full of everyday details about working bailiffs ("The Red Petticoat"), hiring fairs ("What Lack I Yet?"), sheep hurdles, rent audits ("The Unbidden Guest"), ploughing matches, ringled pigs ("Sevens"), carting dung ("A Box of Sweets"), the value of proper drainage ("Squire Pooley"), new ways of fattening stock ("Circe Truggin"), the difference between mustard and charlock—a kind of wild mustard deemed a weed when growing among crops ("Found Wanting"), and the helpful ways of rooks in pecking maggots out of the backs of sheep ("The Baked Mole"). One can also find some specific, albeit incidental, references to East Anglia in the short fiction, where it perhaps suggests some sort of Housman-like "land of lost content". Miss Straw is the daughter of a Suffolk Squire;[2] Ann Fell "expects to find a house with a high-pitched roof, and people as simple and as talkative as those she had left behind" when she journeys from Suffolk to Maidenbridge to be a teacher ("Sweet Suffolk Owl"); Mr Hayhoe decides John Death must be from a Suffolk family (*Unclay*); Paradise is said to be "like Norwich

---

1 TFP to JCP, 15 October 1916; HRHRC   2 "Captain Patch"

Cathedral" by Jane Nutbeam "who, as a child, had once stayed in the Close and played hide and seek in the cloisters"—certainly a memory of his aunts who lived in the Close ("Like Paradise"); and Farmer Anton is rumoured to have "gone to Norfolk" ("Soppit's Sabbath").

Far more interesting and important are a group of stories which, though not set in East Anglia, are centrally concerned with farming and contain protagonists who, unsurprisingly enough, share many of TFP's particular obsessions. First, we need to recognise that two kinds of farmer inhabit the pages of TFP's novels and stories: the good, poor, farmer and the bad, rich, farmer. Sometimes, the poor man becomes rich; in which case he usually ends up committing suicide. Sometimes he is pre-occupied with books, and sometimes with God; in either case, his farm will fail. *The Left Leg* offers a paradigm example. James Gillet is the poor man who "had lost all his interest in the soil, because he had found a more terrible idea, God;"[1] he "sought in the ecstasy of prayer for the meaning of life."[2] After hearing the voice of God while in the fields hoeing mangel, "he never drove a straight furrow again"[3] and his farm began to fail. Farmer Mew is Gillet's avaricious and evil counterpart, whose "habit of life was to crush all" and for whom "living was a matter of continual getting."[4] Inevitably, Gillet is ruined by Mew, whose cows eat his hay and whose sheep are one night driven in to eat his young corn. But Mew, "the giant of Madder", is not really to blame; for he is more than a man, he is an elemental force who "drew all things, the grass, fields, houses, sweet cows, and women, into himself."[5] And Gillet, caring nothing for worldly prosperity, experiences the numinous:

> Grave mould was not plain mould to Gillet now. He saw all Madder afire with the Spirit. Life and death, the creatures, even ants under a stone all burning. The queer presence within had opened his eyes. He saw every blade of grass, every leaf, every movement of the wind, every little red worm, as possessed of God.[6]

The religious experience of the "good" farmer is not always represented in such transcendental terms. Humour often finds a place in the account. "When Thou Wast Naked", for example, features Mr Priddle, "an ordinary man, a little inclined to sadness,

---

1 *The Left Leg*, p. 14   2 *Ibid.*, p. 5   3 p. 15   4 p. 5   5 p. 18   6 p. 47

perhaps", who forgets the cattle he has just bought at auction for £58 in his excitement at buying a "great family Bible", for a shilling, and has to return for them. The cattle are to stock the "moderate-sized farm" he has just rented or "hired" (the very term TFP uses in "This is Thyself" with reference to White House Farm). However, he becomes preoccupied with the Bible, and comes to see the world through it; he "found it so much to his taste, that he could hardly bear to be away from such a book. He delighted in the stories and the language that was sometimes like an old wolf howling in a dark forest."[1] His farm prospers in spite of him, and because of World War One; so, happily, and unlike TFP's real-life experience, he can sell for £40 cows that he bought for £14. But after four years he gives up farming and retires to Little Dodder on the proceeds of the sale, because his son "of a sensitive nature grew ill through the smell of farmyard manure."[2] There Mr Priddle would venture "out alone into the fields, where he would be sure to see some of the scenes and some of the people that moved in the pages of his great book."[3] Two figures in the sunset are transformed into Moses and Jehovah; Mr Shattock's large horsepond becomes the Sea of Joppa; and a lost boy, asking directions to the church, is recognised as the young Jesus and shrewdly referred instead to the Inn, "where the most learned clergy were always to be found." Mr Priddle's wife is tolerant of such eccentricity, and can readily translate his biblical references into English equivalents. She explains at one point: "When he says 'Egypt,' he really means the Maidenbridge workhouse."[4] In this touching eccentric behaviour of Mr Priddle, we observe TFP's fictional *alter ego* doing what he himself so often does in his fiction: re-viewing, even re-constituting, the world he inhabits in terms of his own idiosyncratic, biblically inspired, vision of it. Among the moderns, perhaps only the artist Stanley Spencer interprets the world in such insistently and comprehensively biblical terms.

There are stories, of course, in which religious fervour does not overwhelm or supplant love of the land; indeed, at times the land itself is deemed holy. Thus, for Mr Tiffin, in "Found Wanting", "his land was his Holy Bible."[5] And yet Mr Tiffin, a widower, simultaneously thinks of his land in more earthly terms; he "loved

---

1 *Bottle's Path*, pp. 42–3   2 *Ibid.*, p. 43   3 p. 44   4 p. 66
5 *The White Paternoster*, p. 124

his fields as though each of them was a kind matron by whom he had had a large number of children."¹ He is not, therefore, easily to be wooed away from them and into marriage by the scheming Mrs Wood, his new housekeeper, and her daughter, Lily. When he first meets them, he thinks of each as a field; Mrs Wood was "a little like a nine-acre field of his", and Lily, "a field of lovely flax flowers".² The two women nearly succeed in persuading the guileless Mr Tiffin of Lily's suitability as a wife on the basis of her apparently encyclopedic knowledge of farming until he discovers that the tit-bits of farming lore with which he is tempted come directly from his own copy of Johnson's *Book of the Farm*. Lily is finally "found wanting" when she fails a crucial test; she identifies barley as oats, and wheat as barley.

In "They Were My Fields", and "The Key of the Field", TFP offers two versions of the same basic scenario: a dispossessed tenant farmer yearns to return to the fields he tended so lovingly. But where the first story is more or less realistic in form, the second comes very close to allegory. John Osborn, the landless farmer of "They Were My Fields" returns compulsively to walk the fields that had once been his until forbidden by a magistrate to enter them again. Then, confined to his cottage and garden, he gazes for hours at a time towards the distant farm, repeating the same phrase: "They were my fields." He is also guilt-ridden over his neglect of one small field, God's Close, which had never been tilled. But when he is given a telescope, he is able to see that the new tenant, George Rodden, is preparing to plough this very field, and so he can die happy. His last words bring us back to the theme of the farmer being wedded to the land: "George Rodden be a good husband!"³

Uncle Tiddy, of "The Key of the Field", is "a good husbandman" too, and the first tenant of "twelve acres of the richest pasture" that belong to Squire Jar of Madder Hall. But through the scheming of the envious Trott family, the field is taken from him and given to them. Uncle Tiddy is left to gaze sadly through the high palings that enclose the field, and to ask: "Will the iron gate be locked against me for ever?" Squire Jar is manifestly a landowning version of the itinerant and god-like Tinker Jar; so we cannot be surprised that Uncle Tiddy's virtue is recognised in the end, and that he is given the Squire's own golden key. *En route* to

1 *The White Paternoster*, p. 122   2 Ibid., p. 127   3 *Captain Patch*, p. 269

the field, Mr Jar talks with him of the crops, recalls Uncle Tiddy's good hay (a nice piece of wish-fulfilment!), and promises: "You have been my tenant for a season: you will now be my guest for ever."[1]

We are no longer surprised to find an author putting himself or some version of himself into his own works. Chaucer may have been the first of our English writers to do it, and he eschewed all disguises. TFP does it in many of his stories. We have already seen him as Mr Priddle in "When Thou Wast Naked", but he is also, among other characters, Mr Pitcher, "a poor poet of Madder" in "The Dove and the Eagle", Mr Pymore, the miller of "The Hill and the Book", John Pie of "Christ in the Cupboard", and James Pinnock of "What Lack I Yet?" Here, however, let us focus briefly upon his frequent appearance as Shepherd Poose, whose name was earlier identified as a Suffolk version of Powys. There are at least nine published stories in which Shepherd Poose appears, and in some of these he is as fleeting a figure as Mr Jar. But in two related stories, "A Pretty Babe" and "Thy Beautiful Flock" (a biblical title from Jeremiah xiii. 20), Shepherd Poose plays a major role. In both cases, Shepherd Poose, the employee of Mr Oliver of Norman Grange, is utterly dedicated to his flock of prize-winning, purebred Dorset ewes; yet the sheep keep dying. "The Pretty Babe" also features the miraculous intervention, on Christmas Eve, of the Christ-child, who tends the sheep when Shepherd Poose is lured into drinking too much by his disgruntled predecessor, and who even restores a dead lamb to life. No such saviour, alas, ever came to the aid of TFP in his farming days. As Gertrude, who had reason to know, told the story: "Almost every day one of the labourers on the farm would come to him and say 'Another sheep has died.'"[2]

When TFP finally settled in East Chaldon, then, he was drawn not only by the tranquillity of this little village but by the resemblance of the surrounding hills to the "delectable mountains" of Bunyan's *Pilgrim's Progress*. He alludes to this perception in two places: in the autobiographical fragment in which he describes the influence of Hazlitt's essay, and in the long, first-person story, "Cottage Shadows". By moving to Lenton (a version of [East] Chaldon), Francis Wingrave, the protagonist, like TFP in real life, "fancied that he had reached those same delectable mountains

1 *Bottle's Path*, p. 25
2 Holloway, "With T. F. Powys at Mappowder", pp. 157–8

whereon the thoughtful and pious shepherds fed their flocks."[1] The conception of self-as-shepherd clearly remained strong with TFP, in spite of his disappointment on the farm. It was part of what his brother, John, liked to call, after Ibsen, his "life-illusion." In his copy of *The Apocryphal New Testament*, for example, TFP marked passages he deemed particularly appropriate to his brothers and to himself. Against a self-accusatory passage in "The Shepherd of Hermas", he wrote his initials; the crucial sentence reads: "You, who being weakened through your worldly affairs, gave yourself up to sloth." And in his later years, he would occasionally quote from Matthew Arnold's "Bacchanalia" a few lines that somehow capture the bittersweet nature of his youthful experience:

> Shepherd, what ails thee?
> Shepherd, why mute?
> Forth with thy joyous song
> Forth with thy flute.

And so we have come full circle; the shepherd has returned, if not to his flock, at least to a place reminiscent of safely fictional pastoral haunts, where he could relive and reshape in fiction the life he had left behind, and from where, moreover, he could hope, like Christian, to see the gates of the Celestial City.

---

[1] Selected Early Works, p. 397

The Powys Family circa 1896-7
Marian Powys, A. R. Powys, Rev. C. F. Powys, J. C. Powys, T. F. Powys
Philippa Powys, Littleton Powys, Mrs C. F. Powys, Mrs J. C. Powys, Gertrude Powys
Llewelyn Powys, William Powys, Lucy Powys
[frontispiece to Louis Wilkinson, Welsh Ambassadors, 1936

Dorchester Grammar School in South Street [*1903 postcard*

White House Farm, Sweffling, in 1986 [*photograph by the Author*

Mrs (Mary) Stracey as a young woman
[*Photograph by Jabez Hughes & Mullins, Ryde, Isle of Wight*

Theodore Powys and his eldest son "Dicky" (Theodore Cowper) *circa* 1910-11
[*courtesy of Theodora Gay Scutt*]

Dicky and Francis (1916) in a photograph sent to Mrs Stracey, their godmother
[*Author's collection*]

Dicky, in a photograph sent to Mrs Stracey (godmother) in 1923
[*unknown photographer, Author's collection*]

Theodore Powys outside Beth Car
[*photograph published as frontispiece to* The Soliloquy of a Hermit *(1916)*]

Beth Car, East Chaldon, 1932
  [*photograph by the late Frank Robinson in Author's collection*

Theodore Powys and American admirer, Elizabeth Wade White, Mappowder, 1949   [*unknown photographer. Author's collection*

David Garnett, 1934
[*photograph originally published in* Familiar Faces

Bernie O'Neill by Reginal Marsh: pen-and-ink drawing
[*courtesy Theodora Gay Scutt*

Violet Powys, Theodore Powys, John Hampson, Charles Lahr, Francis Powys and Alec Bristow, September 1932   [*photograph by Frank Robinson*

two photographs of Theodore Powys and "Susie" *circa* 1938
[*courtesy of the late Kenneth Hopkins*

Portrait of T. F. POWYS, a carving in Purbeck stone by ELIZABETH MUNTZ, G.M.C.

portrait of T. F. Powys in Purbeck stone by Elizabeth Muntz, 1949–50
[*photograph from brochure in Author's collection*

4

Theodore Powys
and the Mysterious Mrs Stracey

Despite the fact that TFP's father was a Church of England clergyman and that there were clergymen on both sides of the family, one encounters a distinct streak of anti-clericalism in the author's fiction worthy of Rabelais or Voltaire. In TFP's novel *Mr Tasker's Gods* (1925), for example, The Reverend Hector Turnbull, Vicar of Shelton, is a materialist and a hypocrite of the worst sort. So it would probably surprise readers otherwise familiar with TFP's fiction to find that at the beginning of his career he put much of his energy into what can only be called religious writing. *An Interpretation of Genesis* (1908), a commentary in dialogue form on the Old Testament book, marked his first appearance in print, though scarcely noticed by the public. One hundred privately printed copies in dark blue cloth—undignified even by a title or by the author's name on the cover—were issued, of which only about half-a-dozen or so are now extant. For TFP, this little booklet represented the first fruits of a much larger undertaking—nothing less than an ambitious plan to "interpret" each and every book of the Bible. The abundant evidence of his progress in this endeavour over a period of years and of the inspiration provided by the remarkable woman to whom he dedicated *An Interpretation* under the initials "M.H.R.S." can be found almost exclusively in the files of the Harry Ransom Humanities Research Center and is the focus of this chapter.

The life of a writer is lonely enough at the best of times. But when he has attended no University, belongs to no club, and has withdrawn from the kind of society that might provide encouragement and criticism, to whom does he turn? In the autumn of 1901, upon his arrival in Studland, a secluded Dorset seaside village, TFP was a bachelor of twenty-five, and knew none of the locals—a predictable assortment of farmers, farm-hands, and village shopkeepers. In Sweffling, Suffolk, where he had farmed for some years, he had made a rather successful effort to involve himself in local affairs, and his farm-hands had provided both a ready-made community of sorts and a link to the community at large. In Studland, and later in East Chaldon, this pattern could not be repeated; in any case, TFP's experience of the working classes had been disillusioning. As he reports in the autobiographical "This is Thyself",

> Their quaint clothes and rustic speech made them seem to me like pictures, and I ought to have left them as pictures, but I was foolish enough to look into their lives. And I found that their lives were marked, scarred, and torn; greed and jealousy and hatred lived in them.[1]

The Powys family was, of course, still ensconced in Montacute, Somerset, some fifty or so miles to the northwest; but TFP was determined to maintain a healthy distance—psychological as well as physical—between himself and his family. One does not need to have been a member of a large family to guess at some of his motives. Thus, as he began his long apprenticeship in the craft of writing, TFP turned for help to someone outside his own circle of family and friends. And his audience, his critic, his Muse even, was a woman whose existence has hitherto gone all but unrecognized. She was no Beatrice, let it be said; her role was rather that played by Miss Eliza Mary Ann Savage in the life and work of Samuel Butler (1835–1902), the author of *Erewhon* (1872) and *The Way of All Flesh* (1903). Behind the initials "M.H.R.S" of the dedication in *An Interpretation of Genesis* we find one Mary Henrietta Rennell Stracey.

None of the commentators writing in the 'thirties, while TFP was still active, mentions her by name, although there are allusions to her in Louis Wilkinson's *Welsh Ambassadors* (1936) that are unrecognizable as such without further specific information. In neither of the substantial family biographies— by Kenneth Hopkins (1967) and Richard Graves (1983) is there as much as a passing reference to her. Only Peter Riley (1967), in

---

[1] Selected Early Works, p. 348

his bibliography of TFP's work, offers information of any sort, saying:

> "M.H.R.S." of the dedication is Mrs Stracey, who was Powys's landlady at Eastbourne about 1900. She became almost the sole audience for his earliest works, and in a correspondence which lasted for many years she encouraged Powys and criticised his work at a time when no one else took any real interest.[1]

Apart from the reference to her as "Powys's landlady at Eastbourne about 1900" (information obtained from a family source), Riley's statement is an accurate, albeit abbreviated, account of Mrs Stracey's role. But how desperate was TFP for criticism of his work? And what sort of turn-of-the-century landlady could have offered substantial criticism of any sort, save perhaps a perfunctory "very nice, dearie, I'm sure?" No, this scenario is an unlikely one; and, as will become clear, quite without foundation in fact. Riley may himself have suspected that there was more to the story, for he tried, but failed, to discover more about the mysterious Mrs Stracey.[2]

Although very few of the letters between Mrs Stracey and TFP survive, considerable evidence of the kind of encouragement and criticism she provided for so long can be gathered directly from his manuscripts in the HRHRC. There are also a few relevant items in the Sterling Library and in the Bissell Collection. All these manuscripts contain pencil annotations, some of them quite lengthy, in what can be identified as Mrs Stracey's distinctive, angular, handwriting.[3] TFP customarily wrote at this time in lined school exercise books; and somewhere on the front or back cover, he would insert the name and address of the person to whom he was sending the work: often "Mrs Stracey, The Dale, Upperton Road, Eastbourne". This address is just one of the clues that render suspect Mrs Stracey's identification as a landlady; for it is not near the station and the sea where most of the boarding houses cluster but rather in a neighbourhood of large and well-appointed middle-class homes. Moreover, even brief perusal of

---

1 Riley, *Bibliography*, p. 14
2 Personal communication from Peter Riley, 1985–6. Through the kindness of Peter Riley and Hedley Morgan, I have been able to consult the inventory of manuscripts made by Riley before the bulk of the collection was purchased by the HRHRC.
3 In the current HRHRC catalogue, these annotations are invariably described as "notes and emendations in unidentified hand".

Mrs Stracey's pencilled comments suggests a figure of far greater substance than the term "landlady" implies. She is revealed as a woman of intelligence, education, and common-sense, who is uncommonly sensitive to the spirit of the work to which she is responding as well as to the man behind it.

TFP never actually lived in Eastbourne. In Studland he had taken one of a row of little cottages, 5 Harmony Cottages, opposite the post-office. Studland lies eight and a quarter miles south-west of Bournemouth and three and a quarter from the smaller resort town of Swanage. With the sea to the west, Ballard Down to the south, and the heath-land stretching north and east to Corfe Castle, Studland must have seemed an idyllic retreat indeed. Even today, Brian Jackman can write of "the secret world of Studland Heath [now a national nature reserve], its chocolate and purple tussocks stretching away to a wilderness of birch and bog myrtle and dense reed beds."[1] Yet, by 1904, TFP felt that an influx of holiday-makers threatened his tranquillity, so his energetic younger brother, Llewelyn, helped him find a new home in East Chaldon—"a quiet, peaceful, hidden-away Dorset village, where he could spend the days of his life in surroundings harmonious to the grave temper of his mind."[2]

TFP would never have met Mrs Stracey, had he not felt obliged to supplement his meagre allowance of £60 with what he could earn from lecturing, and begun making weekly trips along the coast to Eastbourne. Although he only had to be away on Thursdays and Fridays, the journey from Swanage was rather a time-consuming cross-country one, involving at least three changes, if he went only by train. In fact, when he was looking for lodgings in August 1902, he "took ship to Brighton" on the way there, and returned by train via Bournemouth.[3] Given his schedule, commuting was out of the question; so it was necessary for him to take lodgings for at least two nights. His expenses would have been quite high in proportion to his earnings—ten shillings for two nights' lodging, and about the same amount for travel—and in practical terms it would have made more sense to move permanently to Eastbourne. But his status as a visiting lecturer gave him no security, and it is inconceivable that he would have abandoned his haven from the world for a relatively busy

---

1 *Dorset Coast Path*, p. 101   2 *Dorset Essays*, p. 111
3 Letter from TFP to A. R. Powys, 27 August 1902; Bissell Collection

resort town like Eastbourne. In any case, confirmation that he kept his Studland cottage is contained in the Bissell Collection in a letter of 17 December 1902 from TFP's sister Katie, redirected from his Eastbourne lodgings to his Studland address.

Without doubt, the most significant and rewarding outcome of TFP's Eastbourne experiment was his meeting with Mrs Stracey. Since she was demonstrably *not* his landlady, one cannot but wonder about the circumstances of their meeting. But first it will be useful to provide a brief biographical sketch of this woman who played such a key role in nurturing TFP's talent. She was born on 3 June 1856, at Walmer, near Deal. Her father, Frederick Byng Montresor (1810–87), was a captain in the Royal Navy at the time of her birth, but rose to become Admiral Montresor, R.N. About her mother, Emily Maria Delafield, little beyond her name is recorded. The Montresors were, as the entry in *Burke's Landed Gentry* (1894) shows, a very old French Huguenot family; the English branch was also very much a military family. Mary was one of seven children, and was twenty-seven when she married the much older Hardinge Richard Stracey (1840–1924) in 1883, the grandson of Sir Josias Henry Stracey, 4th Baronet, and a Lieutenant-Colonel in the 98th Regiment. The couple moved to Eastbourne in the year of their marriage, but only took up residence at The Dale (no. 35), Upperton Road, in 1895. They had five children: four girls—Constance Mary, Elizabeth Julia, Ruth, and Margaret Diana—and a boy, Wilham, who died in infancy. Mary lived at The Dale until 1940, and died during the war, on 4 October 1944. Her eldest daughter, Constance Mary ("Maidie"), who never married, returned to the house in 1946, and lived there at least until 1957. She died in an Eastbourne nursing home on 25 June 1964.[1]

TFP began lecturing in the autumn of 1902, but the earliest reference to Mrs Stracey comes in a letter from his brother, John, at home in Burpham, who reports: "Mrs Stracey can talk or think of nothing but you—She wrote to the Catholic's sister that she had 'learnt more from you than from any one else'—but this is very private as it comes out of a letter to Margaret."[2] Here we have a clue as to how TFP might have met Mrs Stracey—through John William Williams ("The Catholic") whose sister knew

---

1 This information has been culled from public records and from the few remaining letters from Mrs Stracey in which she discusses her daughters.
2 Letter from JCP to TFP, 25 May 1903, Bissell Collection

Margaret, John's wife. In any case, what an intriguing snippet of third-hand gossip! It unequivocally demonstrates the impact of TFP's distinctive personality upon Mrs Stracey. But when one person "can talk and think of nothing but [another]," romance is usually in the air. However, what is the likelihood of there being an affair blossoming between a shy and reclusive twenty-seven-year-old bachelor and a forty-six-year-old mother of four? TFP would not be the first to fall for an older, married woman with children. In 1912 another twenty-seven-year-old, D. H. Lawrence, eloped with thirty-three-year-old Frieda Weekley, who left her three children to be with the man she loved. There were many reasons, as we shall see, why TFP would have been drawn to a woman like Mrs Stracey, and she to him; but an affair of the heart is unlikely to have been among them. Indeed, according to Francis Powys, TFP may have been enamoured of one of Mrs Stracey's daughters.[1] If so, it is likely to have been the eldest, "Maidie", who was born in 1885, and would have been seventeen in 1902.

In his perceptive introduction to a reissue of *Mr Weston's Good Wine*, David Holbrook argues that TFP was afraid of women, and that "they must be kept either as child-women, or as playmates—a way of divesting them of mature femininity, which was to Powys (unconsciously) too dangerous."[2] This is a subject that deserves far more discussion than it can receive here. Holbrook is surely right enough about TFP's fear of women, but, in fact, two types of women need to be considered: there are the "child-women" of whom Holbrook speaks, represented by the profusion of attractive seventeen- and eighteen-year-olds that inhabit his stories—and there are what Michel Pouillard calls "middle-aged or elderly matrons...whom Powys himself systematically calls 'old women'".[3] Pouillard sees the two types as "antagonistic" and cites substantial evidence from the novels in support of this viewpoint: the innocent and beautiful Tamar Grobe of *Mr Weston's Good Wine* at one end of the spectrum, and the procuress, Mrs Vosper, at the other. In the novels in particular the preoccupation with the poles of good and evil is reflected in TFP's depiction of women: the good are usually young, innocent, and often naïvely eager for love, while the bad tend to be relatively old and beyond love and loving. But

---

1 Personal communication from Francis Powys, 5 September 1987. Francis Powys, TFP's younger son, recalls being told this.
2 Introduction to *Mr Weston's Good Wine*, p. xiii   3 *PR* 12, p. 8

the novels, even the early ones, have a distinctly allegorical bent where such polarization of character may be appropriate. The world of the short stories is somewhat more diverse and naturalistic, and consequently depicts a greater range of womankind. Some of the "old women" of the stories, though never more than sketches, are, in fact, sympathetic and attractive characters: Mrs Balliboy gives away her wedding dress to a servant girl ("I Came as a Bride"), the ninety-year-old Dowager Lady Bullman leaves Valentine Cuff three thousand pounds ("Valentine Cuff"), Charlotte Bennett dispenses "loving-kindness" wherever she goes ("Charlotte Bennett"), and Lady Daisy Diller is a rich widow and "a fine woman of forty years old with a free independent nature" ("The Kingfisher").[1] There are, indeed, enough of these good "old women" to offset the Mrs Vospers of the Theodorian world, and to show TFP's interest in the type. No simple binary opposition between young / good versus old / evil can be established. However, only in some of the early fiction do we find fictional, or rather fictionalized, characters that approach the real Mrs Stracey.

There are three extant stories specifically labelled "Old Women", each also with a title of its own: "Miss Edwards", "Miss West", and "Mrs Cern".[2] In each story, we see the central character through the eyes of an unidentified first person narrator, who is in fact providing a perspective on his own life. The autobiographical slant of the stories is reinforced by certain internal clues, and by the fact that in one manuscript, following these three stories, is an early version, perhaps the first, of "Mr Thomas", a narrative later incorporated into *The Soliloquy of a Hermit*.[3] The

---

1 Versions of "I Came as a Bride" (published in *The House With the Echo*, 1928), "Valentine Cuff," and "The Kingfisher" (both of the latter published in *Rosie Plum*, 1966) are present in the HRHRC collections; a fair copy of "The Kingfisher" is in the Feather Collection, as is the sole extant manuscript of "Charlotte Bennett" (published in *Captain Patch*, 1935).

2 All published in Selected Early Works. Versions of "Miss Edwards" and "Mrs Cern", both in inscribed exercise books, are in the HRHRC Collections; slightly different versions in a single notebook, together with "Miss West", are in the HRHRC and in the Bissell Collection. These were among the stories sent to Frances Wilkinson (née Gregg) in 1913, while she was staying with her parents-in-law in Aldeburgh, Suffolk. The exercise book at the HRHRC containing "Miss Edwards" is inscribed on the front cover: "To Mrs Stracey / The Dale / Upperton Road / Eastbourne" [in upper right corner, marked through, and below it] "Mrs Louis Wilkinson / Deepdene Aldeburgh"; in the lower left: "From Powys / East Chaldon / Winfrith / Dorchester". The exercise book at the HRHRC containing "Mrs Cern" is inscribed on the front cover: "To / Mrs L Wilkinson / Deepdene Aldeburgh" (upper right corner); "From / T. F. Powys / East Chaldon Dorchester" (centred at bottom of cover).

3 The manuscript in question is the "notebook" identified in note 2, above.

voice of Mr Thomas, who is the narrator and the fictional *alter ego* of TFP himself, sometimes is merged with the voices of the women characters, and one becomes aware that a single consciousness is in control, the women mere mouthpieces for the narrator's views. Nowhere is this impression stronger than in "Miss West", in spite of the very precise details provided about her by the narrator —her maxims, her love of the rain, her hatred of the clergy (a giveaway!), her ability to make a great deal out of a little. "Like all great women," we are told, she is religious, "but she always kept a free mind." The narrator praises her as "quite a Woman Pantagruel", and as one who "turned all my old ideas upside down" and "forced me to respond to the world's movements."[1] One suspects that TFP is here paying tribute to a real individual, to Mrs Stracey in fact, an "old woman" of a very different sort from the later Mrs Vospers and Mrs Fancies of his novels. The sketch of Miss Edwards, "a little lady in black", also depicts the kind of good, strong, independent-minded woman so rare in TFP's novels. To the people of the town she appeared "quiet and peace-loving", and she loved reading and talking philosophy; yet she also "loved women to rebel," arguing that Christ was the greatest rebel.[2] Most important here is Miss Edwards's influence upon the narrator, best summarized in the following passage:

> . . . Miss Edwards touched life lightly like a fairy, and I fear that I often used to pain her by what I said. . . . She loved plainness of speech, I was in those days proud of being called a mystic. . . . She just pulled me out of all this nonsense in time.[3]

The narrator's admission that he had once been a mystic anticipates a similar admission in *The Soliloquy of a Hermit*, where he tells us: "In the old days I used to tie myself up in a mystic knot, that I never could undo; neither could I ever explain what it meant."[4]

The undoer of that knot in real life was Mrs Stracey. Given the passage cited above, we can see Miss Edwards as another fictional representation of Mrs Stracey. That is not to say, of course, that every detail of Miss Edwards's appearance and character can be correlated with some aspect of Mrs Stracey; but what shines through in the portrait is the love for humanity common to both. There is something curiously symbolic about a manuscript that

---

1 Selected Early Works, p. 305   2 *Ibid.*, p. 295   3 p. 294
4 *The Soliloquy of a Hermit*, pp. 43–4

begins, as this one does, with a cancelled seven-page essay called "Hate", but ends by testifying to the power of love.

TFP began his ambitious project to interpret the Bible in 1905 by tackling the New Testament, first The Book of Revelation (The Apocalypse), that prophetic and enigmatic work traditionally attributed to the apostle John. No manuscript survives, but a 1905 letter from TFP's brother, John, confirms that this bold enterprise was under way.[1] Between February and May 1906, TFP worked successively on the Gospels of Matthew, Mark, Luke, and John. Only then did he turn to the Old Testament, and began, *this* time, at the beginning, with Genesis, writing his commentary during June and July 1906. He worked his way, deliberately, even obsessively, through the Old Testament books: Joshua in May 1907; Job in November 1907; The Song of Solomon in April 1908; and, finally, the twelve minor prophets, in December 1908. Manuscripts, most of them dated, for almost all thirty-nine Old Testament books are in the Powys Family archive at the HRHRC; only two are missing, those for Chronicles I and II. The last notebook with any biblical material, "Interpretations of Biblical Books", is dated 1909. In all, there are well over two thousand manuscript pages of biblical interpretation.

Confronted with this mass of material today, it is hard to understand why anyone would commit himself to such an undertaking. TFP could not have imagined that such writing would provide a better income than the lecturing he had given up; for there was nothing "popular" about his writing. The language of his interpretations, reflecting the totality of his immersion in the Bible, was resolutely archaic, essentially that of the Authorized version itself; and the mode of presentation was a dialogue between "The Lawgiver of Israel" (Moses) and one "Zetetes", TFP's *alter ego*. One clue to his motives may be obtained from an inscription he liked to write on *An Interpretation of Genesis,* after it was reissued by Chatto and Windus in 1929: "This book was written between the years 1905–1907 *when the Bible was my chief study*" (italics added). This inscription suggests that TFP saw his work on the Bible as an investment of sorts, an extension of that programme of self-education he had begun while farming in East Anglia.[2]

1 Letter from JCP to TFP, 1905, Bissell Collection: "I shall be anxious to read what you have to say about the Book of Revelations."   2 See Chapters 2 and 3.

The work also served then as a kind of apprenticeship in writing, a necessary prelude to his more mature work. One of his problems from the outset was his difficulty in shaping the real world into an appropriate fictional mode. Certainly, his experience with these commentaries set an indelible mark upon his style, though it would take many years of assimilation—and all the efforts of Mrs Stracey—before the benefits would become wholly apparent.

In any case, TFP would probably have been mildly surprised that anyone would deem him obsessively preoccupied with the Bible; he saw it very much as a book of life itself. In studying the Bible, he would have claimed, he was studying Humanity, which is every writer's domain. In an unpublished essay on the Bible, contemporary with his interpretations, he is explicit on the matter, calling the Bible a "symbol of man", and warning against those who "believe these black letter signs are inspired, and every word writ by a being above man."[1] In fact, he says:

> Little do they think that it is their own history here, written by themselves.... In the Bible man sees his own mind, even as in a mirror he beholds his face. Should he blame the mirror if he sees a scar there?

He presents essentially the same point of view some years later in *The Soliloquy of a Hermit*:

> The Bible tells us all we can ever know about ourselves.... All the cruelty, all the terror, all the poetry of the Bible is acted in our lives.... The book of our tragedy is in our doors, open it and know what we are and how we shall end.[2]

Although such heterodoxy—his rejection of the Bible as the inspired word of God—would have made many clergymen of the Church of England, including his evangelical father, distinctly uncomfortable, TFP believed he was fulfilling his role as self-appointed "priest", as a kind of secular preacher. So even if we accept that one of TFP's motives for his four-year preoccupation with the Bible was his own development, intellectual and spiritual, we cannot overlook the possibility that he just as earnestly desired to preach his idiosyncratic version of the Word to the community at large.

---

1 This item by TFP is catalogued at the HRHRC under "Essays" as part of Works 4, which includes an exercise book containing "The Bible". For the quoted phrases and a subsequent passages see the next-to-last page of the exercise book.
2 *The Soliloquy of a Hermit*, pp. 30–1

Almost every writer wrestles with the problem of finding an appropriate "voice", a vehicle for communication in which the self may be dynamically sublimated. TFP was no exception; indeed, there is some evidence that his predilection for and susceptibility to religious and philosophical works adversely affected his development as an author. Like many another aspiring writer, he began by writing poetry, for which he had no talent, then shifted to a kind of poetic prose, before "finding" the dialogue form in which all his biblical commentaries were written. The dialogue is, of course, a mode of discourse with a venerable tradition, though hardly to the modern taste. The classical or Platonic dialogue was given something of a new direction by Renaissance humanists such as Roger Ascham, Thomas Elyot, and Thomas More, who found in it a way of representing the interior world of thought and emotion. By the eighteenth century, writers as different as Matthew Prior (*Dialogues of the Dead*) and David Hume (*Dialogues Concerning Natural Religion*) had made the dialogue a familiar and well-accepted form. To the contemporary reader, however, TFP's choice of the dialogue may appear to be further evidence of his perverseness, of his self-destructive tendencies, as well as of his marked preference for the old over the new. In fact, at the end of the nineteenth century, the dialogue was still a respected and viable form, particularly for philosophical and religious subjects. For TFP, Schopenhauer's *Religion: A Dialogue* (1899), a book he bought and signed in August 1904, was probably the immediate source of inspiration, but John Bunyan's *Pilgrim's Progress*, much of which is in dialogue form, cannot be excluded as a partial model.

The original title for *An Interpretation of Genesis* was "Dialogue on Genesis", and, on the evidence of a three-page fragment in the HRHRC, the interlocutors were originally to be "M[oses]" and "T[heodore]."[1] The Pentateuch, of which Genesis is the first book, is traditionally attributed to Moses, the first prophet—which accounts for his role in the dialogue; in the final version, he is identified only as "The Lawgiver of Israel". TFP then hides himself behind the mask of Zetetes, a less transparent disguise, for there is no biblical figure of this name. Zetetes comes from the Greek verb *zetein*, "to seek", and hence is best glossed as "The

[1] This item by TFP is catalogued at the HRHRC under Works as "[Dialogue between M(oses) and T(heodore)]." The interlocutors are indicated by M and T in the left margin of the manuscript.

Seeker". This invented name is specifically associated with the school of Sceptics called Pyrrhonists, whose founder, Pyrrho, questioned the validity of perceptions, and therefore taught that external circumstances of life should be of no consequence to the wise man, who should preserve tranquillity of mind at all costs.[1] Even had we no knowledge of the early manuscript fragment in which "Zetetes" is revealingly given as "Theodore", it would not be hard to recognize the appeal of the Pyrrhonian world-view to the real TFP.[2]

Even when first issued, *An Interpretation of Genesis* probably had little general appeal; it is less a literary document than a religio-philosophical tract and makes difficult reading. Moreover, The Lawgiver of Israel and Zetetes rarely emerge as voices distinctive enough to justify the dialogue format. Sometimes one offers an "interpretation" and sometimes the other, but there seems to be little substantive disagreement between them. However, behind the over-wrought language of this biblical commentary are discernible some of TFP's later preoccupations—with darkness and light, with self-pride, with the role of women—and thus there is good reason to acknowledge its place in the evolution of TFP's particular obsessions and idiosyncratic style. Exemplary of the topical connections that can be made is the Lawgiver's claim, in the course of a discussion about Cain and Abel, that "the wise are regarded as outcasts by all mankind." Zetetes seizes upon this remark and elaborates:

> By reason of Cain's deed the wise are joined unto the lowest class of men, those that are the very beginnings of men. The wise are the companions of beggars and of those that have no home, and if it be that the wise by any means attain unto the full life, wisdom goeth from them, and pride and fatness enter into them, and they that were good become evil.[3]

The fate of "the wise" represented here has no particular biblical sanction; on the other hand, it is perfectly consistent with TFP's later view of himself—particularly in his fictional projections—as an outcast from society, condemned for ever to associate with "the lowest class of men". He is, then, in the very process of

---

1 TFP's Pyrrhonism may have come to him via Montaigne, whose work he very much admired.
2 The name "Theodore" is found in "Genesis 1", the first of four exercise books in the HRHRC for *An Interpretation of Genesis*, 1929.
3 *An Interpretation of Genesis*, pp. 13–14

transmuting his perceived "failure" in life—leaving school at sixteen to farm and thus never qualified to follow his brothers to Cambridge University and his father into the Church—into a philosophy of quietude and solitude, the fullest exposition of which is to be found in *The Soliloquy of a Hermit,* a quasi-spiritual autobiography that deserves to be better known. In *The Soliloquy* TFP represents himself as one of the "priest" class in whom "God practises His divine moods." Though he has "tried to hide amongst grassy hills," he has not escaped, for "the proper place for a priest is in a cave, a narrow cave where he lies with his back against a sharp rock."[1] Nothing he does passes un-censured: "Whatever I do is a criminal offence. I must not even water my flowers, or walk down the road, or throw a stone at a rat."[2] In TFP's fiction, such "victim" characters abound—for example, Mark Andrews, the hapless protagonist of *Mark Only,* who is cheated out of his inheritance and loses his wife to his own brother. In its sharpest formulation, the victim becomes a scapegoat, as in the two versions of the short story entitled "The Scapegoat", or that curious Celtic equivalent, the sin-eater about which he wrote a play, unaware at the time of the existence of the story by the same name published by William Sharp under the pseudonym "Fiona Macleod".[3]

When, in later years, TFP brackets the composition of *An Interpretation of Genesis* within the years 1905–07, we must recognize it as very much an approximation—like much of his post-compositional dating. The earlier of two manuscripts of *An Interpretation of Genesis* at the Sterling Library is dated June and July 1906 on the front covers; these dates are absolutely consistent with what we know from other dated manuscripts. Immediately beforehand, TFP had worked on the four Gospels (February–May 1906), and immediately afterwards on The Book of Job (November 1906). Although the second manuscript of the book at the HRHRC is undated, collation against the first shows unequivocally that it is a revision closer to the final form. On the other hand, the earlier manuscript provides abundant evidence of the editorial role played by Mrs Stracey—reason enough for the work ultimately being dedicated to her. Throughout, in the top and bottom

---

[1] *The Soliloquy of a Hermit,* pp. 2–3   [2] *Ibid.,* p. 48
[3] "The Scapegoat", pp. 12–16; see also the manuscript by this title in the HRHRC. TFP's play *The Sin-Eater,* written with the help of Stephen Tomlin, the manuscript of which is in the Bissell Collection, is in the Selected Early Works.

margins and between lines, are pencil annotations in what we soon recognize as Mrs Stracey's angular hand. Substantive comments, usually a line or two but sometimes amounting to half a dozen or so lines, are to be found on 39 of the 109 pages. In addition, in her role as copy-editor, Mrs Stracey adds punctuation, corrects spelling, strikes out redundancies, and so on. Since TFP's spelling was often inconsistent—a family weakness consistent with early learning difficulties, on the evidence of some of the manuscripts of Llewelyn and John—and his punctuation was quite idiosyncratic, these tasks were by no means trivial. All in all, Mrs Stracey is forthright and confident in her remarks, and one gains a very distinct impression of a strong, intelligent, and thoughtful personality. Without the biographical data now available, one would be tempted to speculate that she was one of the "Sussex headmistresses" for whom TFP or JCP had once worked.[1]

The seriousness of Mrs Stracey's commitment to Theodore's writing can best be gauged by the scope and duration of her involvement. Of the thirty-seven books of the Old Testament for which Theodore wrote "interpretations", no fewer than twenty-nine, all but one at the HRHRC, have annotations by Mrs Stracey. But her efforts were by no means confined to TFP's biblical works; there are half a dozen early fictional and autobiographical pieces that have also been annotated by her. Indeed, the very first manuscript upon which she worked was a novella of 28,000 words, *Under the Bondage of Fear*,[2] an allegorical fantasy, and of particular interest because it shows that TFP's attraction to allegory was there from the beginning of his writing career.

Mrs Stracey wrote to a number of publishers, including Duckworth and John Lane, in June and July 1904, about the novella. However, her enthusiasm failed to arouse any interest; "none of these saw it," she notes on the manuscript itself. For a second novella, *Workers of the Will*,[3] she felt confident enough to supply a six-page alternate beginning. By January 1905, TFP had something different to send his friend in Eastbourne—a series of mini-essays on such topics as "Mammon", "Deformity", "Blasphemy",

---

[1] JCP mentions a number of these headmistresses by name. See a letter from JCP to TFP, Burpham, 25 May 1903, Bissell Collection.

[2] published complete in the Selected Early Works; manuscript in the HRHRC dated January–March 1904, consisting of four exercise books containing chapters II, IV, V, and VII; variant in the Bissell Collection

[3] Manuscript in the HRHRC dated November 1904, consisting of three exercise books containing chapters I, II, and III; extracts in Selected Early Works

and "The Bible". He had evidently been reading Bacon's *Essays,* for he alludes to Bacon a number of times, and one of his own essays is also "On Friendship" (Bacon's was "Of Friendship"). In an accompanying note to Mrs Stracey—the earliest and one of the few surviving items in their correspondence—Theodore frankly admits his uncertainty about the quality of his essays and the need for revision: "There is a good deal that should be cut out from them, but their shortness makes this impossible; for were I to cut out, they would be quite extinguished."[1] Finally, he cites Johnson, from Boswell, in support of what he has produced: "I fancy mankind may come, in time, to write all aphoristically." Undeterred by these remarks, Mrs Stracey drastically pruned the essay on "The Bible", and returned her version to TFP along with the original.

It takes considerable tact—a blend of encouragement and constructive criticism—to help an insecure and unpublished writer, and Mrs Stracey appears to have known instinctively the right combination. Sometimes she would write a marginal "I like this bit best yet," or a "this is true," or, more extravagantly, "I like this —it is true good." This last comment, incidentally, occurs at a point in TFP's "Ezekiel" where he makes an observation that could not help but appeal to a strong-minded woman like Mrs Stracey: "Open the door to the woman, O thou son of man, lead her forth, the night shall not hold her for ever." On the other hand, some of TFP's comments about women provoked a more negative reaction. When he ventures to write that "the virgin must be defiled before she can become a Mother," Mrs Stracey responds with: "Why say this? Walt Whitman would not agree with you."[2] She can also be very firm and direct in her criticism—especially where she sees him lapsing into the kind of obscurity of language to which he was all too prone. In his Bunyan essay, commissioned by Ralph Shirley for *The Occult Review,* but never published there, TFP writes of the soul that it "forms itself in a new birth."[3] With this, Mrs Stracey is manifestly impatient: "You can't *form* a new birth—the imagery is wrong—Shall we say 'bears within it the seed of the New Life'?" She is equally forthright in asking whether it is "right to say man *became* a feeling—a feeling is an attribute, not a thing in itself."

1 This item is in the Bissell Collection.
2 This item is catalogued in the HRHRC as "Ezekiel (1st part)" under "Powys, Works". All Mrs Stracey's comments appear on unnumbered pages, although some bear roman numerals.
3 Cf. Selected Early Works, p. 171; manuscript in one exercise book of 38 pages, catalogued in the HRHRC under "Powys, Works".

And we have an opportunity to see just how she helped "untie the knot" of TFP's self-confessed mysticism. When he refers to "the danger to the mystic that is an especial danger for us", Mrs Stracey objects sensibly: "not for the general public. I think very few feel or understand this," and puts her pencil through more than a page of writing. And she responds to a characteristic passage about man's loving the darkness more than the light with: "You know I don't think this quite true—though it is true to you—many will not believe it." Her resistance to TFP's concept of darkness is reaffirmed in "Interpretations of Biblical Books" where she argues: "I think it is very difficult to imagine darkness as a thing in itself...."[1] On this point, however, she would not prevail; the dichotomy of darkness and light, which derives ultimately from Genesis, is a pervasive theme in TFP's writing. It is, for example, central to his "Darkness and Nathaniel" in *Fables* (1929).

The straightforward narrative of TFP's first biblical efforts, which included the lost work on Revelation, had evolved into dialogue format by the time he came to "The Story of John. A Dialogue" in May 1906. John and TFP are the interlocutors, but Mrs Stracey is drawn into the dialogue as well. When, for example, TFP observes rather enigmatically that "Thought is the dove that bringeth the green leaf to the ark of the body," Mrs Stracey asks "In this symbol of the dove—does it mean that thought inhabits for a time the ark of the body but flies out bringing back good news?"[2] And when "John" evades the issue of the nature of sin by saying "Surely thou knowest what I mean," Mrs Stracey intercedes to say "No, John. We do not yet know what sin is." Elsewhere, she remonstrates with TFP over his characterization of Nathaniel: "I think your opinion of Nathaniel is inadequate. I think Jesus had the gift of seeing the naked souls of all around him."

Inevitably, TFP did not act on all Mrs Stracey's suggestions. Comparison of the rewritten version of the Bunyan essay with the original shows less evidence of change than might have been expected.[3] On the other hand, the published version of *An*

---

[1] "Daniel," section VI, in "Interpretations of Biblical Books", exercise book dated 1909 and containing sections on Ezekiel, Daniel, Hosea, Joel, Amos, and Obadiah, catalogued in the HRHRC under "Powys, Works 3"

[2] "The Story of John. A Dialogue", manuscript dated May 1906. There are versions of this work in the HRHRC Collections and in the Bissell Collection, both with comments by Mrs Stracey.

[3] There is a draft version of the Bunyan essay in the Bissell Collection; the rewritten version, dated March 1908, is in the HRHRC Collections and is now published in Selected Early Works.

Interpretation of Genesis is discernibly, if not dramatically, different from the two manuscripts; and many of the changes of omission, correction, and clarification in the printed work can be attributed directly to Mrs Stracey.

That TFP continued to send his work to Mrs Stracey from 1904 at least until 1912 is the best indicator that he valued and benefited from her efforts. There are also a few early letters in the Bissell Collection from TFP to Mrs Stracey, all from 1906, which help shed some light upon their relationship. One of these, dated 1 April 1906, apparently refers to "The Story of Mark" which had just been returned by Mrs Stracey; and TFP's pessimism about his work is apparent in his response to her: "I will read the story again, though I doubt if too many words are good." Apart from telling her that he is reading Milton's *Paradise Regained,* there is nothing personal in the letter, which is in large part written in the same archaic style he was then using in his work. Another letter in the Bissell Collection, undated but probably late in 1906, is an attempt to clarify some of the points raised by Mrs Stracey about something of his that she had been reading. He begins:

> I think my idea was this—the poor widow being the soul impregnated by the Truth in man, she gives birth to the second child, but the famine is grevious [sic] in the land, so the Truth in the soul wills her child to hide in death, because he could not live in the famine unless he first died.

No wonder Mrs Stracey was puzzled![1] Some two pages later—perhaps realizing the opacity of his "clarification", TFP admits that "It is hard when you write a symbol inside a symbol that it should not seem strained. I wonder how we can make it better." Obviously, he is both willing to explain at length and to work with Mrs Stracey in improving what he has written.

We have very little evidence from which to arrive at any substantive estimate of Mrs Stracey's views of the world, beyond her responses to TFP's work, and a few late letters. We do know that her approach to religion had some of the same unorthodoxy as TFP's. In passing on some lines of a prayer from the Psalms she liked to recite in the morning, she assures him in an undated letter in the Bissell Collection that she takes the lines "in my own way,

---

1 For the biblical context and the significance of "the second child" in TFP's fiction, see the very useful summary in Elaine Mencher's edition of T. F. Powys: Selected Early Works, p. xxix.

not as the Church does—the ideas in them are from the Psalms which were written hundreds of years before the Church." On the other hand, one of her grandsons remembers her in her last years, when she was confined to a wheelchair with arthritis, as "a kindly if straight-laced person" who once sent a maid to stop him rolling about on the lawn with a neighbour's little girl because she was showing her knickers.[1] Undoubtedly, her legacy, and the fullest expression of her views, is found among the marginal comments in TFP's manuscripts. There, for example, we find that she agrees "fundamentally" with TFP's statement in *An Interpretation of Genesis* that "the law of marriage hath made all flesh one, and therein shalt thou find the Truth," while recognizing that "the modern woman scorns the idea."[2] Nonetheless, she raises an important practical point that had real meaning to her as the mother of four daughters: "How is woman to find the Truth if there are not enough men to marry all—she must find it in some other way." Although she distances herself from "the modern woman" or feminist, we can detect some sympathy for the feminist position too. Abram's request that his wife lie to the Pharaoh provokes her scorn "Note how weak these old Hebrews are about their women—it seems their weak point." And her response to the vision of "man playing the wanton and the harlot" is perfectly in accord with TFP's attitude towards middle-class hypocrisy: "Yes, and telling lies about it too, especially in respectable England pretending to know nothing about lust and its fruits."

Nowhere does TFP treat middle-class hypocrisy more fully and caustically than in his first novel, *Mr Tasker's Gods* (1925). The "gods" celebrated in the title are actually the pigs of Mr Tasker, "dairyman of distinction" and churchwarden. These "gods" play but a single role in the novel: to devour Mr Tasker's drunken father, when he falls unconscious into their sty. TFP writes here with uncharacteristically Swiftian savagery—as befits, perhaps, a work originally composed in 1915—and the focus throughout is upon the darker, animal side of man. Henry Turnbull is easily identifiable as the Theodorian victim-hero, anomalous by his virtue in a singularly unpleasant family. His "failure" in life exactly parallels that of TFP himself "the third son had never gone beyond the

---

1 I am very grateful to P. T. Garner-Richardson, Mrs Stracey's grandson, for responding to my appeal in the *Eastbourne Herald* of 20 July 1985, p. 9, with information and photographs.

2 *An Interpretation of Genesis*, p. 53

third form of a rather poor preparatory school. And at sixteen, his ignorance being still in such evidence, the head master returned him to his father . . . and suggested farming."¹ The father, vicar of Shelton, who "was well clad in the righteous armour of a thick and scaly conscience that told him that everything he did was right,"² in fact dies chasing a seventeen-year-old servant-girl around a brothel bedroom. Here the sense of righteousness sounds like his own father, but certainly not the escapades with the servant! The two brothers, John (a curate) and George (a doctor), are money-grubbing sensualists who inherit everything and turn the reclusive and scholarly Henry out of the family home.

With the help of Mrs Stracey, TFP largely purged himself of the archaic biblical language and style of his earliest phase; in its place he developed a style of limpid clarity in which the biblical element was thoroughly assimilated. It is a style whose simplicity, in fact, may owe more than a little to his father's manner of locution. The Bible would not, however, be neglected: as Louis Wilkinson, one of his closest friends, sagely remarked, "To TFP, the Bible is about the inhabitants of East Chaldon [his Dorset home]."³ It is ironic, then, that TFP's fiction drew the ire of some critics as all too realistic. Reacting to TFP's depiction of Shakespearean "country matters" in *Mr Tasker's Gods,* the critic for *The Spectator* charged that "Mr Powys continues to blacken rusticity"—as though it were a travelogue under review—and assured readers that "villagers are generally kindly, decent, ordinary people, much like the rest of us."⁴ Contemporary critical comment might have been more acute had it observed that Bunyan and the Bible remained powerful influences upon TFP's work, and asked what mode of fiction such models suggested. Henry Turnbull's expulsion from the paternal home, for example, is equated, in a chapter entitled "The Sword of Flame", with that of Adam from the Garden of Eden:⁵ "He must leave the garden, there was no staying there for him now. . . . The angel with the sword of flame bade him begone."⁶ This event had earlier been foreshadowed in "Truth out of Satan's Mouth" (Chapter VIII) when, in a dislodged copy of

---

1 *Mr Tasker's Gods,* p. 19   2 *Ibid.*
3 *Welsh Ambassadors,* p. 17. He was evidently paraphrasing a comment by Rebecca West; in an essay on Theodore Powys in *Seven Friends,* p. 99, Wilkinson observes: "Rebecca West once remarked that to Theodore, Old Testament characters (including, she may have meant, God) were the villagers of East Chaldon."
4 "Men Like Beasts", *The Spectator,* 28 February 1925, p. 333
5 Genesis iii.24   6 *Mr Tasker's Gods,* p. 228

Paradise Lost, Henry Turnbull lights upon Satan's speech which asks "For what God after better worse would build?"[1] Already Turnbull sees that "he too was being turned out of the garden by a remorseless angel, and he had begun to take his first steps in that outside desert place."[2] Here we have not realism but something approaching realistic allegory, a mode most fully and powerfully realized in *Mr Weston's Good Wine* (1927), wherein God takes the guise of a travelling wine salesman, dispensing, as the occasion demands, the light wine of love or the dark wine of death. The epigraph for *Mr Tasker's Gods is* drawn from *The Pilgrim's Progress,* and there are allusions to the book throughout the novel. The bestial drover, for example, transformed by his encounter with the saintly Henry Neville, confronts the tramp "with as good a will to victory as ever Christian had shown Apollyon."[3] Clifton Fadiman is one critic who appreciated what TFP was about in the novel:

> In him is that painful uprightness of soul that distinguished his favourite author, John Bunyan. It is this very fury of moral salubrity that drives him, as it does James Joyce, to delineate a universe of the septic.[4]

TFP's marriage in 1905 did not interfere, as it might well have, with his relationship with Mrs Stracey—something for which his young wife, Violet, must be given proper credit. It is easy to see how a newly-married young woman of eighteen might have felt threatened by an older woman with whom her husband seemed to enjoy a special kind of intellectual intimacy from which she was excluded. In any case, the bonds of friendship between the two families were strengthened when Mrs Stracey agreed, in 1906, to become godmother to Theodore Cowper ("Dicky"), the first child born to TFP and Violet, and, in 1909, to Francis, the second son. Louis Wilkinson, whom TFP had known since his Aldeburgh school-days, agreed to stand as godfather. Henceforth, Mrs Stracey would typically be referred to not as "Mary", nor even as "Mrs Stracey", but as "Babe's Godmother", or plain "Godmother". It is in this guise that she customarily appears in TFP's early letters—including those excerpted by Louis Wilkinson in *Welsh Ambassadors.* TFP's confidence in the "Babe's Godmother" extended in a number of directions. Asked to read a sample of the work of his younger sister Katie, he offers gentle encouragement,

---

1 *Mr Tasker's Gods*, p. 78   2 Ibid., p. 79   3 Ibid., p. 248
4 "Novels by Two Brothers", *The Nation*, 24 June 1925, p. 720

and suggests Mrs Stracey as an appropriate person from whom to seek a second opinion.

The role of Louis Wilkinson and John Cowper Powys in seeing *An Interpretation of Genesis* printed in 1908 has been documented —and perhaps overstated—but that of Mrs Stracey is not generally known.[1] The little book was, of course, dedicated to her in recognition of her encouragement and editing. But TFP consulted her also about the printer's quotation; and, when Louis Wilkinson failed to dispose of the copies he had taken to America, she suggested that E. S. Fowler, an Eastbourne book-dealer on Cornfield Road, not far from her home, might be interested. Louis, however, was asked to conduct the actual negotiations. He also agreed to write an introduction of some sort for the book, but might have balked at submitting it to Mrs Stracey, as TFP asked him to in a letter of July 1907: "Would you mind writing your introduction and sending it to Godmother at Eastbourne, and will you ask her to send it on to me, and then I will pin it into the first page of the m.s."[2]

From about 1913, then, Mrs Stracey deliberately withdrew into—or was assigned—only the more conventional role of godmother. TFP still found occasion to seek her advice and help—for example, in securing a baby book for Frances and Louis Wilkinson before the birth of their son Oliver in 1915—but not about literary matters. TFP stayed with the Stracey family for three days in January 1912, after travelling with Llewelyn to Folkestone, and Mrs Stracey visited the Powys family in East Chaldon at least once before the First World War, but otherwise maintained contact primarily through Violet, who, like many wives, was the family correspondent. In one informative (undated) letter to Violet written during the war, Mrs Stracey expresses relief that "my godchildren are not likely ever to have to fight like the men of our days," and pleasure at hearing of "Theodore reading the lessons in the church".[3] She also alludes to the Zeppelin raids on London of 1915 and to some of the wartime conditions Violet had evidently described to her—the scarcity of meat and the downs put under the plough. From time to time, she received

---

1 See Wilkinson, *Welsh Ambassadors*, pp. 76–81, and Riley, *Bibliography*, p. 13.
2 Letter from TFP to Louis Wilkinson, July 1907, HRHRC; cited, in part and inaccurately, in *Welsh Ambassadors,* p. 78, and misdated "June"
3 Letter from Mrs Stracey to Violet Powys, undated but (on internal evidence) before Easter 1915; Bissell Collection

photographs of her growing godchildren. In 1916, there was one of the two boys proudly posed with their air-rifles, and inscribed on the back in TFP's hand "With love from Dickie and Francis".[1] Then, shortly before Dicky left for Africa, there was a portrait of an almost grown-up Dicky, looking, as his brother Francis says, like Cousin Ferrers. Mrs Stracey replied warmly to the long letter Violet had written to accompany the photograph:

> Thank you too for Dicky's photo; it is very nice & I feel quite proud of my godson. It is a splendid thing for him to have this opening to free country life—just what he would like—instead of having to go through more schools and colleges. I expect he will enjoy the voyage, but I know it is a great trial for you and Theodore to have to part with him—so far away—but it seems as if parents always have to suffer a bit for their children.[2]

Alas, no letter survives that records her sense of loss when Dicky was murdered in East Africa, seemingly by poachers, in 1931.[3] The last two extant letters are addressed to TFP himself in response to other misfortunes. TFP's stroke in the spring of 1938 brought an odd but cheerful letter from "Godmother," as she usually signed herself, in which she hoped that "I shall appear to you as you last saw me—and the long course of years will pass away!"[4] She brings him up to date on the lives of her daughters, including Maidie, pursuing an artistic life in London, and "very nice-looking still with her bright colour and lovely grey eyes". News of the recent death of Llewelyn brought a more conventional letter of sympathy "from yr. old friend", and this would prove to be the last communication between them.[5]

Mrs Stracey was not, strictly speaking, the only person who paid any attention to Theodore's work during these early years. His brother, John, Louis Wilkinson, and Bernie O'Neill were all very concerned that TFP be given every encouragement in his work, and their letters show that they did their part conscientiously from the first. Yet they all had their own lives to lead, and John and

---

1 The original was most generously sent to the author by Mr Garner-Richardson, 18 February 1986.
2 Letter from Mrs Stracey to Violet Powys, *ca.* September–October 1923; Bissell Collection
3 Elspeth Huxley provides a detailed account of this gruesome ritual murder in chapter 10 ("The Powys Saga") of *Out in the Midday Sun* (1987).
4 Letter from Mrs Stracey to TFP, 28 June 1938; Bissell Collection
5 Letter from Mrs Stracey to TFP, 5 December 1939; Bissell Collection

Louis were still struggling to establish themselves as writers. Moreover, for a good half of each year, John and Louis were in America, maintaining extraordinarily demanding lecture schedules. What TFP needed was someone who had both the time, the inclination, and the patience to devote to a sustained dialogue about just those religious and philosophical issues that then mattered most to him. Mrs Stracey filled the bill perfectly! The real-life dialogue—and we are surely entitled to call it that—between the two of them was, then, every bit as crucial to his development as the fictional dialogues between Theodore Zetetes and Moses, the Lawgiver of Israel.

5

Getting into Print

In his 1936 interview with Claude Luke ("Why I Have Given up Writing"), TFP flatly claims that neither the generation of ideas nor writing itself were hard work. Kenneth Hopkins, for one, did not accept this claim, observing that "Writing, with Theodore, was work, and he must always have felt a stronger incentive to stop than to start."[1] Here it is likely that Hopkins is drawing upon Louis Wilkinson who asserted that "he always disliked any work except writing; and he disliked the act of writing which he found laborious. It was only the strength of impulse to express his thought and to exercise his invention that made him undergo the task of putting pen to paper."[2] The comments by Hopkins and Wilkinson thus suggest one kind of answer to the question of why TFP gave up writing. In his letters TFP occasionally gave indications that whatever book he was working on would be his last—evidence that would seem to support the Hopkins–Wilkinson position. Writing—good writing—invariably requires the considerable labour of rewriting; it is hard work. D. H. Lawrence had reached his fourth complete rewriting of "Paul Morel" (later *Sons and Lovers*) by the summer of 1912, but the prolix manuscript (some 180,000 words) still required the ministrations of Edward Garnett to "trim and garnish" it, as Lawrence admitted;[3] and between 1908 and 1915—some of the very years in which TFP was trying to establish himself as a novelist—Virginia Woolf was writing and rewriting *Melymbrosia* until it found shape as *The Voyage Out* (1915). Leonard Woolf recalls that she burned five or six drafts of this, her first, novel.[4] But creative considerations apart, "getting

---

1 *The Powys Brothers*, p. 21   2 *Theodore*, p. 10; see also *Welsh Ambassadors*, p. 65
3 D. H. Lawrence to Edward Garnett, 12 January 1913; Letters, Vol. 1, p. 501
4 *Virginia Woolf, Interviews and Recollections*, p. 150

into print" may be aided or inhibited by a myriad other factors. Although, for example, Woolf's first novel was published by Duckworth, her half-brother's firm, she was so traumatized by the experience that she and her husband set up their own Hogarth Press. In a letter to David Garnett, dated 26 July [1917], she wrote: "I don't like writing for my half brother George [Duckworth]."[1] This is an odd slip—in fact, it was Gerald Duckworth who was the publisher. When Duckworth asked Evelyn Waugh to delete objectionable passages from his first novel, *Decline and Fall,* he refused and took it to Chapman & Hall, where his father was managing director.[2]

In this chapter the focus will be the trials and tribulations of TFP as he struggled to get into print, and to document how, "with a little help from some friends", he was able to overcome that omnipresent inclination to stop. Two novels in particular will be scrutinized, though other works will be drawn into the discussion as well. The two novels are *Mr Tasker's Gods* (1925), TFP's first full-length novel, the publishing history of which has never been fully unravelled; and *Mr Weston's Good Wine* (1927), his most admired and commercially successful novel.

TFP was remarkably lucky, as a writer, in his friends and acquaintances. In spite of his aversion to travel and his sometimes taciturn exterior, he attracted the attention, often amounting to devotion, of such people as Louis and Frances Wilkinson, Stephen Tomlin, Sylvia Townsend Warner and David Garnett (these last three are grouped together as the dedicatees of *The Left Leg*). Apart from his family, especially brothers John and Llewelyn, these individuals constituted Theodore's first real audience, and were, in different ways, instrumental in getting him published. But the road to publication was, nonetheless, hard and long; and, as his son Francis remembers, his cupboards became filled with manuscripts copied and recopied laboriously in longhand.[3] Much of TFP's work exists in at least two or three manuscript versions. In later years, items deemed ready for submission would be sent off for typing by Dora Choules. These manuscripts and many related letters—the majority of which are now in the archives of the HRHRC, or in the complementary archives of The Powys Society (Bissell and Feather Collections) in the Dorset County Museum—provide the raw materials for the chapter.

1 Letters, Vol. 2, p.168
2 Christopher Sykes provides the full details in *Evelyn Waugh: a Biography*, p. 84.
3 "The Quiet Man of Dorset," cited in Coombes, *T. F. Powys*, p. 17; the essay by Francis Powys was first published in The *Adelphi*, 1954, and was reissued separately by The Powys Society in 1994.

The Long and Troubled History of Mr Tasker's Gods

Mr Tasker's Gods has a special importance in the Theodorian canon. It was his first "real" novel, and TFP naturally had a considerable emotional stake in its success. The original title, *The Moods of God*, reminds us of the novel's lineage—as stepchild of *The Soliloquy of a Hermit,* where this phrase first occurs—and alerts us to its preoccupations.[1] For into this book, TFP had poured all his resentment, all his frustrations, and—yes—all his *anger* at the world in general, and perhaps at his family in particular.

Initially, "success" for TFP was coterminous with "publication" and, not long after completion of the novel, publication seemed to be assured. The redoubtable Arnold Shaw, neophyte publisher, had invested heavily in the Powys brothers, and had already produced TFP's *Soliloquy of a Hermit* (1916) along with no fewer than seven of John's books in 1915–16.[2] We cannot be sure why Shaw agreed to advertise—and subsequently to publish—*Mr Tasker's Gods*. He may have been bullied into over-hasty acceptance of the novel by the formidably persuasive team of John Cowper Powys and Louis Wilkinson; or he may simply have had faith in an author who could produce a work as profound and readable as *The Soliloquy of a Hermit*. The only clue we have to Shaw's opinion—in the absence of his archives[3]—is the "Publisher's Note" included on the verso of the half-title page of *The Soliloquy*:

> In issuing this little volume adapted to such readers as are interested in original religious psychology, the publisher wishes to announce his intended publication of an extraordinary realistic novel by the same hand entitled *Mr Tasker's Gods*, which should appeal to a far wider public. Such publication, however, must necessarily depend upon the interest excited by the present little work.

On the evidence of this statement, Shaw's real familiarity with the novel at the time remains uncertain. But he has clearly provided himself with an escape clause: the fate of *Mr Tasker* would depend upon the sales of *The Soliloquy*. Since there are no figures available

---

   1 On the first page of the exercise book containing this manuscript fragment in the Bissell Collection, the title, *The Moods of God*, was crossed out, and *Mr Tasker's Gods* substituted.
   2 Eight books in total by JCP from 1914 to 1917
   3 The best source of information about Shaw is Paul Roberts's scrupulously researched work *The Ideal Ringmaster*.

on the number of copies of *The Soliloquy* issued or the rate of sales, we might reasonably conclude from the fact that he did *not* publish *Mr Tasker* that not much interest was excited by *The Soliloquy*. It only received three brief reviews in America, to the best of my knowledge, and TFP mentions one in England. But, as we shall see, there were other factors that contributed to Shaw's decision.

An important clue to the genesis of *Mr Tasker's Gods* is to be found in a fragmentary essay, labelled by the cataloguer "An untitled essay upon the novel". The title is quite misleading, for this is essentially an autobiographical piece, dateable on internal evidence to pre-September 1925.[1] TFP writes:

> It is easy to get hold of the characters for a novel, no one need worry over that. I was once a great walker and during one of my country walks I passed a village, the name of it I never paused to enquire. I went by the Rectory gate and looked, as I passed, into the garden. Two young men were sitting under an elm tree in the garden and in the garden I saw a bearded figure working in the hot sun. I watched him as I went by. He looked like one who lived in a world of contemplation and he certainly wasn't the gardener. He put the plan in my Mind, and when I began to write Mr Tasker he was there as Henry [Turnbull].[2]

Now we can safely date the composition of *Mr Tasker* within the period 1911–16 (1911 was the date of the National Insurance Act mentioned on page ninety-two as "the new Insurance Act"), the very dates during which TFP himself wore a beard, as evidenced in the photographic frontispiece to *The Soliloquy of a Hermit*, 1916.[3] So TFP has seen in the mysterious figure a reflection of himself—a bearded contemplative in a rectory garden. TFP— unlike John Pardy in the fable—shared Voltaire's belief that "the only true happiness was to be found in cultivating a garden."[4] It was Candide's overwhelming experience of the world at large—a world of horrifying violence and injustice—that led him to seek refuge from it in his garden.[5] In TFP's terms It was "a wild, mad world . . . a world that cannot quietly tend its garden".[6] His most sympathetic characters seek, though they rarely find, similar refuge from a modern version of Candide's world. In *Mr Tasker's*

---

1 The internal evidence is the reference to then unpublished *Mockery Gap*, published on 10 September 1925.

2 Selected Early Works, pp. 442–3; the only extant manuscript is in the HRHRC.

3 There is a pencil sketch, dated May 1912, of TFP with a beard, in Gertrude Powys's sketch book.   4 *Fables*, p. 82

5 "I know also," said Candide, "that we must cultivate our garden," *Candide*, p. 77

6 *The Soliloquy of a Hermit*, p.12

Gods, friends Henry Turnbull and Henry Neville to some extent share the characteristics of the Theodorian scapegoat figure destined to suffer and die. But it is Henry Turnbull, the "idiot son"[1] of the clergyman who is virtually a self-portrait, at times bordering on caricature, of the author.[2] Henry's voice reveals "a natural melancholy";[3] he had "never got beyond the third form of a rather poor preparatory school" and had left at sixteen;[4] he grows a beard and reads the Church Fathers,[5] as well as *Paradise Lost*, Jeremy Taylor's *Holy Living and Dying*,[6] and *Pilgrim's Progress*;[7] he is patronized by his older brother John;[8] and, like Candide "his experience of the world's humour taught Henry to love the vicarage garden." However, these lingering autobiographical traces should not blind us to what we have in the novel: a signal artistic step beyond the merely personal—as in "This is Thyself"—and beyond the arbitrarily transformed self of Mr Thomas[9] in *The Soliloquy of a Hermit*, into the realm of fiction. The transformation from the first-person of Theodore Powys to the third-person of Mr Thomas (the doubter) is a kind of artistic shape-shifting that allowed TFP to develop a proper artistic perspective on and distance from himself—"the other side of myself", as he put it.[10]

Peter Riley dates the composition of *Mr Tasker's Gods* "between the winter of 1916 and the summer of 1917",[11] presumably on the evidence of TFP's own notes on the end-paper of his copy of Moffat's *New Translation of the Bible*, which is quite explicit: "This book was written during the winter of 1916 and completed the following summer."[12] There is an almost identical statement, usefully dated 12 September 1929, on the flyleaf of a copy of the novel inscribed to Fred T. Bason, the bookseller and diarist.[13] Decisive as these may appear, the dates are off by a year, as a number of letters—dated and undated—reveal. In *The Powys Brothers* (1967), Kenneth Hopkins makes a stab at sorting out the confused history of *Mr Tasker's Gods*, and locates the first reference to *Mr Tasker* in TFP's January 1916 letter to Louis Wilkinson.[14] In

---

1 *Mr Tasker's Gods*, pp. 49 and 52
2 In *The Powys Brothers* R. Heron Ward asserts that Henry Neville is a rare self-portrait of TFP, without, apparently, recognizing the overwhelming evidence favouring Henry Turnbull.
3 *Mr Tasker's Gods*, p. 27   4 *Ibid.*, pp. 19 and 23   5 p. 23   6 p. 77   7 p. 89   8 p. 53
9 "I am transformed." (*The Soliloquy of a Hermit*, p. 58)
10 See further my introduction to "This is Thyself" in *PR* 20, p. 6.
11 *Bibliography*, p. 20   12 Cited Coombes, *T. F. Powys*, p. 169
13 See *Fred Bason's Diary*. The inscribed copy is now in the Bissell Collection.
14 Hopkins, *The Powys Brothers*, p. 53

fact, there are earlier references by TFP and others. For example, John mentioned to Llewelyn from Rochester, N.Y. on 19 October [1915]—Malcolm Elwin's dating of the year—that TFP reported being "half way through his novel, Mr Tasker". Then there is an undated letter from TFP to John discussing the novel, which—internal evidence demonstrates—predates the 1916 reference:

> I did so hope that the Confessions would be published this autumn [1915]. I had so counted on them, it is a weary business writing with no hope, and Lord Derby saying "Why the bloody hell can't you shoot Germans" just behind . . . try my dear to get Arnold to publish them in the spring . . . I work at Mr Tasker, I shall have the rough copy finished perhaps by January and then I shall copy it out on sheets [about 100,000 words]. My writings are too disagreeable. . . . It is an ugly book.

Since the so-called Derby Scheme to which TFP is alluding was only operative from 11 October 1915 through December (conscription was approved by Parliament in January 1916), this letter must fall within that time period. TFP is also under the impression that he still has a stake in "Confessions"—which had already shrunk from the original conception of six brothers to three—and that it would be issued by Arnold Shaw. Of course, the joint production appeared as *Confessions of Two Brothers* in February 1916, under the imprint of Claude Bragdon's Manas Press.[1] A later letter to John from TFP dated only 16 December must also be from 1915. It reports "a most splendid letter from Arnold enclosing £10–10" in advance royalties and adds "I still go on harmlessly copying out very carefully Mr Tasker just as you told me. Arnold even talks of that. What a divine fellow! This copying out will take two or three months."

The first complete manuscript of the novel, in thirteen Longman exercise books in the Bissell Collection, records the transition from *The Moods of God* to *Mr Tasker's Gods*.[2] The later "fair-copy" manuscript at the HRHRC from which the novel was to be typed is in an unusually large and careful hand of a sort that always signals a "finished" piece of work. Although now bound into a single buckram-backed volume, it clearly falls into four sections, each with TFP's name and address. The first section of seven chapters

---

[1] The rejection of the joint production by John and Llewelyn is puzzling. Roberts usefully speculates that "it may be that the atypically gloomy and extremely cynical persona he [John] presented and the negative reactions to lecture audiences he displayed were seen as too potentially damaging to business." (Roberts, *The Ideal Ringmaster*, p. 23)

[2] Cf. above, p. 117

was posted to Shaw on 10 January 1916, without insurance or registration. Since he had received no reply, TFP wrote anxiously to John for information. Yet his nonchalance—perhaps feigned—about potential changes is striking: "I think the novel will stand a good deal of cutting out; it won't bleed. Let Arnold and Wilkinson decide. Ho ho! Well what does it matter?"[1] This would not be the last time he expressed such sentiments, and one can only conclude that his anxiety to get into print, to earn something from his writings, outweighed any concerns about the artistic integrity of the work itself. Yet it is hard to imagine many contemporary writers—Katherine Mansfield for example—conceding control so readily. When Michael Sadleir wanted to cut certain putatively offensive passages in "Je ne parle pas Français" to sanitize it for inclusion in the Constable edition of *Bliss* (1920), Mansfield objected vehemently on the grounds that it would blur the outline of the story and asked rhetorically "Shall I pick the eyes out of a story for £40?"[2]

TFP also wrote to Louis about what he blithely called his "domestic novel", explaining that "Jack thinks you would not mind preparing it for the press"[3] and giving him *carte blanche* to "cut out chapters, pages"[4] or even to "leave out half the chapters if you like."[5] John collected all three sections of *Mr Tasker* that had been sent by February 1916 and delivered them to Louis and Frances in Philadelphia for typing and editing. In the letter to TFP of 22 February [no year] reporting delivery, he urged TFP to "send the whole thing over" so that Louis and Frances could determine what alterations might be necessary, "even to cutting out whole chapters here and there."[6] Since the HRHRC manuscript includes a note from TFP indicating that the final section ("last seven chapters") was sent on 1 March 1916, John's letter must pre-date TFP's note and was therefore written in February of that year. John also let his brother know that Shaw was vacillating over publication: "Arnold seems unable to decide definitely himself just at present." Shaw's "hesitating mood", according to John, stemmed from being "still rather

---

1 TFP to JCP, 22 January 1916; HRHRC
2 Katherine Mansfield to John Middleton Murry, 6 April 1920, The Collected Letters, Vol. III, p. 273. TFP's attitude was more prevalent among Victorian authors. Valentine Cunningham cites Charles Kingsley's unabashed pragmatism, "I am aiming altogether at Popularity, and am willing to alter or expunge wherever aught is likely to hurt the sale of the book," in his article "Unto him (or Her) that Hath". (*TLS*, 11 September 1998, p. 12)
3 TFP to Louis Wilkinson, 26 January 1916; Colgate
4 TFP to Louis Wilkinson, 3 February 1916; Colgate
5 TFP to Louis Wilkinson, 9 March 1916; Colgate
6 Colgate

heavily in debt" from *Wood and Stone*. At the time of writing, money might well have been the only obstacle, but by midsummer a more substantive threat had materialized. It was in July 1916 that another Theodore—Theodore Dreiser—ran foul of John S. Sumner and the New York Society for the Suppression of Vice, when the publisher John Lane was forced to withdraw Dreiser's novel, *The Genius* (published in October 1915) from circulation. Given the publicity surrounding this affair and JCP's friendship with Dreiser and his involvement in the fight against censorship, it is inconceivable that Arnold Shaw would have been unaware of the case and its implications for a new and struggling publisher. There can be little doubt that had he given TFP's manuscript anything but the most cursory attention, he would not have hesitated at all—he would have refused it outright. Nonetheless, he included *Mr Tasker's Gods* on his list of publications forthcoming in September printed at the back of *Blasphemy and Religion*. Yet he was still undecided in September, according to John.[1] Knopf, another neophyte publisher at this date, *did* read *Mr Tasker's Gods* carefully when it was subsequently offered to him and declared himself "nervous" about it "because people 'have' one another in it too openly and Americans won't 'stand for that.'"[2] So no matter what the structural or other shortcomings of TFP's novel, no matter what magic Louis and Frances might have worked upon it, it is unlikely in the repressive environment then current that any American publisher would have been bold enough to risk issuing *Mr Tasker's Gods*. In effect, it was doomed even before the entire manuscript had been delivered!

In spite of TFP's willingness to submit his manuscript to wholesale revision, there is surprisingly little evidence of any such activity on the manuscript itself. Sentences, sometimes paragraphs, have been marked out in pencil, and a few marginal corrections and desultory changes in punctuation have been made—all apparently in Louis' hand. One thus gets the general impression that only portions of the manuscript were actually subjected to editorial scrutiny. The busy Louis seems to have found the task larger and more time-consuming than expected, and turned it over to his wife, Frances. John—who had his own motives for promoting Frances—could not resist retailing this information to TFP:

> By the way do you realize that it was not Louis at all who revised and typed Mr Tasker but Frances? Louis had nothing

---

1 JCP to LlP, 14 September [1916]; *Letters of John Cowper Powys to his Brother Llewelyn*, vol. 1, p. 212   2 JCP to LlP, October 1916; *Ibid.*, p. 213

to do with it. If you want to commend anyone for that piece of work the praise is entirely due to Frances . . . you'd better let Frances be the person to do that same sort of thing over the other books that she did for Mr Tasker.[1]

But Arnold Shaw would disappoint them all, and never did publish *Mr Tasker's Gods,* although he remained loyal to John's work. TFP's account of the whole affair was characteristically simple: "Mr Shaw changed his mind [and] returned the ms to me."[2] Shaw's aversion to controversy is further reflected in his refusal to take two hundred copies of Louis Wilkinson's novel *The Buffoon* from Knopf —an agreement he had entered into *before* reading the novel—in which Jack Welsh is a transparent caricature of John Cowper Powys.[3]

By November 1916, John and Louis were trying other publishers[4] to no avail: Huebsch and perhaps Mitchell Kennedy, who would hardly have been a likely taker, given his own 1913 experience with censorship. TFP received the bad news and wrote back to Louis, "Is Mr Tasker really such a terrible book?" Knowing full well the kind of passage likely to provoke censoriousness, he suggested "cut out the frolics of the clergy if you like"—referring to the scandalous behaviour of Edward Lester and Hector Turnbull. In light of his one-time admission that Mr Tasker was in truth "an ugly book", one can only interpret as tongue-in-cheek his final remark: "I thought the story was extremely modest and innocent."[5]

This seems an appropriate point to revisit TFP's earlier puzzling description of his novel as "domestic". Once we recognise TFP's autobiographical investment in the novel, we can gloss it as "concerned with matters of the *domus,* i.e. home". If this is the case, we cannot ignore the possibility that his father, the Reverend Charles Francis Powys, was the private target behind the fictional Hector Turnbull. Louis Wilkinson's suggestion that the Powys *paterfamilias* was the model for the errant clergymen, and his more general insistence upon the father's "sadism", brought a strong—if not altogether convincing—denial from TFP.[6]

If friends and family had so far failed TFP, it was certainly not through lack of effort. For the time being though, *The Soliloquy* alone would have to represent him in America. So he asked for *Mr*

1 JCP to TFP, Wed 21 March [1917]; Bissell Collection
2 TFP to Andrew Melrose, 23 October 1925; Bissell Collection
3 See JCP to LlP, 28 April [1916]; Letters of John Cowper Powys to his Brother Llewelyn, vol. 1, p. 202   4 JCP to LlP, 9 November 1916; *Ibid.*, p. 215
5 TFP to Louis Wilkinson, 16 December 1916; Colgate
6 See *Welsh Ambassadors,* p. 24.

Tasker to be returned,[1] and now in typescript and manuscript, it made the long journey back across the Atlantic, to East Chaldon, by early October 1917.[2] Henceforth he always referred to it as "the typed novel *Mr Tasker's Gods*", as if it had acquired a dignified suit of clothes. It was obviously time for a new approach, for professional help; so TFP turned to Frederick Chard of Curtis Brown Ltd, a representative of one of the best of the newly ascendant literary agencies. The contact was made through the good offices of Arnold Shaw who must have been anxious to smooth any ruffled Powys feathers.[3] In one of TFP's earliest references to Chard, he identifies him as "Arnold's agent in this country".[4] Ten days later, Theodore eagerly sent his most recent work, still in manuscript—*Amos Lear*, a novel, and *Hindcliff Tales*— to the man he hoped would be his latest champion. TFP's naïveté about contemporary literary trends is exemplified by his solemn pronouncement in his letter to Chard: "I fear that the most likely fault found will be that they [the stories] are breaking new ground in literature." His further optimistic description of the stories as "rather in the Russian fashion" echoed his words to John.[5] He had read his Dostoevsky[6] and his Tolstoy —or at least *My Religion*; but it may have been John's gift of Constance Garnett's translation of *The Darling and Other Stories* (1916) by Chekhov that prompted the questionable claim of Russian influence. On the fly-leaf of this volume (now in the Bissell Collection), TFP had written "very important, not to be lost". "Gloom", the title of what he deemed one of the best of these stories, pinpoints the only characteristic of Russian fiction salient in his work. Another highlighted story was "Sammy"—the autobiographical significance of which might easily be overlooked, unless one is aware that in a later version in the HRHRC it is re-titled "Theodore". This juxtaposition of his own name with "Gloom" reflects his general disposition at the time, and so do the stories. In "Sammy/Theodore", for example, the wall which the protagonist strikes with his hoe symbolizes the psychological barriers that oppress him, that constrict his life: "The wall was made of flint, its colour was a dirty freckled grey. The wall hemmed Theodore in, he could not go out to the world

1 TFP to JCP, 9 July 1917; HRHRC   2 TFP to JCP, 7 October 1917; HRHRC
3 See TFP to Andrew Melrose, 22 October 1925; Bissell Collection
4 TFP to JCP, 19 May 1917; HRHRC   5 TFP to JCP, [October 1916]; HRHRC
6 TFP owned a copy of the Everyman (Dent) edition of Constance Garnett's translation of *The Brothers Karamazov* (now in the Bissell Collection).

beyond the wall . . . it expressed to him his whole life."[1] Material like this tells us more about the "mood of God" afflicting TFP than about his development as a writer; but the image of the wall is a recurring one, as in "This is Thyself", which dates from the same period as *Mr Tasker's Gods*.

Frederick Chard's efforts on TFP's behalf were partially successful: he negotiated a contract with Andrew Melrose for *Amos Lear* and for an English edition of *The Soliloquy of a Hermit*. However, Melrose wanted some changes, and TFP's reluctance to do the work himself may have proved a fatal error. To some extent the solicitousness of John, Louis and Frances had led him to ill-founded ideas about the role of agent and publisher. He dragged his feet at an invitation to visit London for consultations about *Amos Lear*, and he was perilously presumptuous in his willingness "to put the matter of 'Amos Lear' freely into Mr Melrose's hands to alter as he thinks best."[2] Though he was sufficiently aware of the scale of the required changes to report to John that "it will have to be altered a great deal, I believe,"[3] astonishingly, he felt no compunction about writing to ask "if it can be put in order for publication by Mr Chard or his friends in London according to Mr Melrose's wishes." His only excuse—relayed to John—was a complacent "You know I can't do that sort of thing."[4] It is not clear whether he assumed that most of the changes needed were low-level mechanical changes (spelling and punctuation)—in which case he was certainly right that he could not do "that sort of thing"—or whether he was acknowledging the difficulties he often had with problems of structure and narrative development. In any case, when *Mr Tasker's Gods* arrived back from America, TFP was initially inclined to forward it to Chard for consideration by Melrose, but the perspective of a year and perusal of the typescript convinced him that it would take considerable work to render it and his other work "more suitable to this market".[5] In the end, he changed his mind and did send it to Chard after all. It was under consideration at the beginning of 1918 and well enough regarded by his agent to become the standard against which TFP's other works were measured. Nonetheless, he was not optimistic, and offered the following incisive self-critique: "If I had not put so

---

[1] Selected Early Works, p. 449
[2] TFP to Frederick Chard, 15 July 1917; Bissell Collection
[3] TFP to JCP, 9 July 1917; HRHRC [4] TFP to JCP, 9 July 1917; HRHRC
[5] TFP to Frederick Chard, 30 November 1917; Bissell Collection

much of God's words in Mr Tasker, if I had not put so much of myself into it, all might have been well."[1] When *Georgina, a Lady* was rejected as "too crude" in 1918,[2] only *Mr Tasker* and *Amos Lear* remained in circulation. Melrose came through to the extent of issuing the re-titled *Soliloquies of a Hermit* in 1918 and, in 1919, signing a contract to publish *Amos Lear*—"only a flimsy bit of paper with Andrew Melrose at the bottom", TFP grumbled.[3] Melrose also assured Louis during a visit in December 1919 that his plans had not changed.[4] A more dyspeptic assessment from Raymond Savage of Curtis Brown at the end of same month could not have encouraged TFP: "Between you and me and the gatepost, I am getting rather fed up with Mr Melrose, who is too slow for words."[5] In another year, even the patient TFP had given up.[6] The pattern of "hope deferred"[7] and then destroyed was being repeated. And to add insult to injury, it would take him another two years to retrieve *Amos Lear* and other manuscripts from the dilatory Melrose.[8]

Upon his return from East Africa to settle in Dorset, and eager to get into print himself, Llewelyn unselfishly took it upon himself to advance the literary career of his struggling brother. Already by September 1919 he had read the *Hindcliff Tales* and *Mr Tasker's Gods*, preferring the short stories to the novel.[9] After reading *Georgina, a Lady* too, he realised that both still needed substantial work, but only tried his hand at editing *Amos Lear* and a few of the *Hindcliff Tales* (there are, for example, annotations on the HRHRC manuscript of "Jane"). Somewhat unfairly, Llewelyn also saw fit to chastise John for merely offering praise: "Both his novels, 'Mr Tasker' and 'Georgina, A Lady' require revising and getting into some kind of order—perfectly useless your shouting 'genius, genius' and being too lazy or foolish to give him honest criticism."[10] But could he have been unaware that Louis and Frances had already put considerable effort into revising *Mr Tasker*? In any case, when Louis and Frances returned to England, they swung into action

1 TFP to JCP, 4 January 1918; HRHRC
2 TFP to JCP, 24 November 1918; HRHRC
3 TFP to JCP, undated but c. 1919; HRHRC
4 Though Melrose once visited TFP in East Chaldon, the visit does not seem to have warmed their relationship.
5 Raymond Savage to TFP, 31 December 1919; Bissell Collection
6 TFP to JCP, 22 December 1920; HRHRC
7 TFP to JCP, 5 December 1919; HRHRC
8 TFP to JCP, 14 October 1922; HRHRC
9 TFP to Louis Wilkinson; *Welsh Ambassadors*, p. 170
10 LlP to JCP, 8 October 1919; Letters of Llewelyn Powys, p. 100

once more. Louis took *Georgina, a Lady* with him to London to read and concluded, as TFP gloomily told John, that "it will require more revising than anything he has seen of mine yet."[1] Bad news indeed! Once again, Louis passed the manuscript to Frances, just to correct and suggest alterations or cross out,[2] as TFP put it disingenuously. That revealingly offhand "just" is, of course, an injustice, however unintended, to Frances and the demands of the editorial process. Meanwhile Frances, who had been reading and editing TFP's work since 1913 had even paid a visit to Curtis Brown in January 1920[3] on Theodore's behalf, which provoked a strained, but polite, request from his agents to inform them in advance of the intervention of others. By March, TFP had become anxious about the fate of *Georgina*, but was reluctant to hurry Frances; he at least had the grace to recognize that "she is really very good at this work."[4] But the intervention and advice of TFP's loyal band of supporters proved futile—*Mr Tasker's Gods*, *Hindcliff Tales*, *Amos Lear*, *Georgina, a Lady*, "A Wolf in Sheep's Clothing", all had been "found wanting".

When Stephen Tomlin, refugee from Oxford and would-be sculptor, discovered East Chaldon in 1921 during a walking tour, he also discovered TFP. He shared his discovery with Sylvia Townsend Warner, whom he had known from his schoolboy days at Harrow, and described for her "a sort of hermit" with "a very fine head"— the sculptor's point of view.[5] Thus began a series of events that would at last lead TFP to a publishing house, Chatto & Windus, willing to show faith in him, and to an editor, Charles Prentice, who would become a friend tolerant of his *modus scribendi*. Yet it would still take some years and the efforts of Sylvia Townsend Warner and David Garnett in particular, before *Mr Tasker's Gods* appeared in print. Upon the recommendation of Tomlin, Warner solicited a copy of the novel from its author and sent him a copy of her unpublished play, *The Sin-Eaters* (which seems to have been the inspiration for the later TFP / Stephen Tomlin collaboration on a play of the same name). Uncharacteristically flattered by the extravagance of what Warner later called "that prim and literary letter",[6] he replied in strangely un-Theodorian language: "It is

---

1 TFP to JCP, 5 December 1919; HRHRC; see also *Welsh Ambassadors*, p. 170.
2 TFP to JCP, 1 March 1920; HRHRC
3 TFP to Louis Wilkinson, 22 January, 1920; Colgate
4 TFP to JCP, 1 March 1920; HRHRC   5 *PR* 5, p. 13
6 Sylvia Townsend Warner to TFP 7 February 1925; Bissell Collection

very charming of you to ask to see *Mr Tasker's Gods*. I hope you won't be frightfully disappointed"[1] and sent her "a very sombre typescript". Her subsequent lengthy written reaction offered plenty of the kind of praise that would warm any author's heart, but some frank criticism too. On the one hand, she said, "I feel battered and excited, dazed as if I had come in from fighting a high wind. You know the feeling one has after *Wuthering Heights*? I feel rather like that;" on the other hand, "it has left me with a feeling of perturbed melancholy." She was, she confessed, particularly reluctant to abandon her conviction that there was some "steadfast virtue" in the countryman that passed "from him into the ploughed field" and to admit that "this last remnant of faith is only the last rag of sentiment."[2] In later years she was blunter, confessing that "I found it hard to stomach the ruthless hatred with which he pursued the peasant characters." Her emerging political views may have been a factor here (she was a longtime member of the Communist Party). But her visceral response was, she felt, the consequence of reading "a blacker and bitterer draught than the final published version".[3] This would have been the already "improved" typescript returned by Louis Wilkinson. It is worth noting that Warner's early—and naïvely romantic—view of life in the country would not endure; indeed with more experience of the reality, it would more closely approximate to Theodore's dark vision. Writing in *The Countryman* (July 1939) she affirms the difference between the rural life as envisaged by a townee and as it really was: "Rape and brutality accompanied the course of true love. ... Worst of all was the indifference of public opinion and the ignorant animal resignation of the victims." This modification of Warner's perspective also alerts us to the fact that the blackness and bitterness of TFP's vision was not just a product of his allegedly melancholic disposition. The rural world was often a harsh and cruel environment. In "This is Thyself", for example, TFP observes that "The suicides in the village where I lived [Sweffling, Suffolk] were abnormal. One man killed himself every year that I lived there," and cites the cases of a blacksmith and a road-mender by hanging, and a carpenter by drowning.[4] Lest TFP's account be dismissed as the selective recollection of a

---

1 TFP to Sylvia Townsend Warner, n.d. but [1921]; Bissell Collection
2 Sylvia Townsend Warner to TFP, November 1921; Bissell Collection
3 *PR* 5, p. 14
4 Selected Early Works, pp. 348–9

melancholic, one only has to point to Llewelyn's poignant anecdote in a letter to John about a case in Dorset:

> Our coal man, aged fifty, has committed suicide. We liked him so much. As he waited behind a heap of "slegren" [local variant of slag-(heap)] near Moreton, he wrote a letter to his wife. It ended "Goodbye, my love. I meant to write more, but I see the train coming." He was cut clean in half—a very generous fellow, full of vitality and spirit, but worried because he had been fined £5 for taking some coke from a government truck at Wool Station.[1]

To solicit help in securing a publisher for TFP, Tomlin, who was acquainted with David Garnett, then a partner in Birrell & Garnett, booksellers, wrote advising him to expect a visit from Sylvia Townsend Warner, to discuss TFP's work.[2] There could hardly have been a better choice. Not only was Garnett, through his parents, very knowledgeable about an array of literary matters, but he had the kind of contacts in the publishing world that could—and would—prove valuable to TFP. David's father was then reader for Jonathan Cape; and the Russian translations by David's mother, Constance, had been published by Chatto & Windus since 1916.[3] His own wildly successful novella, *Lady into Fox*, was about to be published by the same firm. The sample Warner carried to the Taviton Street bookshop, however, was not *Mr Tasker's Gods* but "Hester Dominy". Garnett took this 35,000-word novella to Charles Prentice at Chatto & Windus with his own recommendation and thereby precipitated the publication of *The Left Leg* in May 1923 and of *Black Bryony* in November of the same year.[4] Not satisfied with a single tack, he persuaded H. N. Brailsford, the editor of *The New Leader*, a new Labour weekly, to accept a number of TFP's stories, beginning with "The House with the Echo".[5] This proved to be a valuable contact, because the magazine published twenty of TFP's stories in the space of four years. TFP's account of his good fortune shows him

1 LlP to JCP, 14 April 1933; Cambridge University Library
2 See Warner's account in *PR* 5.
3 *The Darling and Other Stories* was the first volume published on 21 October 1916. See further Richard Garnett, *Constance Garnett. A Heroic Life*, p. 305.
4 TFP subsequently asked the Cambridge Literary Agency—which had been unsuccessful in placing any of the various manuscripts in their possession—to forward "Abraham Men" directly to Chatto & Windus. In fact, they sent it back to him and he forwarded it to the publishers himself. He sent *The Left Leg* to the publishers himself.
5 See H. N. Brailsford to TFP, 22 August 1922. (Bissell Collection)

comprehending the connection to another member of the Garnett family—the translator whose edition of Chekhov's stories he deemed so valuable. "Constance Garnett's son," he proclaimed proudly, "gave the editor my name."[1]

Meanwhile, a year after Warner read *Mr Tasker*, David Garnett tackled it at TFP's request.[2] Happily, Garnett seems to have experienced less trouble digesting "the sombre typescript" than Warner—no doubt because it had by then been revised and retyped at Stephen Tomlin's urging.[3] TFP was obviously relieved: "I expected you to advise a burning fiery furnace for Mr Tasker and you suggest pins . . . I will pin him up so that his own mother won't know him. You have done a great deal for me and I am very grateful. Yes, I'll unfrock those clergy."[4] Prentice was apparently almost as grateful to Garnett as TFP was. In one phone conversation, Prentice "burst out with renewed thanks to David for having recommended your work to them," according to Tomlin.[5] Garnett also spoke of *Mr Tasker* in approving terms to his father, Edward. Thus alerted by his trusted reader and talent-scout, Edward, Jonathan Cape himself wrote to TFP about *Mr Tasker*, saying: "I have heard something of it and what I have heard interests me very much."[6] At the time, David Garnett actually had possession of the typescript; so Theodore asked him to pass in on to Cape "after the medicine you have given him". There could hardly have been more propitious circumstances; for Cape would inevitably refer the novel to Edward for his professional opinion. In fact, this process was short-circuited: David simply handed the typescript to his father! Alas, Edward Garnett was not one to be stampeded by his son's enthusiasms and wrote a very direct letter to TFP:

> I should have written before this is to give you my opinion of the novel. I am much interested in your outlook on rural life & congratulate you on the strength of certain scenes; but "from the point of view of a publisher" you have accentuated the darker side of the picture to a degree that would alienate or indeed terrify the ordinary reader. I think that if you ever rewrote the novel mitigating the insistence of the harsher

1 TFP to JCP, 14 October 1922; HRHRC
2 In a letter of 10 October [1922], Stephen Tomlin wrote "I shall be excited to see your criticism of 'Tasker's Gods'." (Bissell Collection)
3 TFP to JCP, 14 October 1922; HRHRC
4 TFP to David Garnett, 1 November 1922; Hilton Hall
5 Stephen Tomlin to TFP, 24 January 1923; Bissell Collection
6 Jonathan Cape to TFP, 14 December 1922; included in letter from TFP to David Garnett, 15 December 1922; Hilton Hall

realism, the publishing firm I represent, viz., Messrs Cape would likely make you an offer. In any case I should be glad to see any future ms you may have to show. I may add that your clerical portraiture is specially interesting.[1]

The last line—"your clerical portraiture is specially interesting"— warrants comment. The scandalous behaviour of some of TFP's clergymen that others—including David Garnett, on the evidence of TFP's "I'll unfrock those clergy"—saw as problematic, the resolutely freethinking and anti-establishment Edward apparently saw as worthy of approbation. But once again, the much-travelled *Mr Tasker's Gods*, by now quite the ugly duckling, was returned to East Chaldon, prompting TFP to write to his new friend, David, in terms of painful resignation: "I am very much indebted to you and to your father. Please thank him for his letter. His opinion for which I am most grateful . . . I will hold carefully and it will inspire me to go on in the way, keeping my hands to the plough."[2] Poor Theodore! A few years later, brother John would get a far warmer reception from the same Edward Garnett who recommended publication of *Wolf Solent* and then called it "not far from a great novel".[3] For his part, John always maintained that "[Edward Garnett] made some excellent improvements," and was characteristically generous in his comments about the Garnett family's role in getting Theodore into print: "It had been left to the Garnet [*sic*] family, those fearless explorers of the *Terrae Incognitae* of Genius to make straight his path."[4] However, Louis Wilkinson, who had worked so hard on TFP's behalf to no avail, was decidedly ambivalent about David Garnett: "Do you really feel that you can safely go by David Garnett's advice. . . . He has written well, but that doesn't mean he can judge well."[5]

It is not at all clear that David, who had already helped secure one publisher, was really intent upon securing a second for *Mr Tasker*. In any case, the possibility of competition over a hitherto unwanted novel evaporated and *Mr Tasker's* fate would rest upon the judgement of Charles Prentice alone. TFP drafted some seven pages of changes in a Sherborne notebook during 1923; by early 1924, Prentice had read the typescript and approved its

1 Edward Garnett to TFP, 19 January 1923; Bissell Collection, laid into ms of *Mr Tasker's Gods*
2 TFP to David Garnett, 20 January 1923; Hilton Hall
3 Review of *Wolf Solent* in *Now and Then*, Summer 1929
4 *Autobiography*, p. 534
5 Louis Wilkinson to TFP, 17 August 1926; Bissell Collection

publication, subject to some changes. TFP replied at once: "I am extremely pleased you admire this one, and that you see, as I hoped you would, that it should stand—with the last suggested alterations—as it is."[1] Subsequently he sent the new typescript of *Mr Tasker,* incorporating "the revisions that you agreed would be a help to the book".[2] The revisions themselves merit scrutiny, not least because they made publication less risky. The decision about whether to keep the original version or select the revisions was left to Prentice, as notes by TFP (in red ink) and by Prentice (in pencil) make clear. Material was excised from "Two Clergymen" (Ch. xxxii) and "Peace and Plenty" (Ch. xxxv); then they were merged as chapter xxxiv under the former title of chapter xxxii. The principle of exclusion can be inferred from this sample: "These wide-awake ministers had recognized long ago one fact about their natures, that one girl was not enough to satisfy their broad-minded and large-hearted belief in women." TFP had meanwhile acquired a new perspective on "The Sap from the Root" (Ch. xxxvii) and suggested: "I think that perhaps it would be best to entirely delete this chapter because it seems to me now only to add unnecessary horror to the story; but I will leave this to the publisher to decide." No doubt with a sense of relief, Prentice wrote simply "Yes, omit." So the reading public was spared the story of the mother who buried her dead children under bushes in the garden, of the old man who boasted of having three hundred rats buried under his French beans, of the carter who lamented the death of his daughter and her child born of incest.[3]

When she received an advance copy of the novel, Sylvia Townsend Warner was delighted: "Your alterations have improved it immensely from the version I read—three winters ago, was it, or four?"[4] The great day dawned on 12 February 1925 and, nine years late, *Mr Tasker's Gods* was published in an edition of 2,500. The jacket bore an attractive woodcut of pigs—the gods of the title—in a farmyard. Here too the Garnett family played a role, since the illustration was the work of Ray Garnett, David's talented wife, who had already done woodcuts for *Black Bryony.*[5] TFP was pleased with her contribution, deeming it "quite one of

1 TFP to Charles Prentice, 5 February 1924; Chatto & Windus Archive
2 TFP to Charles Prentice, April 1924; Chatto & Windus Archive
3 The cancelled chapters are now published in Selected Early Works.
4 Sylvia Townsend Warner to TFP, 7 February 1925; Bissell Collection
5 See *PR* 10, pp. 9–28.

the best things you have done."[1] Compared to TFP's earlier books, initial sales were encouragingly strong. Within six weeks of publication (i.e. by 31 March 1925) 785 copies had been sold in the British Empire. "Despite the lugubrious reviews," boasted Prentice, "[It] has done best of all."[2] There were, of course, some good reviews. Liam O'Flaherty, in particular, waxed enthusiastic in *The Irish Statesman*:

> In order to be a work of genius, a novel must offer something more than a perfect style, the imprint of a cultured mind and that gentleness of soul which makes everyone love Mr Powys. It must be a relentless picture of life . . . it must have the power to invoke great beauty and great horror in the same breath as it calls forth laughter from the lips. It is because *Mr Tasker's Gods* draws such a relentless picture of life and because it possesses that peculiar, magical power, that I claim it to be a work of genius.[3]

O'Flaherty rather undercuts the rhetorical force of his review of the work by admitting to his admiration of, and personal acquaintance with, the man. But he genuinely found in *Mr Tasker's Gods* a work that resonated with his own "temperamental predilection for violence, hatred or horror and—artistic conviction of its validity".[4] Unfortunately, O'Flaherty's position seems to have been very much a minority one. Writing to his old friend, Louis Wilkinson, TFP observes "Mr Tasker appears to be a red rag to most of these British reviewers. I should like Douglas Goldring's opinion—and yours and Nan's [Ann Reid, Louis' second wife]."[5] David Garnett conveyed his feelings about one reviewer to Charles Prentice: "What an old idiot Sydney Waterlow is about Theo's book in *The New Statesman*."[6] But TFP took consolation in the fact that: "even with all this butchering Mr Tasker has gone better than any of the others, so my enemies may lick the dust."[7]

Soon, interest in *Mr Tasker* was being shown from some unlikely quarters. David Garnett had, not implausibly, suggested to one Madame Vergerova, London representative of Mospoligraph Publications in Moscow, that *Mr Tasker's Gods* "might be a success in Russia." Although TFP was willing to settle for the £15 flat fee,

---

1 TFP to Ray Garnett, 9 February 1925; Hilton Hall
2 Charles Prentice to TFP, 29 June 1925; Bissell Collection
3 *The Irish Statesman* iii, no. 26, 7 March 1925, p. 827; cited on the jacket of *Mockery Gap*   4 Kelly, *Liam O'Flaherty the Storyteller*, p. 82
5 TFP to Louis Wilkinson, March 1925; *Welsh Ambassadors*, p. 191
6 David Garnett to Charles Prentice, 25 February 1925; Chatto & Windus Archive
7 TFP to David Garnett, 14 March 1925; Hilton Hall

the Russian publishers eventually decided against the project. However, *Mr Tasker's Gods* did appear in Russia in 1927 in a translation by Lydia Slonimsky.[1] Writing from Leningrad, the translator was able to report a remarkable event: "The first edition of *Mr Tasker's Gods* is already out of print and in autumn will come out in a second."[2] Despite his earlier, seemingly fatal, objections, Alfred Knopf had by this time agreed, on a book-by-book basis, to publish TFP's work in America. The backing of a distinguished publisher such as Chatto & Windus must have been reassuring to him, but whatever happened to those objections about the indecorous behaviour of some of the characters? The evidence is ambiguous, but some of the revisions in *Mr Tasker* may have originated with Knopf. There is also some evidence that Knopf's continued support was in doubt. Prentice seems to have pressed him to set up *Mr Tasker* himself from the start, but he declined.[3] His normal, conservative, practice was to import sheets —apparently one thousand in the case of *Mr Tasker's Gods*—and then reprint, if a book succeeded.[4] In fact, Knopf never had any reason to reprint *Mr Tasker's Gods:* it did not sell well in America and TFP's sales had gone steadily downhill there since *The Left Leg*.[5] But at least in England TFP's loyal circle was enlarged by new admirers, some of whom made themselves known. One such was the popular novelist, Dennis Wheatley, who boasted that he had a complete set of TFP's books but that "I like *Mr Tasker's Gods* best, and I am happy to say that I have given quite a number of copies of it to various friends. . . . Your simplicity of style combined with depth of feeling always makes me think of you as the English Tolstoy."[6] A very different reaction came from the founder of an informal TFP club at an RAF base near Sheffield. In an otherwise enthusiastic letter, Corporal Frederick Peele Yates wrote: "But, really Mr Powys, you should never have written *Mr Tasker's Gods*. Does all this sound presumptuous to you? Even if it does, we still think *Mr Tasker's Gods* unworthy of you."[7]

1 copy in the Bissell Collection
2 Lydia Slonimsky to TFP, 30 July 1927; Bissell Collection
3 TFP to Charles Prentice 11 June 1924; Chatto & Windus Archive
4 Knopf took one thousand sheets of *The Left Leg* and *Black Bryony*, but only five hundred of *Mark Only. Innocent Birds* seems to have been the one book set up for Knopf in America.
5 Chatto & Windus to TFP, 29 June 1925; Bissell Collection
6 Dennis Wheatley to TFP, 8 December 1934; Bissell Collection
7 Frederick Peel Yates to TFP, 12 January 1943; Cambridge University Library

Mr Weston's Good Wine: *A Curious Chapter*

Alfred Knopf once claimed in conversation that his firm gave up publishing TFP's books because it "got tired losing money on him."[1] In fact, there was far more at issue than money. Perhaps Knopf had forgotten the circumstances surrounding the decision twenty-five years earlier, but there is a curious relationship to the trials of *Mr Tasker's Gods*. When Prentice first read *Mr Weston* in 1925, he was overwhelmed by the poetry, the vision, and the sheer good writing, and deemed it the best of TFP's novels by far: "I put it with 'Innocent Birds' and 'Mr Tasker'—for I'm growing to regard *Mr Tasker's Gods* with ever-increasing respect; but above them both decidedly."[2] His only substantive objection was to the ending —a not infrequent problem in TFP's work—which left him "vaguely, dissatisfied somehow", in part because it seemed so rushed: the Mumby brothers are chased but abruptly forgiven, Tamar disappears, and Mr Weston "drives away so very curtly." In response, three months later, TFP sent his revised version—including an additional chapter.[3] However, Prentice was still unhappy with the treatment of Mr Weston and—though usually reticent about matters of content—sketched out a possible ending: "My expectations lead me to a longer epilogue in which, say, Mr Weston reaches the top of the hill again, looks back on Folly Down, and subsequently disappears."[4] The actual ending follows this outline, but the details are exquisitely Theodorian. Alfred Knopf's objections were of a very different nature. While he recognized the high quality of the work and was inclined to take the book, he was troubled by "a feeling that it might in places be too strong for the ordinary conventional Christian morality".[5] To make matters worse, Prentice admitted that similar sentiments had been "raised also in this office." In order to "get over any possible criticism of the silly sort" he advocated issuing *Mr Weston* initially in an expensive (fifteen-shilling) limited edition "with illustrations by some suitable artist" —exactly the strategy adopted in England. (Nobody mentioned that this was the sort of treatment customarily afforded erotic literature!) Riley's explanation—that "this was an experiment on

1 Alfred Knopf to Martin Steinmann, 9 April 1951; Steinmann Collection
2 Charles Prentice to TFP, 1 December 1925; Bissell Collection
3 TFP to Charles Prentice, 15 March 1926; Chatto & Windus Archive
4 Charles Prentice to TFP, 24 March 1926; Chatto & Windus Archive
5 Charles Prentice to TFP, 15 July 1926; Chatto & Windus Archive

the publisher's part following the disappointing sales of *Innocent Birds*"¹—must now be discounted. Knopf also considered the possibility of such a limited edition, only to reject it outright, and thus severed his connection with TFP. Behind his decision lay an explosive legal opinion solicited by his staff. The report by lawyer Ben Stern (of Stern and Reubens) concluded that the first half of the book contains numerous passages which make it legally objectionable, particularly Mrs Vosper's conversations (Ch. xiv) and the Mumby brothers' near-rape of Jenny Bunce under the oak tree (Ch. xv). Yet in Mr Wilson, Knopf's editor, TFP had found an admirer; in the letter accompanying the legal opinion, he confessed that "the general drift and significance of the book won me completely" and "if you decide to take the chance and go ahead, with the little verbal and phrasal expurgations that can be easily and quickly done, the possible ensuing fight is one which we can sustain with a good conscience."² Knopf, of course, listened to his lawyer.

Once again, TFP's supporters had to rally round and find another American publisher. Charles Prentice proposed that David Garnett broach with his father, Edward, the possibility that they might try Viking, for whom Edward had been appointed English representative in April 1925.³ In this delicate matter David doubted that he could help, as he explained: "No, my father dislikes Theo's work and he certainly would not recommend him unless strong pressure would be put on him to do so."⁴ However, he promised to see what he could do, while warning "he dislikes Theo's work and has a grouse against it." It is not unlikely that the "grouse" was linked to *Mr Tasker's Gods* and derived from the embarrassment he surely felt in recommending *against* a manuscript he had recommended reading in the first place. In any event, David did not open the subject because, as he put it, "my father blew off steam at his name." In all likelihood, Prentice himself approached Edward in his role as Viking's English representative, and Edward dutifully forwarded the manuscript. However, conscious of his father's opinion, David took no chances and wrote to Ben Huebsch (who had merged his own business with Viking's in 1925) to make the case for *Mr Weston* and to warn him that "my father dislikes Powys, a curious aberration of taste."⁵ Just a few

---

1 *Bibliography*, p. 27   2 Wilson to Alfred Knopf, 19 August 1926; HRHRC
3 Jefferson, *Edward Garnett*, p. 205
4 David Garnett to Charles Prentice, 29 June 1926; Hilton Hall
5 David Garnett to Ben Huebsch, 8 August 1926; HRHRC

days earlier Sylvia Townsend Warner had fired off a strongly worded letter to Huebsch as well. Viking had been her American publisher ever since *Lolly Willowes* (1926). Perhaps unwisely, she revealed that Knopf rejected the novel "on the grounds that it is improper and blasphemous, and would render him liable to prosecution". However, she emphasized its allegorical nature and waxed indignant at TFP's detractors:

> Mr Powys is not a writer for everybody, but I am sure that he is a writer for posterity. . . . *Mr Weston's Good Wine* is the maturest and most profound of his books, and that it should have been sniffed at and turned over as though it were an indecent work is nothing short of an affront to the whole profession of letters.[1]

The rhetorical powers of Garnett and Warner proved triumphant. Notwithstanding the cautiousness of Prentice and the faint-heartedness of Knopf, Viking set up and published *Mr Weston's Good Wine* as a regular trade edition and, since it preceded Chatto's limited edition of 660, theirs became the true first edition. Somehow the New York Society for the Suppression of Vice missed an inviting target—perhaps because it was so busy in 1927 obtaining convictions against twenty-eight other individuals for violation of obscenity statutes. If America failed Theodore in the case of *Mr Tasker* in 1916, it did not with *Mr Weston*. In England the whiff of something improper lingered. An amusing example is the letter TFP received in 1934 from one Peter Howes:

> The "Good Wine" I interpreted as "the attributes of God" in general, but I understand . . . that this is quite wrong and that the Good Wine is "sex". "Sex", however, may cover so much. . . . You are not advocating indiscriminate sex-relationships (forgive the suggestion, but as you know it is one of the charges against you by certain people) but the very opposite.[2]

In the same year, Grant Richards expressed his regret that he had never followed up on his plan to visit TFP: "Had I done so I might possibly have been the publisher of *Mr Weston's Good Wine*, which is to me one of the wonder books of its decade . . . Vlaminck, with a touch of Greco, translated into English narrative prose."[3]

---

1 Sylvia Townsend Warner to Ben Huebsch, 5 August 1927; The Letters of Sylvia Townsend Warner, pp. 12–13
2 Peter Howes to TFP, 4 February 1934; Bissell Collection
3 Richards, *Author Hunting*, pp. 263–4

The obdurate worldliness of the Reverend John Turnbull and his like in *Mr Tasker's Gods* was a natural target of the unworldly TFP who was disdainful of "the getting mood" as he labelled it in *The Soliloquy of a Hermit*.¹ It is no contradiction, however, that he hoped to make a modest living from his writing. So the reception of ten guineas in advanced royalties for *The Soliloquy* in 1916 was an occasion for real celebration and modest hope. Four years later and nary a penny richer, he wrote to Louis Wilkinson a little plaintively: "I should like to earn a little out of these damned writings, that is all. I have a certain lust for plum jam."² The sad fact is, however, that none of his books sold well enough to provide a comfortable living. From the limited edition of *Mr Weston's Good Wine* he earned just £67—but called it "a great help."³ His total income thus rose from £170 to £225 for the year. In 1932 he told his brother John that "America does not put much in my purse. Royalties for six months amounting to ... not quite £2-0-0."⁴ If disappointment at his poor sales emerged from time to time, envy—the ugliest of the moods of God—at the phenomenal success of his major benefactors, David (with *Lady Into Fox*) and Sylvia (with *Lolly Willowes*) never did.⁵ But as a supplement to his meagre income, TFP began to sell some of his manuscripts. The typescript of *Mr Tasker's Gods* that had been so painstakingly made by Frances Wilkinson was one of the earlier items put on the market. Douglas Clayton, a book-dealer and cousin of David Garnett, had secured a little over £10 for TFP for the typescripts of "Archdeacon Truggin" and "The Dewpond",⁶ and so proposed asking £25 from "two rich collectors in America" for the typescript of *Mr Tasker*, together "with the letter, and extra chapter and numerous corrections."⁷ In *The Bookman*, 75, April–December, 1932, p. vii, there is an advertisement by Melrich V. Rosenberg of New York for "T F. Powys's Autograph MSS. Published and unpublished ... priced for resale by the trade". The

---

1 "He is the people, and his dominating mood is the getting mood." (*The Soliloquy of a Hermit*, p. 4

2 TFP to Louis Wilkinson, January 1920; cited in *Welsh Ambassadors*, p. 171

3 TFP to Louis Wilkinson, 7 January 1928; Colgate

4 TFP to JCP, 4 May 1932; HRHRC

5 When Prentice was casting around desperately for another mode of publication that would boost TFP's sales for *Black Bryony*, he hit upon something that had worked well in the case of Garnett's *Lady Into Fox*—woodcut illustrations by Ray Garnett.

6 Douglas Clayton to TFP, 13 August 1929; Bissell Collection

7 Douglas Clayton to TFP, 19 November 1929; Bissell Collection. Alas, this important typescript has vanished, possibly in America.

manuscript for *Mr Weston's Good Wine* went to Percy Muir at Elkin Matthews for £50[1]—almost as much as TFP had made in royalties for the first edition! Such sales helped, but could not compensate for the lack of a regular income. Finally, David Garnett rallied TFP's friends and admirers, collected £92. 2s 0d, sent him £30, and put the rest, "on deposit" at Chatto & Windus to be paid quarterly.[2] Many of the same people also banded together to help win Theodore a civil list pension. The petition to the Prime Minister made a strong case, pointing out that while "T. F. Powys has always been extremely poor, his present circumstances are deplorable."[3] He was initially awarded £60, which was raised in 1940 to £100, and, finally, £130 in 1950.[4]

In telling us something of his taste in books, TFP confessed: "I like an author who has seen—who has lived, what he is writing about."[5] In fact, he endured as much in life as any of his long-suffering characters ever did in fiction. He overcame his failures at school and as a farmer, he conquered his melancholy by accepting it as a "mood of God", he learned to write his way out of religion ("the only subject I know anything about"[6]) and into life, he suffered poverty and the disappointment of rejection. But, sustained by the richness of friendship, he learned to cultivate his own garden with patience, and his books are the eternal blooms thereof.

1 Percy Muir to TFP, 16 June 1936; HRHRC
2 TFP to David Garnett, 23 September 1933 and 27 March, 1940; Hilton Hall
3 H. J. C. Grierson to Prime Minister [Ramsay Macdonald], 3 November 1933; copy forwarded by Charles Prentice to David Garnett; Hilton Hall
4 TFP to David Garnett, 3 March 1950; Hilton Hall
5 *The Soliloquy of a Hermit*, p. 23   6 *Ibid.*, p. 5

6

Theodore Powys and John Death

"He, under Whom I have my dominion and my power, is a dark star. Who can escape Him?" (*Unclay*)

While Theodore Powys was in bed with flu on 28 March 1929, Sylvia Townsend Warner paid one of her frequent visits. She enjoyed reading to him and feeding him titbits of information likely to provoke his morbid curiosity—on this occasion the initial instalment of a grave-digger's diary in the latest issue of *The Countryman*.[1] After praising her contribution to *Kindness in a Corner* (1930), he asked: "Do you think it would be proper for me to introduce Death into a story?" and began to share his "first thoughts" for a work he had already entitled *Unclay*.[2] The next day, Good Friday, Sylvia's text was Norman Ault's recently published *Seventeenth Century Lyrics* (1928), a copy of which had been presented to TFP by their publisher and friend Charles Prentice in November 1928. Later she noted in her diary that "the poems Theo marked [were] nearly all about death."[3] One of them, "The Prayer" by Jeremy Taylor, from the festival hymns included in *The Golden Grove* (1655), is unequivocally the source of the unusual title TFP had mentioned the day before. For in TFP's copy, the relevant page number (285) has been written in pencil on the fly-leaf and the neologism "unclay" has been underlined in the poem:[4]

---

1 J. W. Robertson Scott, ed., *The Countryman Book*, 1948, includes a reprint of "The Grave Digger's Diary" from the 1929 *Countryman*.
2 The Diaries of Sylvia Townsend Warner, p. 33; *Recollections of the Powys Brothers*, p. 133
3 Sylvia Townsend Warner Diary ms; see also *Recollections*, p. 133.
4 TFP's copy is now in the Bissell Collection.

> My soul doth pant towards thee,
> My God, source of eternal life.
>   Flesh fights with me:
>   O, end the strife,
> And part us, that in peace I may
>   Unclay
> My wearied spirit, and take
> My flight to thy eternal spring,
>   Where, for his sake
>   Who is my king,
> I may wash all my tears away,
>   That day.

Of course, TFP had long been familiar with Taylor's work. As early as 26 April 1906, he told Louis Wilkinson: "I have been reading Jeremy Taylor and recommend him to your notice; he is a cock of the right kind."[1] So he must have been re-reading Taylor's *Rule and Exercises of Holy Dying* (1651) in preparation for writing *Unclay*. While outlining the plot of the novel for Sylvia, he also mentioned "that sad Mr Taylor", observing that "It is a little terrible to be with him. One sees him in his pit of despair and feels that one has but to take a step to be in it too."[2] One other early trace of the genesis of *Unclay* is to be found at the back of TFP's copy of the Book of Common Prayer,[3] where he scribbled a few pencil notes—unfortunately not dated: "Unclay / Facey of Dodder / the small farmer / who loves Susie Dawe".[4]

That John Death as protagonist is introduced only in TFP's *last* novel, the realistic allegory, *Unclay* (1929), cannot be deemed accidental. He had already reinvented God in his own image in *Mr Weston's Good Wine* (1927) and now presented Death as a friendly forgetful fellow of uncertain occupation with whom the innocent clergyman, Mr Hayhoe, is quickly on first-name terms. Could it be that in thus confronting "the last enemy" in fictional form and reducing him to a mere character in a novel TFP completed his self-administered remedy and rid himself of his fear of death? Though the question cannot, of course, be answered definitively, it is the case that in later years he *was* capable of joking about his own death. He told his wife, Violet, for example, that should he die from eating the mushrooms he liked to gather,

---

1 *Welsh Ambassadors*, p. 76   2 *Diaries*, pp. 41–2
3 a present from his mother in 1895   4 TFP's copy is now in the Bissell Collection.

she could keep as many cats as she liked after she buried him.¹ But he also liked to remind everyone that there was no escaping John Death. His obsession is evident even in his reply to John's birthday letter in 1946: "all I can think of and consider now is Master John Death" he writes.² And sometimes JCP enters his brother's domain: "Mrs Playter [Phyllis's mother] comes next in line for *Master J. Death* being 83 and next comes Brother John in his 78th year."³

This chapter attempts to explore the roots of TFP's obsession with death, to register the significance of those moments when death intruded upon his quiet life—notably the murder of his eldest son, Dicky—and, finally, to reconstruct the story of his own death from documentary sources, especially family letters and diaries.

Roots of Obsession with Death

Although we know all too little about TFP's early life and less still about the forces that shaped his mental life, there are tantalizing glimpses of evidence in his writings. *Under the Bondage of Fear*" (1904), one of his first and most autobiographical pieces, offers a picture of a sensitive and guilt-ridden child, here called Jake, exposed to a stern Old Testament God and to the terrors of hellfire and damnation: "As a babe, he lived ever in a vale of tears, and growing older his terrors increased. Being very delicate and weakly, and loving no noisy or rough games, he was despised of his brother." In church the boy is terrified by the "harsh words" of the priest whose references to "deep and dark sins" convince him that "he was defiled by them." He finds some consolation in an "old book" (*Pilgrim's Progress*) but is haunted by nightmares in which demons mock him or he is "a martyr of the olden times and . . . bound naked to a stake" while those lighting the pyre repeat "This is the righteous judgement of God."⁴ This brief account of the mental afflictions of TFP's fictional *alter ego* has the ring of truth to it and accords well with what we know about TFP himself. In fact, he *was* troubled by nightmares all his life—Theodora Scutt recalls how "through two thick walls his cries would wake me"—

---

1 *Cuckoo in the Powys Nest*, p. 15   2 TFP to JCP, 22 December 1946; HRHRC
3 JCP to TFP, 19 December 1949; cited Riley, "T. F. Powys at Mappowder", p. 17
4 Selected Early Works, pp. 36, 38, 39; the manuscript of *Under the Bondage of Fear* is in the HRHRC.

and he suffered something akin to a nervous breakdown while quite young.¹ Bunyan's allegory is, of course, recognized, along with the Bible, as a seminal influence upon his fiction; but no other account exists, to the best of my knowledge, of the psychological reasons for its importance to him, save that to be found in *Under the Bondage of Fear.* Young Jake's nightmare death at the stake which is equated with "the righteous judgement of God" is given gentler fictional shape in TFP's published novels and stories as "God's Gift". There are a number of possible sources for this conceit, but TFP may first have encountered it in *The Rule and Exercises of Holy Dying* (1651) where the emphasis is slightly different: "And because eternal life is the gift of God, I have less reason to despair."² Nonetheless, the full significance of this singular vision of death can only be appreciated when we recognize that the phrase "God's Gift" is also a gloss upon TFP's first name, "Theodore", from Greek *theos* = God + *doron* = gift. The anglicized form of the Hebrew equivalent is Nathaniel, a name that occurs most notably in TFP's sombre fable "Darkness and Nathaniel".³

As we have seen, it was from his mother's side of the family that TFP seems to have inherited his melancholic, even morbid, disposition. His mother, Mary Cowper Powys, was the daughter of a clergyman, the Reverend W. Cowper Johnson of Yaxham, who discouraged frivolity on the part of his daughter in favour of "making very serious work of prayer & Bible study, and rejecting all reading that is inconsistent with such habits."⁴ In many points of character, then, TFP resembles his distant kinsman on his mother's side, the poet William Cowper (1731–1800): both suffered from lifelong fits of depression, and both sought relief in "a retired and quiet life of simple domestic and rural pleasures".⁵ It is also hard to read Cowper's letters without recognizing sentiments that TFP would have endorsed and might even have articulated. In the end-pages of his disbound copy of Cowper's Private Correspondence (1824), TFP has jotted down "155 style" in evident approval of Cowper's observation on page one hundred and fifty-five that

---

1 *Cuckoo in the Powys Nest,* p. 244
2 Jeremy Taylor, *The Rule and Exercises of Holy Dying* (1651) 1845, p. 228
3 For etymology, see Farrar, *The Proper Names of the Bible,* p. 177.
4 W. Cowper Johnson to Mary Cowper Johnson, 17 January, 1869; in Mary Barham Johnson Collection
5 Margaret Drabble, *The Oxford Companion to English Literature,* 5th edition, Oxford, 1985, p. 236

"there is a certain *style* of dispensations maintained by Providence in the dealings of God with every man, which, however the incidents of his life may vary . . . is never exchanged for another."[1] It was *his* fate, Cowper believed, to be subjected to "sudden, violent, unlooked-for change". TFP, it would appear, saw himself as similarly afflicted. In her journal for 26 September 1932, Alyse Gregory noted that "He sleeps and wakes always with his mistress —death . . . ."[2] and that he revealed that "FEAR had been the whole centre and driving force of his life."[3]

Death in the Family: the Death of the Son

A death in the family provokes many emotions: grief, of course —but also anger, bewilderment, despair. Sometimes these emotions are exorcized by action of one sort or another, and, in the case of an artistic temperament, creatively exorcized. The death of Katherine Mansfield's brother, Leslie, in World War One in 1915 "completely changed the balance between her cynical side and the other, and so released her main creative stream."[4] D. H. Lawrence, perceptive as ever, wrote to her consolingly:

> Do not be sad. It is one life which is passing away from us, one I is dying; but there is another coming into being, which is the happy creative you. I knew you would have to die with your brother; you also, go down into death and be extinguished. But for us there is a rising from the grave, there is a resurrection.[5]

Here, of course, Lawrence goes beyond consolation in trying to get Mansfield to embrace his own phoenix mythology. When Rudyard Kipling lost his son, John, in the same war in the same year, he plunged himself into work for the War Graves Commission and into writing that was far more spiritual, recognizing both the redemptive value of suffering, as in "The Gardener" (collected in *Debits and Credits*, 1926) and also—in a few stories—the healing power of the English countryside. But the persistence and intensity of his personal loss is heard most poignantly in the refrain to his poem, "The Children", which asks the world the always unanswerable question: "But who shall return us our children?"

---

1 This copy is in the author's collection.
2 *Recollections of the Powys Brothers*, p. 146   3 24 May, 1942; *Ibid.*, p. 147
4 Alpers, *The Life of Katherine Mansfield*, p. 183
5 20 December 1915; coincidentally TFP's birthday! (The Complete Letters of D. H. Lawrence, Vol. 2, p. 481)

The war affected the Powys family less than many—largely because John, Theodore, and Llewelyn were all at one time or another declared unfit to serve—though Bertie was taken prisoner on the Western Front and Willie served as a sergeant major in the East African Service Corps. None of the three, however, went unscarred by its effects. Llewelyn, for example, who took Willie's place on the farm while his brother was in the army, found conditions grim and his situation not without its dangers. In a letter to JCP on 23 September 1917, he refers to a nearby settler murdered in the night by natives and confesses that "sometimes when I sit alone at night . . . I think this may be my end."[1] TFP, who could claim little success after years of writing, was humiliated by his poverty, experiencing marital troubles, and almost suicidally depressed, sometimes yearning for "the peace that passeth understanding"[2] and sometimes expressing fear of death: "True is it, as Dr Johnson said We shall receive no letters in the grave . . . But I'm terrified of it."[3] He was twice summoned to Dorchester Barracks for possible induction into the army (D. H. Lawrence too was made to appear twice, to his humiliation)—the last on 26 May 1917, and one suspects that, had he passed his physical, he might have gone to war with something of a sense of relief. Ironically, his escape from the army came at the price of unwanted intimations of mortality; for the examining doctor detected a disqualifying heart condition which led TFP—cautious as ever—to abandon swimming. Small wonder then that even the end of the war failed to shake his gloom, and he could imagine himself dead all too easily:

> What a queer thing too it is to think of, that in a very short time we shall be dead, quite dead. Fancy a person standing by the bed and saying quite loudly so that anyone really ought to hear—Theodore. And there would be no reply, only silence.[4]

Both JCP and TFP were destined to lose sons. JCP's, Littleton Alfred, would die as the indirect result of a motorcycle accident; but, in October 1931, TFP's son, Theodore Cowper Powys or Dicky, as he was generally known, met a death that surpassed in violence and grotesqueness the worst excesses of his father's considerable imagination. At first glance, it seems surprising that

---
1 Cited in Elwin, *The Life of Llewelyn Powys*, p. 133
2 TFP to JCP, 16 March 1918; HRHRC
3 TFP to JCP, 29 September 1916; HRHRC
4 TFP to JCP, 5 December 1919; HRHRC

the obsessively cautious TFP should ever have allowed a son of his to venture so far from home. When Dicky was ten, he was scheduled to go off to Sherborne Prep, just as his father had. So painful were TFP's memories of the experience that he could not even contemplate delivering Dicky to the school himself. Instead, he wrote to his sister, Gertrude: "If Dicky does go to Sherborne next Autumn, if I bring him to Montacute, would you take him? ... I think I might cry and cry if I took him up that road."[1] The key to understanding TFP's willingness to send the same son to Africa that he had been unwilling to take to school in England lies in Dicky's desire to be a farmer, particularly a sheep farmer. The frustrated hopes of Theodore, the father, of becoming good shepherd to his own flock might yet be realized through Theodore, the son. So Dicky, still a youthful seventeen, sailed for East Africa aboard the *Gloucester Castle* on 6 December 1923 bound for life as a sheep farmer under his uncle, Willie. But TFP's acquiescence— it was probably never much more—in Dicky's emigration did not mean that he stopped worrying about him. For example, on the date of his first birthday abroad, TFP wrote to JCP: "I do pray that he will be careful when he rides the motor bicycle. He had a number of adventures when he looks, like Saul, for the lost asses of the King."[2] Only one of Dicky's early letters to his father survives; there he describes himself, almost triumphantly, as "busy with 20,000 sheep".[3] He must also have tried to allay his father's well-known anxiety, for Sylvia Townsend Warner records in her diary for 5 August 1928 that "At tea Theo spoke of Dicky knowing no fear in Africa. Theo said in a harmless country full of lions and tigers there would be little opportunity to learn that useless lesson."[4] Irony is in evidence here, alongside anxiety. It would be six years before Dicky returned home for a visit. His father wrote to Sylvia Townsend Warner on 8 October 1929 recording the event and concealing his relief just as he had his earlier fears:

> Dicky does not seem to have altered in the least. He arrived rather suddenly with the same overcoat that he went away in six years ago. His hat was different that was all. He does not take all the cream for breakfast, which is what I expected him to do, and so I am very pleased with him.[5]

1 Bissell Collection   2 26 October [1924]; HRHRC
3 10 November 1926; Bissell Collection. Theodora Scutt cites "2,000 sheep" in *Cuckoo in the Powys Nest*, p. 94.
4 Sylvia Townsend Warner manuscript diary   5 Bissell Collection

He quickly won the affection of his father's now-established circle of literary friends, especially Valentine Ackland and Sylvia Townsend Warner. He went to Dorchester with Sylvia in late October 1929, and visited her in her Bayswater flat a couple of times during January 1930. She was struck from time to time by his marked resemblance to TFP whom she had been observing with the eye of the inveterate story-teller, "Theo's upper-lip, and Theo's nose set on at Violet's angle",[1] and "a tone strangely like Theo in Dicky".[2] On 7 January Dicky and Sylvia went to the London Zoo and then to dinner with Charles Prentice, TFP's and Sylvia's editor at Chatto and Windus, who then reported to TFP: "Sylvia, Dick and I had a very happy dinner last night. Afterwards we went a walk along the south side of the river between Hungerford Bridge and London Bridge, through desert streets, past still blank towering buildings, and the strange secret noises of hidden machines . . . ."[3] The following evening Valentine Ackland—with whom Dicky had flirted in Chaldon—escorted him around town. She describes him as "shy and amorous" in her account of their near-affair in *For Sylvia*.[4]

The first news of Dicky's death came in a cable from Willie Powys on 21 October 1931—not a month after the publication of *Unclay*—saying that Dicky had been killed while out riding. This was soon corrected by another cable to the effect that he had been killed by a lion, the initial conclusion of the police report. Bad as that must have seemed, the truth seems to have been far worse: Dicky had actually been murdered—speared, beheaded, and his head and testicles carried off as trophies by Samburu warriors fulfilling a manhood initiation rite of spear blooding. This ritual had a dual function: to demonstrate courage against traditional enemies and to win the favour of young women. Although the practice was forbidden by colonial authorities and had been discouraged by three executions in the mid-'twenties, incidents increased dramatically in 1929 again when the administrative centre was moved outside Samburu territory proper. Dicky was thus working in a long-contested border area in which tribal and colonial systems collided fatally. He had ridden out on his white pony as usual on the morning of 19 October to inspect the flocks

---

1 Sylvia Townsend Warner, Diaries, p. 47; 25 October 1929
2 Sylvia Townsend Warner, ms Diary, 4 January 1930
3 Charles Prentice to TFP, 8 January 1930; HRHRC
4 Valentine Ackland, *For Sylvia: An Honest Account*, pp. 117–18

around Il Pinguan in Northern Laikipia and his pony had returned riderless a few hours later. He was only twenty-five. The fate that Llewelyn—who, curiously enough, also rode a white pony in Kenya—had imagined for himself had befallen another member of the family, his nephew.[1]

The day after he received the news, TFP sat down and dutifully wrote letters to family and friends, informing them of Dicky's death. His letter to his brother Bertie outlines no more than the painful facts; his letter to Sylvia Townsend Warner adds that "Violet, though of course terribly upset, goes on just as usual" and asks her to inform Charles Prentice; the letter to Francis has a quintessentially Theodorian edge to it: "Well, I remember Dicky falling down a bank once and saying That's done for him. This time it has."[2] In replying to a letter of sympathy from Charles Lahr, the bookdealer, TFP's anguish is barely suppressed: "Perhaps God is treating us less kindly by letting us live than Dicky who he has killed."[3] Some days later, he is particularly revealing in a letter to Bertie:

> I certainly never knew before that one could feel quite so strangely as Violet and I feel—Violet is a little better—but I don't expect that the world will ever be the same world to her again now that Dicky has ceased to live. She looks strangely about her, missing something.[4]

Meanwhile, in East Africa, British Colonial rule proved itself totally inadequate to dealing with a ritual killing such as that of which Dicky was the victim. In December 1931, Kiberenge, a former soldier in the King's African Rifles, tipped off the police that the death was a spear-blooding and the work of six *morans* (young men of warrior age) who had been incited by one Leaduma, a Samburu *Laibon* or seer. Unfortunately, his allegations were discredited and he was convicted of perjury. However, on other evidence, five Samburu warriors who had allegedly been heard boasting of their feat were eventually brought to trial in Nairobi in 1934, but were acquitted for lack of evidence. Theodora Scutt mentions the case briefly and says "fifteen or so were executed."[5]

---

1 The fullest accounts of this gruesome episode are to be found in Elspeth Huxley's *Out in the The Midday Sun* and in Jack Smith-Hughes's earlier account, "Songs of the Vultures or Samburu Witchcraft, The Powys Mystery, 1931".
2 23 October 1931; HRHRC
3 24 October 1931; Bissell Collection
4 29 October 1931; Bissell Collection   5 *Cuckoo in the Powys Nest*, p. 95

Nothing in the official record supports this claim. In this matter Theodora Scutt's source is simply wrong.[1]

On behalf of the family, Willie commissioned "a proud casting in bronze" to mark Dicky's lonely grave, with words from Isaiah xxix.10 selected by his father.[2] The plaque read:

HERE LIES
THEODORE COWPER POWYS
OCT 26 1906
OCT 19 1931
FOR THE LORD HATH POURED OUT
UPON YOU THE SPIRIT OF DEEP SLEEP

As the anniversary of Dicky's death approached, TFP wrote to JCP in terms that—importantly, from a biographical point of view—seem to connect Dicky's death with TFP's abandonment of writing: "It is now almost a year since Dicky was killed. . . . It is now too nearly a year since I wrote any fiction. And I begin to wonder how I ever came to do such a thing. I am sure I could never do so again."[3] The implicit linking of these two events looks very like *prima facie* evidence. On the other hand, one of the few surviving letters from Dicky to his father—dated only 5 December but probably 1930—seems to constitute possible counter-evidence. Dicky wrote: "The Kukes [Kikuyu] pinch a lot which always makes everybody furious . . . . I am awfully sorry you are going to stop writing books as I love reading them."[4] Now the reference to "books" may simply mean that TFP had given up writing novels or it may mean that he was declaring his intention to give up *all* writing at least ten months before Dicky's murder. Even if we accept the latter reading, we may wish to explain it—and a number of other such statements made after the completion of *Unclay*—as the kind of thing that an author often says at the end of his latest creative struggle. In the face of this ambiguity, we need evidence of a different sort. Llewelyn's letter to John dated 12 February 1933 would appear to confirm TFP's abandonment of writing, at least soon after he and his wife had adopted Susan (later Theodora) in January 1933: "Theodore is very fond of his Susie. He is in fair

---

1 Compare Huxley, *Out in the Midday Sun*, p. 143.
2 Willie Powys to A. R. ("Bertie") Powys, 15 August, 1932; Stephen Powys Marks Collection
3 14 October 1932; HRHRC
4 Bissell Collection

spirits but drawing himself back to his old way of living and has given up writing."[1] Yet, only seven months later, we find TFP writing to Charles Prentice of Chatto & Windus to promise that "In about two months time, I hope to have enough of these new short stories that I have been doing, almost enough for a book" (17 September 1933).[2] At best, then, we can say that TFP vacillated and that his inclination to give up writing extended over a considerable period of time. But what are "these new short stories"? The three long stories in *The Two Thieves* (1932) were all written by September 1931, as were "The Better Gift" (originally intended for *The Two Thieves*, but not published until 1937 as *Goat Green*), and "The Sixpenny Strumpet"; so the book in question could only have been *Captain Patch* (1935). Now one of TFP's surviving notebooks[3] contains the manuscript of an essay on "Summer"—one of his rare non-fiction publications—which appeared in the *Daily Herald* on 2 June 1933. In all likelihood, this occasional piece was written that year; thus the ten stories in the same notebook (five of which were included in *Captain Patch*) can also be assigned to the same period. Such indirect dating by association is necessary, since TFP eschewed, for the most part, any effort to date stories. If we remember the reason he offered in "Why I Have Given up Writing" for having begun—"At one time I hoped to find happiness in writing, like Burton of *The Anatomy of Melancholy*, who professed to discover in writing a cure for depression"—we may even venture to suggest that perhaps, after all, he meant what he said about giving up writing in his letter to Dicky, and that, in fact, it was Dicky's death that led him to *resume*. In any case, this last burst of creative energy faded within a year or so, and there is not much disputing TFP's statement of 1936 that "I have written nothing for two years. . . . A writer should know when to stop, when he has said enough." Louis Wilkinson's comment in a letter to TFP dated 18 December 1937 that he was "pleased to see in the papers that you were writing again"[4] was probably prompted by the recent public-ation of *Goat Green* by the Golden Cockerel Press. Wilkinson no doubt assumed that the work was newly written, when, in fact, as we have seen, it was written six years earlier.

1 12 February 1933; HRHRC
2 Chatto & Windus archives, Reading University
3 Francis Feather Collection. This notebook is item number 73 in Peter Riley's checklist.   4 Bissell Collection

For TFP, the memories of his first-born were buried with him: Dicky at Sherborne, Dicky on his motorbike, Dicky "at the same table with me learning Swahili" (24 December 1922)—so that in later life he rarely mentioned the son he lost to Africa and his own dream. But Violet kept his photograph by her bed and kissed it each night before retiring.[1] Little wonder that when Willie Powys volunteered to let Susie / Theodora live with his family in Kenya, Violet "nearly went into hysterics, saying that Africa had taken too much from her already."[2] Did she ever know the full story of her son's death? It is impossible to say. But TFP chose to present—to casual acquaintances at least—the more palatable account of Dicky's death given in Willie's second cable. Thus, in his letter to the composer Christopher le Fleming of 15 February 1932, he apologizes for being unable to offer hospitality as his wife was still recovering from the death of their eldest son who was killed by a lion in Africa. And four years later, the evidence of her diary for 23 January, 1935 suggests that his sister, Gertrude Powys, may have been shielded from the truth as TFP knew it. She notes there: "Dicky's friend Carpenter was killed by a rhinosaurus [sic]. I wonder if his horse that shied was the one Dicky rode & that shied with him?"[3] His memory haunted her. When she went to tea with her brother, Littleton, and his wife, Mabel, in Weymouth just before World War Two, they strolled by the former family residence in Greenhill Terrace and Gertrude wrote in her diary, "I thought of Dicky's head at his bedroom window so often."[4]

Final Days: the Death of the Father

The churchyard of St Nicholas in East Chaldon is now full of individuals from the Powys circle—among them Katie Powys, Bob and Flo Legg of the *Sailor's Return* Pub, Farmer James Cobb of West Chaldon Farm, and Betty Muntz, sculptor of the head of TFP now in the Dorset County Museum. The words on her tombstone—"I will lift up mine eyes unto the hills"—echo one of TFP's oft-quoted lines from the Bible, and suggest his influence upon her. Others in the churchyard include Valentine (Molly) Ackland (1906–69) and Sylvia Townsend Warner (1893–1978), both good friends of TFP who left valuable impressions of him in their writings. Strangely

---

1 *Cuckoo in the Powys Nest*, p. 93   2 *Ibid.*, p. 223
3 HRHRC. This is one of a series of Gertrude's pocket diaries in the collection.
4 Thursday 23 March 1939

absent from this company is TFP himself whose final journey to his resting place in Mappowder churchyard is here recounted.

The heart problem detected by the army doctor in 1916 when TFP was forty-one led him to claim hyper-sensitively that "I have felt that organ rather prominent of late."[1] In fact, the problem was probably no more than an innocuous irregularity, a murmur, and it never again features in reports on his health. But for a while he could, with some satisfaction, set his heart problem against John's ulcer and Llewelyn's consumption in the family list of complaints. His fear of death, of course, never needed any sanction from reality and was omnipresent. Writing to David Garnett in 1927 about TFP's attitude to death, Sylvia Townsend Warner observes:

> It is the judgement of a child to compare him with Donne and Webster . . . for they could not keep away from the thought of death, it was like pressing the sore tooth to them, but with Theo it is the only tooth that will not fail him.[2]

Two years later, after an afternoon walk with him during which they discussed *Unclay*, Sylvia came to appreciate for the first time just how real his fear was: TFP confessed that "I never go to bed without thinking of my death."[3] Llewelyn was, in his own way, every bit as obsessed with death as his older brother, though his very real illness undoubtedly gave him more justification. Inevitably, when the two brothers got together—one the creator of John Death, and the other given to exclaiming "Timor mortis conturbat me" (an epigraph from William Dunbar used in Llewelyn's *Love and Death*, 1941)—the conversation often turned morbid. Llewelyn wrote to John describing TFP's reaction to a conversation with one of the locals, old Dickon. Llewelyn had asked bluntly "Are you afraid of death?" and the old man had replied sagely, "No . . . *Because it is natural.*" "It was the word natural," says Llewelyn, "that provoked the humourous malice of Theodore, who after all has always distrusted nature and is to his very marrow bone a puritanical visionary."[4]

By 1938, TFP was sixty-three and well into his retirement from writing. He suffered from headaches and high blood pressure, and his hand trembled somewhat; and, after Bertie, who was six years younger than TFP, died in 1936, death must have seemed far from

1 TFP to LlP?, 22 June 1916; HRHRC
2 Sylvia Townsend Warner to David Garnett, 25 September 1927; Hilton Hall
3 3 April 1929; Diaries, p. 33
4 LlP to JCP, January 1933; Colgate

a distant prospect. During this period, Gertrude usually went to tea at Beth Car on a Tuesday, and reported him "not at all well" on 11 January 1938. But it was not until Monday 28 March 1938 that she reported: "Theodore felt giddy when he got up and fainted. He has to be kept quiet in bed. It was like a stroke."[1] In fact, his good friend Dr Charlie Smith confirmed this diagnosis, as Llewelyn wrote to H. Rivers Pollock, an old friend from his Cambridge days: "Theodore has given us all anxiety. He fell in his kitchen and the doctor seemed to think he had had a slight stroke. He is in bed, his mind and body unaffected I am thankful to say." (20 April 1938)[2] Llewelyn in Clavadel heard of his brother's "alarming attack" from Littleton, and in his reply quoted back Littleton's remarks about "that white head that has harrowed so many hells of which you & I know nothing, lying so white upon a white bed." (April 1938)[3] TFP's recovery was very slow, so that he was still complaining about his head in October, and in 1939 Violet wrote to David Garnett's wife, Ray, that "Theodore is far from well. Last March he had a stroke & it's taking such a time for him to get better. His head is still bad & he can't talk but for a few minutes."[4] His brush with death together with the start of World War Two inevitably brought him to contemplation of it, so that, upon receipt of a knitted pullover as a birthday present, he wrote to his sister Lucy in melodramatic terms: "I took off rags to put on a whole garment. May I do the same when I come to die." (21 December 1939)[5] By October of that year, however, he was well enough to walk with Gertrude on High Chaldon, the hill overlooking the village, when she came for her usual Tuesday tea on 17 October 1939.[6] Unfortunately, neither the world news nor the news from Switzerland about Llewelyn's health was good: in mid-November he had a stomach hemorrhage and 2 December brought a telegram from Alyse Gregory, his wife, to say "Darling Lulu died this morning."[7] A few days later TFP, who had grown very close to Llewelyn while he lived nearby at Chydyok, spoke fondly of his brother visiting White House Farm, Sweffling so many years ago. Gertrude recorded in her diary: "Theodore said today he never saw anyone so happy as when as a boy Lulu arrived at Saxmundham [Suffolk] to stay with him & ran out of the station in his Eton coat to him."[8]

1 Gertrude Powys, pocket diaries, HRHRC
2 Letters of Llewelyn Powys, p. 252   3 *Ibid.*, p. 251   4 Hilton Hall   5 Bissell Collection
6 JCP to Gertrude Powys, 2 December 1939; Gertrude Powys pocket diaries
7 Alyse Gregory to JCP, 2 December 1939; HRHRC   8 5 December 1939

TFP's sense of personal loss lingered and, even years later, was still strong. Thus, on 5 August 1948, he wrote sadly to Penn Kine: "Llewelyn has now been dead nearly nine years. I have no words to say how much I miss him."[1] For Llewelyn, confronted with the same fears as his elder brother, had responded in a way unthinkable to TFP: he had chosen to rush out and embrace life, to celebrate the glory of life, to seize not love *or* death (the two vintages of wine available to Mr Weston's clients) but love *and* death (as in his autobiographical novel of that name). When Llewelyn died, so died the risk-taker, the womaniser, the *bon vivant* that a secret TFP would dearly have liked to be. TFP's recognition of the contrast between his timidity (something akin to Joyce's paralysis) and Llewelyn's boldness came early in life, as we see from the self-accusing words he puts in Louis Wilkinson's mouth in one of his dialogues (28 August, 1911): "You dare not taste the apple because you fear the worm in the core."[2]

A few months after Llewelyn's death, TFP was shocked to learn of the death of Ray Garnett, who had done woodcuts for a number of his books, including *Black Bryony*, *Mark Only*, and *Mr Tasker's Gods*. The Garnett family had also visited Chaldon in the 'twenties; and Ray, then a young mother of two boys, got on famously with all the inhabitants of Beth Car. TFP wrote a remarkable letter of consolation to his friend David[3] in which he recalled happier days: "It seems only like yesterday, when she was at Lulworth with Richard and William. And I remember earlier playing with her and Richard near Jar's Stone [on High Chaldon]. When your letter came I had taken up a book of poems":

> 'Tis true—with shame and grief I yield—
> Thou, like the van, first took'st the field;
> And gotten hast the victory
> In thus adventuring to die
> Before me, whose more years might crave
> A just precedence in the grave.
> But hark! my pulse, like a soft drum
> Beats my approach, tells thee I come;
> And slow howe'er my marches be
> I shall at last sit down by thee.[4]

1 Bissell Collection
2 Selected Early Works, p. 216; HRHRC
3 For the full text see Richard Garnett's article in *PJ* 11, p. 41.
4 Henry King's "Exequy" as in *The Oxford Book of English Verse*, ed. A. T. Quiller-Couch

For TFP, poetry offered a special kind of consolation. That is why John Death very much approves Mr Hayhoe's choice of poet in *Unclay*: "I believe that you have Keats' *Odes* in your pocket. He's a fine poet and knows whom to praise when he listens in a darkening evening to the song of a nightingale."[1] In *Still the Joy of It*, Littleton Powys, the athletic schoolmaster of the family, recalls with bewildered amusement the letter of sympathy *he* received from TFP on the death of his second wife, Elizabeth Myers: "My brother Theodore . . . introduced this quotation from the Arabic: In the Garden of Life a bird sang on the highest branch, and then soared away."[2]

Violet was a devoted wife to TFP and, especially after his stroke, a good nurse who danced attendance on his every need. However, from time to time, she had health problems of her own. At the beginning of July 1949, TFP related how "Poor Violet had a dreadful bleeding of the nose the other day, though it may have saved her from a stroke. We were very frightened. She is better now but still feels her head rather bad and is sometimes giddy."[3] The account Theodora Scutt gives of the same incident, is both funny and indicative of TFP's desperate dependency: "At the sight of the ghastly blood-stained apparition that was his wife . . . Daddy completely lost his head; he dived down between the sheets and called out 'Oh, don't die, Violet! Don't die!'"[4]

Since TFP, Violet and Susan had moved to Mappowder in 1941, they had lived in The Lodge, a damp and cramped cottage right next to the churchyard. As Peter Riley put it so well: "He ate and slept on the horizon of the dead."[5] Given this locale and his naturally morbid predisposition, his thoughts increasingly turned to his own demise. Eyeing an old oak-tree for which he had particular reverence, for example, he once remarked to his neighbour, Vera Wainwright: "Enough wood for a coffin." Yet here he found real peace too and even befriended the rector, Dr Samuel Francis Jackson—"old Frank" to TFP—who shared some of his bookish interests. TFP is said to have been instrumental in the revival of Compline and would recite the responses from the back of the church. But his health was not good—especially since the effects of his stroke lingered on. Violet reported to Alyse Gregory, Llewelyn's widow, that her husband complained a great deal

---

1 *Unclay*, pp. 155–6   2 *Still the Joy of It*, p. 268
3 TFP to JCP, 4 July 1949; HRHRC   4 *Cuckoo in the Powys Nest*, p. 280
5 *PR* 3, p. 77

about his head and that "he has numbness in his arm & can't use it very well. I have to help him on with his clothes."[1] In fact, it seems to have been his ill-health rather than anti-social inclinations that caused him to worry about visitors and to "hide away from them" whenever he could. His favourite retreat was atop one of the oldest flat-top gravestones under the yew tree where he might read a little William Barnes or Shakespeare or just sit in silent contemplation. It was at this time that "he began to refer too frequently to the time when he would be 'underneath the grasses' in that same churchyard."[2] One of those visitors he could *not* escape was the American Elizabeth Wade White, Valentine Ackland's friend, who insisted upon a photograph to mark the occasion. In the photo of them arm-in-arm, TFP looks as grim as Elizabeth looks gleeful at cornering her prey. She later sent him a copy of Christina Rossetti's *Poems* inscribed "For Dear Theodore, with Elizabeth Wade White's love, & remembering Sunday 10 April 1949".[3] In 1950 Jack Clemo, something of a disciple, visited (23 August)—though he later claimed "I never shared his pathological obsession with death."[4] There exists a photograph of the two of them, with TFP apparently holding Clemo's hand.[5] In the summer of 1951, Gerard Casey would prove far more welcome to TFP, especially in the light of his readiness to indulge discussion of the Theodorian canon of writers: Richard Baxter, Jacob Boehme, Meister Eckhart, William Law and, of course, Jeremy Taylor. James Stern, another visitor, provides a vivid word picture of TFP, based upon a visit in February 1953:

> Yesterday was a Red Letter day: Theodore Powys. Fascinating. He and his wife ("Vilutt") & adopted daughter Susie, 20, live in what was once the school of the village of Mappowder, which is near absolutely Nowhere. . . . He has not written anything for sixteen years. "I am out of business." "Writing makes my head ache." From pictures I always thought he looked like a prehistoric grandmother; he doesn't at all. He looks like a sage with a ruddy complexion, huge white eyebrows, the hooked nose, a mane of white hair, & black eyes which stare at you.[6]

1 Violet Powys to Alyse Gregory, 17 November 1942; HRHRC
2 *Cuckoo in the Powys Nest*, pp. 226–7
3 This photograph is in the author's collection, laid into Elizabeth Wade White's inscribed copy of *Mr Weston's Good Wine*.
4 *Recollections of the Powys Brothers*, p. 164
5 Included in *Still the Joy of It*, opposite p. 113
6 *James Stern: a Life in Letters*, p. 151

The year 1952 was not a good one for the Powys family. Gertrude died quite suddenly in April, and TFP was not well enough to attend the funeral in Montacute. The brother and sister had always been close, a closeness forged in their youthful days together at White House Farm in Sweffling. John's son, Littleton Alfred, was terminally ill, and TFP's younger sister, Lucy was in a sanatorium at North Allington, Dorset. TFP's sight was now failing, probably on account of cataracts—another ailment to which the family seemed vulnerable. Responding to John's usual birthday gift of money, TFP wrote: "I don't see very well. But I rather like not seeing very well. You don't want to see everything."[1] The last line is vintage TFP—"You don't want to see everything." In fact, one of his troubles in life had been seeing too much, the skull beneath the skin. The combination of grief and dimmed vision seemed to precipitate a slow withdrawal into himself, the hermit without the soliloquy, now walking in the footsteps of his father. He would sit cradling some familiar volume like an old friend without turning as much as a page, or he would take up the knitting he had begun as therapy (his father had taken to netting). He certainly would not have wanted to see very clearly what lay before him.

When Sylvia and Valentine visited TFP in mid-July of 1953, they found him alone, looking "marked for death" and "terrified of falling into the hands of a hospital"[2]—just as brother Bertie had been in 1936. Five days later they heard from Violet that Dr Smith had told her the nature of TFP's malady—it was cancer of the bowel. Upon their next visit on 31 July 1953, "Theo wore his guise of 17th cent[ury] stoicism."[3] The following day they called to drive him to Sherborne Hospital. Theodora could not remember who took him, but her description of the sick man is evocative: "He went, beautifully dressed in his best suit and looking like the dying Merlin."[4] At the hospital, he was admitted to a private room with a pleasant view. After Valentine returned with string she had bought for his dressing gown, she was overcome by emotion. When Violet later entered the empty house, she burst into tears and Sylvia wrote in her diary "it is a time for autumn sowing, whether T. F. lives or dies" (consciously or unconsciously echoing her own epigraph for *Summer Will Show*). On 8 August he was discharged

1 TFP to JCP, 20 December 1952; HRHRC
2 17 July 1953; The Diaries of Sylvia Townsend Warner, p. 198   3 *Ibid.*, pp. 199
4 *Cuckoo in the Powys Nest*, p. 288

and Valentine drove him home to Mappowder. He had been given drugs to take at night and was scheduled to return on 9 September for an operation. When Sylvia next saw him on 11 August they chatted about her latest novel (*The Flint Anchor*) and "somehow we got round to God being a shy being, in agonies at public appearances... but behind all this peaceable chatter, I saw his eyes roving to next month."[1] In fact, ten days before the date set for his operation, he mustered enough will-power to refuse to undergo it, choosing what he was told would be "a year of life rather than two years perhaps with tubes in his belly" (4 September 1953).[2] Harold Raymond, who had replaced Charles Prentice as TFP's contact at Chatto & Windus, sent Violet a reassuring letter when he heard the news:

> Yes, I am sure you are right. The choice lies with Theo. It is his life & his mind is clear, and capable of making a decision. Whatever some doctors may think of the decision he has come to, I am positive that many of them, if they themselves at his age were faced with the same dreadful choice, would decide as he has done.[3]

But the choice was no easy one for TFP. At times he would be calm and resigned, at others he would be overcome by intense fear and melancholy, on 7 September 1953 even threatening to hang himself. Dr Charlie Smith had meanwhile retired and the new doctor, Eccleston, prescribed no pain-killing drugs, saying somewhat callously that "when the pain began, Theo would be willing enough to go back to hospital."[4] On her visit of 18 October Sylvia kissed his forehead while he lay asleep. He awoke and she said: "We have loved each other for such a long time" and he replied "Yes, my dear, we have loved for a very long time." This may have been the last coherent exchange between the two old friends.[5]

When the stress of coping with a dying man became too much for Violet, even with Theodora's help, his daughter-in-law, Sally Powys, took over some of the duties. Of course, at this point, TFP was well aware that his life was ebbing away. By this stage, word had spread about his condition, and a procession of relatives and old friends began to appear at Beth Car or to write. Littleton came in October and discreetly gave Violet £100. The two brothers "had a delightful talk for an hour, both knew it was the last," according

---

1 Warner, manuscript Diary 2 Warner, Diaries, p. 200
3 Harold Raymond to Violet Powys, 22 October 1953; Bissell Collection
4 18 October 1953; Bissell Collection 5 Warner, manuscript Diary

to Littleton.[1] One childhood friend, Marjorie Phelips, formerly of Montacute House, wrote in a shaky hand from Hampshire: "Those old days at Montacute are still very happy recollections & I can remember a lot of amusing incidents... I shall think of you."[2] Louis Wilkinson, who lived close by in Hazelbury Bryan, paid more than one visit and wrote to JCP with details. Later he wrote: "When I last saw him, very soon before his death, of which he had thought and written so much, he was serene, he was at peace and content."[3] This statement, repeated for a booklet in the Mappowder Church in 1967, smacks more of reassurance than reality. In fact, TFP's attitude to death had never been consistent. As Valentine Ackland told his sister Lucy many years later:

> <u>Sometimes</u> he saw it [death] as most desirable: sometimes as an escape & a safety... but many times it was a terror to him, and I think he often went in great fear because of it.... But also I THINK I have known him become quite tranquil in his spirit—whether acceptance or just resignation, I don't know.[4]

Angus Davidson had heard the news from Sylvia Warner and visited early in September; he told David Garnett over dinner in London who then wrote to TFP on 6 November asking to visit on Thursday, 12 November. By then, TFP was too weak to reply and his son, Francis, did so instead, reporting that his father was getting frailer every day, though his mind was alert: "He is at present without much pain, and our only hope is that he will not have to suffer."[5] Alas, by the time of David's visit, the situation had deteriorated and TFP was confused and slipping in and out of consciousness. At one point he evidently refused communion from the Rector, from whom he had become increasingly estranged. It must have been around this time that he allegedly cried out "Belle! Belle!" But whether this was a reference to the long-dead wife of his friend, Bernie O'Neill, or to a church bell, a favourite motif, we simply cannot say.[6] He lapsed into a coma so that when his sister Katie visited from East Chaldon on 26 November it was too late for farewells.[7] Later she wrote to Lucy who had accompanied her: "I feel glad I went. But oh what a sad

---

1 Littleton Powys to Vera Wainwright, 27 December 1953; Vera Wainwright Collection
2 Bissell Collection   3 *Theodore*, p. 13
4 1 November 1967; Louise de Bruin Collection
5 8 November 1953; quoted by Richard Garnett in *PJ* 11, p. 43; Hilton Hall
6 See Peter Riley, *PR* 3, 1978.
7 "Katie" Powys to Louis Wilkinson, December 1953; Bissell Collection

sight it was . . . I was grateful that we both could stand together at his feet, knowing what he has been to us and what we lose by losing him."¹ Sylvia Warner was reading David Garnett's autobiography when Valentine took the phone call that TFP was "sinking", so she had trouble sleeping:

> That night—there was a wind—I woke many times thinking of Theo; and once, hearing him say [in] that familiar voice of quiet violence, "A leaf has been blown away." I knew it was part of a sentence about an autumn morning in Madder or Dodder, and one morning seeming like another. But A Leaf has been Blown Away. After that I slept, as I hope he does. But I wish he had read my book.²

Sylvia may have been remembering the fable of "The Withered Leaf and the Green" where the chestnut represents the false optimism of youth and the oak represents the pessimistic fatalism of age. In any case, she gave a rather different version of the story to Katie Powys in a letter, saying that she dreamed she was reading a manuscript by him of how "one morning looks like another, but is not the same" and then "I heard Theo's own voice continuing the sentence and saying A leaf has been blown away."³

TFP died the next day, Friday, 27 November 1953 at 6.45 in the evening, just before it was time for his favourite service, Compline. There are two versions of who was present at the moment of death. Theodora Scutt recalls that only his wife, Violet, and two local women, Lottie Garrett and Bess Trevett, who had been helping, were there. But Francis Powys recalls being alone in the room with his father at the time of death. In any case, the two women took on the task of laying him out. When his death was announced on the BBC, he was misidentified as a novelist and poet, a mistake which suggests some confusion with John Cowper Powys. Oddly enough, in far-off Corwen in Wales, John first got the news from this announcement. Writing to Lucy, he says:

> We were not a little startled by the news of his death last night, <u>Friday night</u> on the wireless. But your heavenly letter to Phyllis came safely this morning and you can believe how we studied every word of it . . . especially those words of his I will . . . come . . . back.⁴

---

1 "Katie" to Lucy Powys, 27 November 1953; Bissell Collection
2 Warner manuscript Diary, 26 November 1953
3 Sylvia Townsend Warner to "Katie" Powys, 27 February 1954; Bissell Collection
4 Bissell Collection

And, just as TFP's thoughts were drawn back to his brother's childhood when Llewelyn died in 1939, John's took him back to schooldays at Sherborne when TFP died, albeit articulated in John's familiar style of tortured particularity:

> Aye Aye how clearly can I see his figure when as a little boy he came down through the field up towards the Yeovil Rd. at Sherborne when L[ittleton] and I came out of Wildman's House and went up that long field to the Yeovil Rd. to meet him on his way to the Trent Lanes from wh[ich] you could see Montacute Hill.[1]

Sylvia Townsend Warner once tried, in 1927, to write TFP's "Life", but had to abandon the project, in part because her would-be subject had serious reservations about it. But he surely would have approved her evocative coverage of his death, especially the funeral on 1 December 1953. A portion of her description was included in Claire Harman's edition of The Diaries of Sylvia Townsend Warner.[2] But a later unpublished section of the Diary itself deserves quotation:

> Susie coming out, just after the coffin, in a pre-raphaelite beauty of entranced sorrow. Violet, as though she would fall into the grave as the coffin was lowered, and Francis with a stern set gravity, holding her back, his gaze averted. Old Mr Jackson [the minister], after the last blessing, standing still beside the grave, his foot on the wooden cross-bar . . . with a most moving air of having broken off a conversation that would later be resumed, of having, only temporarily, the last word; and old Mrs Lucas, delivering Katie's bunch of bay-leaves into the grave.[3]

At last, TFP, the creator of John Death, had found rest in God's Acre, as he liked to call the churchyard. Like Matthew Hurd in *Black Bryony* (1923), "the perfect stillness had called him, and he had accepted it . . . as the kindest of God's gifts to man."[4] He had never wanted a tombstone, telling Violet during the war: "No Violet, I know you cannot afford a tombstone for me; indeed I hate tombstones. I won't have one."[5] But he got one anyway— such memorials are for the living. It is in the shape of an open book, upon the left-hand page of which is inscribed

---

1 JCP to Lucy Powys, 28 November 1953; Louise de Bruin Collection
2 p. 203   3 Sylvia Townsend Warner, manuscript Diary
4 *Black Bryony*, p. 183   5 TFP to JCP 25 December 1941; HRHRC

IN LOVING MEMORY OF
THEODORE FRANCIS
POWYS
AT REST
27 NOVEMBER 1953
AGED 77 YEARS

Upon his grave in spring celandines sometimes grow; these were among his favourite flowers because of their link with Wordsworth's poem.

In *The Rule and Exercises of Holy Dying* one of Jeremy Taylor's precepts is that "He that would die well must always look for death, every day knocking at the gates of the grave."[1] In this matter, TFP followed the advice of the seventeenth-century divine, as a way of conquering his fear of death. But he remembered, too, Nietzsche's advice in *Thus Spake Zarathustra* on how to survive life: "Creating—that is the great salvation from suffering, and life's alleviation."[2] Reflecting upon his career, he once said with characteristic humility: "When I look back I wonder that I ever wrote at all. I suppose it was fright. Fright that when God says to me Show me your work I should have had nothing to show."[3] We can only be grateful for the bondage of fear that drove him to such a productive response.

[1] *Ed. cit.*, p. 37
[2] Friedrich Nietzsche, *Thus Spake Zarathustra*, translated by Thomas Common, New York, 1926, p. 99
[3] "Why I Have Given up Writing"

Works Cited

Ackland, Valentine, *For Sylvia: an Honest Account*, London: Chatto & Windus, 1985
Alpers, Antony, *The Life of Katherine Mansfield*, New York: Viking Press, 1980
Bentley, Nicolas, ed., *Fred Bason's Diary*, London: Wingate, 1950
Betty, J. H., *Dorset*, Newton Abbott and London: David & Charles, 1974
Biddell, H., contr., in Page, William, ed., *The Victoria History of the County of Suffolk*, Vol. 2, 1907
Blaen, Angela, "The Wisht Hound Tradition and T. F. Powys's *Mark Only*", *PR* 18, 1986, pp. 66–8
Blythe, Ronald, *Characters and their Landscapes*, San Diego, New York and London: Harcourt Brace Jovanovich, 1983
Bridgewater, Paul, *Nietzsche in Anglosaxony: a Study of Nietzsche's Impact on English and American Literature*, Leicester: Leicester University Press, 1972
Cavaliero, Glen, *The Rural Tradition and the English Novel*, London: Macmillan, 1977
Churchill, R. C., *The Powys Brothers*, London: Longmans for the British Council and the National Book League, 1962
Cirlot, J. E., *A Dictionary of Symbols*, New York: Philosophical Library, 1962
Coombes, Harry, *T. F. Powys*, London: Barrie and Rockliff, 1960
Crabbe, G., The Poetical Works of George Crabbe, with Prefatory Notice, Biographical and Critical by Edward Lamplough, London: Walter Scott, 1888
Crabbe, G. [Jr], *The Life of George Crabbe by his Son*, Introduction by Edmund Blunden, London: The Cresset Press, 1947
Draper, Jo, *A Dorchester Camera*, Stanbridge, Wimborne, Dorset: The Dovecote Press, 1984
Elwin, Malcolm, *The Life of Llewelyn Powys*, London: Macdonald, 1947
Fadiman, Clifton, "Novels by Two Brothers", *The Nation*, 24 June, 1925, p. 720
Farrar, John, *The Proper Names of the Bible*, 4th edn, London: John Mason, 1948
Foss, Peter, *Wessex Memories: Country Essays by Llewelyn Powys*, Gloucester: The Powys Press, 2003
Garnett, David, *The Familiar Faces*, London: Chatto & Windus, 1962
―― "T. F. Powys", *The Borzoi 1925; being a record of ten years of publishing*, New York: Alfred A. Knopf, 1925
Garnett, Edward, Review of *Wolf Solent*, *Now and Then*, No. 32, Summer, 1929, pp. 11–12
Garnett, Richard, *Constance Garnett: a Heroic Life*, London: Sinclair-Stevenson, 1991
Garrett, Eric, *Bradford Abbas: The History of a Dorset Village*, Yeovil: Haynes Publishing, 1989
Gatrell, Simon, *Hardy the Creator: a Textual Biography*, Oxford: Clarendon Press, 1988
Gourlay, A. B., *A History of Sherborne School*, Sherborne: Sawtells, 1971
――"The Powys Brothers at Sherborne School", Reminiscences read by

Kenneth Hopkins from a script prepared by A. B. Gourlay at Powys Society meeting, 26 October, 1974

Graves, Richard Perceval, *The Brothers Powys*, London: Routledge; New York: Charles Scribner's Sons, 1983

Greene, Graham, "Henry James: The Private Universe", Collected Essays, Penguin, 1970, pp. 21–34

Hanson, Clare, *Short Stories & Short Fictions, 1880–1980*, London: Macmillan, 1985

Hazlitt, William, "On Living to One's-self", Selected Essays of William Hazlitt, ed. Geoffrey Keynes, London: The Nonesuch Press, 1930, pp. 24–39 [TFP used the Bohn Library edition.]

Hill, Susan, Introduction to *The Distracted Preacher and Other Tales*, Harmondsworth: Penguin, 1970

Holbrook, David, Introduction to T. F. Powys, *Mr. Weston's Good Wine*, London: Heinemann, 1974

Holloway, Mark, "With T. F. Powys at Mappowder", in Humfrey, *Recollections of the Powys Brothers*, q.v.

Hone, William, *The Apocryphal New Testament, being all the Gospels, Epistles, and other Pieces now Extant*, London: William Hone, 1820

Hopkins, Kenneth, *The Powys Brothers: a Biographical Appreciation*, New Jersey: Fairleigh Dickinson University Press, 1967

Huddlestone, Miles, ed., *James Stern: A Life in Letters, 1904–93*, Wilby, Norwich: Michael Russell, 2002

Humfrey, Belinda, ed., *Recollections of the Powys Brothers*, London: Peter Owen, 1980

Hutchins, John, *The History and Antiquities of the County of Dorset*, 3rd edn, 1861–70, cor., augm., and improved by William Shipp and James Whitworth Hodson, Westminster: J. B. Nichols and Sons, 1861–70

Huxley, Elspeth, *Out in the Midday Sun*, New York: Viking, 1987

Jackman, Brian, *Dorset Coast Path*, London: Her Majesty's Stationery Office, 1979

Jefferson, George, *Edward Garnett: a Life in Literature*, London: Jonathan Cape, 1982

Johnson, Joe, *Shirley Village*, Shirley, Derbyshire: Shirley Millennium Committee, 2nd edn, 2000

Johnson, Mrs John, Diary of Mrs J. Johnson, ms, Mary Barham Johnson Collection

Johnson, Mary Barham, "The Powys Mother", *PR* 8, 1980–1, pp. 57–64

Jones, Irene, *The Stalbridge Inheritance, 1780–1854*, Dorchester: Larkwood Publishing, 1993

Kelly, A. A., *Liam O'Flaherty, the Storyteller*, New York: Barnes and Noble, 1976

Kelly's Directory of Norfolk, 1896

Kelly's Directory of Suffolk, 1904

Lawrence, D. H., The Tales of D. H. Lawrence, London: Martin Secker, 1934

——Zytaruk, George, and Boulton, James, eds., The Letters of D. H. Lawrence, Cambridge: Cambridge University Press, Vol. 1, 1979; Vol. 2, 1981

Lewis's Topographical Directory, 1845

Luke, Claude, "Men Like Beasts" (review of *Mr. Tasker's Gods*), *The Spectator*, 28 February, 1925

Mackenzie, Robert, *America: a History*, London: T. Nelson and Sons, 1887

Mansfield, Katherine: O'Sullivan, Vincent, and Scott, Margaret, eds., The Collected Letters of Katherine Mansfield, Oxford: Clarendon Press, Vol. 1, 1903–1917, 1984

Marlow, Louis [pseud. Wilkinson, Louis], *Seven Friends*, London: The Richards Press, 1953

——*Swan's Milk*, London: Faber and Faber, 1934

——*Welsh Ambassadors: Powys Lives and Letters*, London: Chapman and Hall, 1936

Miller, Henry, "John Cowper Powys: a Living Book", from *The Books in My Life*, Norfolk, CT: New Directions, 1952; reprinted in Humfrey, *Recollections of the Powys Brothers*
Millgate, Michael, *Thomas Hardy: a Biography*, New York: Random House, 1982
Perry, P. J., *British Farming in the Great Depression 1870–1914*, Newton Abbot: David & Charles, 1974
A Pictorial and Descriptive Guide to Weymouth, Portland, Swanage, and South Dorset, 4th ed., revised, London: Ward Lock & Co., Ltd, n.d.
Pouillard, Michel, "T. F. Powys Conferencier à Eastbourne 1902–03", *Études Anglaises*, XXII, No. 4, 1969
——*T. F. Powys (1875–1953): La Solitude, Le Doute, L'Art*, Tomes 2; Thèse presentée devant l'Université de Grenoble III, le 20 Mai 1978, Service de reproduction des Thèses, Université de Lille III, 1981
——"Woman and Women in T. F. Powys's Novels" *PR* 12, 1983, pp. 7–16
Powys, Francis, "The Quiet Man of Dorset", *The Adelphi*, Vol. 31, No. 1, 1954
Powys, John Cowper, *Autobiography*, New York: Simon and Schuster; London: John Lane, 1934. The London: Macdonald 1967 and Picador 1982 editions have the same pagination. The London 1934 edition is used for reference.
——Elwin, Malcolm, ed., Letters of John Cowper Powys to his Brother Llewelyn, London: Village Press, 1975
——Wilkinson, Louis, ed., Letters of John Cowper Powys to Louis Wilkinson, 1935–1956, Hamilton, New York: Colgate University Press, 1958, reprinted The Village Press, 1974
Powys, Littleton, *The Joy of It*, London: Chapman and Hall, 1937
——*Still the Joy of It*, London: Macdonald, 1956
——Illustrated fishing notebook (ms), n.d. (gift of JCP to LlP), Bissell Collection
——"My Hermit Brother", *John O'London's Weekly and Outlook*, 11 December 1953
Powys, Llewelyn, "Corfe Castle", *Dorset Essays*, revised edn, Bristol: Redcliffe Press, 1983
——"Stalbridge Rectory", *The London Mercury*, vol. XXXI, no. 184, February, 1935
——*Dorset Essays*, London: John Lane, The Bodley Head, 1935
——*Earth Memories*, New York: W. W. Norton, 1933
——*Skin for Skin*, New York: Harcourt Brace & Co., 1925
——*Somerset Essays*, London: John Lane, The Bodley Head, 1937
——Wilkinson, Louis, ed., The Letters of Llewelyn Powys, with an Introduction by Alyse Gregory, London: John Lane, The Bodley Head, 1943
POWYS, THEODORE FRANCIS, *Black Bryony*, New York: Alfred A. Knopf, 1923
——*Bottle's Path and Other Stories*, London: Chatto & Windus, 1946
——*Captain Patch*, London: Chatto & Windus, 1935
——Diary, ms, 1892, HRHRC
——*Fables*, London: Chatto & Windus, 1929
——*Father Adam*, Gringley-on-the-Hill: Brynmill Press, 1990
——*God's Eyes a-Twinkle*, London: Chatto & Windus, 1947
——*The House with the Echo*, London: Chatto & Windus, 1928
——*Innocent Birds*, New York: Alfred A. Knopf, 1926
——*An Interpretation of Genesis*, London: Chatto & Windus, 1929
——*The Left Leg*, New York: Alfred A. Knopf, 1923
——*Mark Only*, London: Chatto & Windus, 1924
——*The Market Bell*, Gringley-on-the-Hill: Brynmill Press, 1991
——*Mockery Gap*, New York: Alfred A. Knopf, 1925

POWYS, THEODORE FRANCIS contd.
—*Mr. Tasker's Gods*, New York: Alfred A. Knopf, 1925
—*Mr. Weston's Good Wine*, London: Chatto & Windus, 1927; reissued by Hogarth Press, with an introduction by Ronald Blythe, 1984
—*Rosie Plum and Other Stories*, London: Chatto & Windus, 1966
—"Rules of the Liberty Farm 145 acres", ms, n.d., Bissell Collection
—"The Scapegoat", *PR* 3, 1978, pp. 12–16
—Mencher, Elaine, ed., Selected Early Works of T. F. Powys, Denton: Brynmill Press, 2004
—*The Soliloquy of a Hermit*, New York: G. Arnold Shaw, 1916; reissued as *Soliloquies of a Hermit*, London: Andrew Melrose, 1918. The London 1918 edition and the London: Village Press edition, 1975, have slightly different pagination. Reprinted Gloucester: The Powys Press, 1993
—"The Story of John, A Dialogue", ms, May, 1906; HRHRC
—"This is Thyself", introduced and annotated by J. Lawrence Mitchell; ed. Belinda Humfrey, *PR* 20, 1987, pp. 5–26; also in Selected Early Works
—*The Two Thieves*, New York: Viking Press, 1933
—Unclay, London: Chatto & Windus, 1931
—"Why I have Given up Writing", *John O'London's Weekly and Outlook*, Vol. XXXVI, No. 915, 23 October, 1936, pp.145–6, 152, quoted in part in Riley, *Bibliography*, p. 63
Raine, Kathleen, *Berkeley, Blake, and the New Age*, Ipswich: Golgonooza Press, 1977
Richards, Grant, *Author Hunting*, New York: Coward-McCann, 1934
Riley, Peter, *A Bibliography of T. F. Powys*, Hastings: R. A. Brimmell, 1967
—"T. F. Powys at Mappowder: a consideration of his fiction in the light of the twenty years of non-writing", *PR* 3, 1978, pp. 17–31
Roberts, Paul, *The Ideal Ringmaster: A Biographical Sketch of Geoffrey Arnold Shaw (1884–1937)*, Kilmersdon, Somerset: The Powys Society, 1996
Scutt, Theodora G., The Potocki typescript: see note 2, p. 40.
—"Theodore Powys, 1934–1953", *PR* 9, 1981–2, pp. 60–80
—*Cuckoo in the Powys Nest: a Memoir*, Denton: Brynmill Press, 2000
Sewell, Brocard, ed., *Theodore: Essays on T. F. Powys*, Aylesford: Saint Albert's Press, 1964
Skeat, Walter W., *The Place Names of Suffolk*, Cambridge Antiquarian Publications, No. 46, 1913
Smith-Hughes, Jack, "Songs of the Vultures or Samburu Witchcraft, The Powys Mystery, 1931"; *Nine Verdicts On Violence*, 1956, pp. 109–38
Stanley, Edward, *A Familiar History of Birds*, London: Longmans, Green and Co., 1902
Stape, J. H., ed., *Virginia Woolf: Interviews and Recollections*, Iowa City: University of Iowa Press, 1975
Sykes, Christopher, *Evelyn Waugh: a Biography*, London: Collins, 1975
Unger, M. F. *Bible Dictionary*, Chicago: Moody Press, 3rd edn, 14th printing, 1967
Voltaire, *Candide: or Optimism*, a new translation, backgrounds, criticism, ed. Robert Martin Adams, New York: Norton, 1966
Ward, Richard Heron, *The Powys Brothers*, London: John Lane The Bodley Head, 1935
Warner, Sylvia Townsend: Maxwell, William, ed., The Letters of Sylvia Townsend Warner, New York: Viking Press, 1983
—Harman, Claire, ed., The Diaries of Sylvia Townsend Warner, London: Chatto & Windus, 1994
—Manuscript Diaries, Dorset County Museum
White's Directory of Suffolk 1891

Wilkinson, Louis [see also Marlow], "Some Memories of T. F. Powys", in Sewell, ed., *Theodore*, pp. 9–14

Williams, John, "Theodore Powys: all good books tell the same tale", *PR* 10, 1982, pp. 29–42

Woolf, Leonard, "Virginia Woolf; Writer and Personality", *The Listener*, 4 March, 1965, pp. 327–8; reprinted in Stape, *Virginia Woolf*

Manuscript and Other Collections

BELLE: Collection of Mrs B. H. [Sylvia] Belle (née Wilkinson); and Orwell Park School (successor to Eaton School) archives

BISSELL COLLECTION: Collection of the late E. E. Bissell: manuscripts, letters, and books from the library of TFP. Includes "Charlie", the fishing notebook of Littleton Powys, TFP's black farming notebook, and other farm records.

Louise de BRUIN collection, Mappowder

CHATTO & WINDUS ARCHIVE, Reading University

COLGATE: Colgate University Powys Collection. Includes Letters from TFP to Louis Wilkinson, and a few from Louis Wilkinson to TFP.

DORSET COUNTY LIBRARY, Dorchester: Powys Collection of Books. Also holds material concerning Dorchester Grammar School.

DORSET COUNTY MUSEUM, Dorchester. Now houses both the Bissell and the Feather Collections on behalf of the Powys Society, and the manuscript Diaries of Sylvia Townsend Warner.

FEATHER COLLECTION: Collection of the late Francis Feather: manuscripts, especially of unpublished short stories—including "The Coward"

GRAVES: Notes and other materials gathered in the course of research for *The Brothers Powys* (1983). Includes typescript of "Portrait of T. F. Powys" from Count Potocki.

HILTON HALL: Garnett Family Collection, Hilton Hall, Cambridgeshire

HOPKINS: Collection of the late Kenneth Hopkins; typescripts, letters, books; now dispersed

HRHRC: Harry Ransom Humanities Research Center, Austin, Texas, Powys Collection: manuscripts, letters, photographs, etc. Includes autobiographical "This is Thyself" and 1928 diary, and the Pocket Diaries of Gertrude Powys.

JOHNSON: Collection of Mary Barham Johnson. Includes many letters from maternal side of TFP's family as far back as the 18th century. Now held by Stephen Powys Marks.

NORFOLK: Norfolk County Records Office, Norwich: electoral rolls for Warham; early county directories

RILEY: Collection of materials not used in Riley's *Bibliography*, entitled "T. F. Powys: Bibliographical Addenda"; now in the collection of J. Lawrence Mitchell

SHERBORNE: Sherborne Preparatory School archives. Includes Littleton Powys's record of admissions from 1880 onwards.

STEINMANN Collection: the correspondence of Martin Steinmann, Jr, with T. F. Powys, Alfred Knopf, in preparation for his 1954 University of Minnesota doctoral Dissertation, *T. F. Powys: a Thematic Study*

SUFFOLK: Suffolk County Records Office, Ipswich: electoral rolls for Rendham and Sweffling; Sweffling Parish Council records; coroner's inquests; large-scale ordnance survey maps; tithe maps

Vera WAINWRIGHT Collection, British Library